MR. BLOK

"I am I – I am unique as any other person
– as any other fingerprint – I don't like it
– but I have no choice."
– Gregor Piatigorsky

Mr. Blok

A novel
by

GREGOR PIATIGORSKY

With An Introduction By Joram Piatigorsky

BOOKS

Adelaide Books
New York / Lisbon
2019

MR. BLOK
A novel
By Gregor Piatigorsky

Published by Adelaide Books, New York / Lisbon
adelaidebooks.org

Editor-in-Chief
Stevan V. Nikolic

For any information, please address Adelaide Books
at info@adelaidebooks.org

or write to:

Adelaide Books
244 Fifth Ave. Suite D27
New York, NY, 10001

ISBN-10: 1-951214-66-8
ISBN-13: 978-1-951214-66-1

Printed in the United States of America

Introduction

My father wrote *Mr. Blok,* a thought-provoking and deeply satirical novel of the times, at the prime of his illustrious cello career, in the late 1940s and early 50s. I was very young and didn't read the manuscript until last year. At some point many years ago I asked Papa why he didn't publish it. "Because if I did," he said, "both you and your sister Jephta would be expelled from school!" Doubtful, I thought, but he said nothing more.

Time passed and Papa died from lung cancer in 1976; he was 73. The manuscript languished in my mother's house for 36 more years. When she died at 100 in 2012, I found several copies of the typed manuscript, which I gathered along with Papa's other writings, including short stories, essays, poems, limericks and even the beginning of a second volume of his autobiography, *Cellist.* He often wrote on scraps of hotel stationery on his numerous travels concertizing.

Papa was well-known for being a spellbinding raconteur, often exaggerating and twisting reality into new shapes and sizes, and this talent jumps out of everything he wrote. *Mr. Blok* has many examples of tangential episodes and scenes that are typical of Papa's storytelling. The story radiates in various directions echoing Papa as he spoke in overlapping circles of free associations. I believe these digressions enrich the novel greatly.

Mr. Blok was written in English and the present version has not been altered. Indeed, some of the language and views reflect the era in which it was written. I am unaware that Papa ever had a professional editor. He read his novel as it progressed to Adele Friedman (today Adele Siegal), who typed the manuscript from her shorthand notes. It is this typed manuscript that is presented here. I asked Adele, now in her nineties, about her experience typing *Mr. Blok*. She said that she first met with Papa to type the beginning of *Mr. Blok* in Philadelphia shortly before we moved to Los Angeles in 1949. Papa would have been 46. She told me that Papa dictated from his notes, and between his accent, the weird story and her awe at being in the presence of the famous musician she was "totally flummoxed." She continued to meet with Papa to type the novel as it progressed in the 1950s. Adele has remained a treasured friend of our family.

Papa also spoke at length to Doris Stevenson, a fine pianist who was his assistant in his master classes at the University of Southern California. I asked her if she would be willing to share what Papa might have confided about *Mr. Blok*. She said, "I've always loved *Mr. Blok*, and I never understood why he wouldn't publish it. He said it was because you children were young. I couldn't see anything controversial about it, being young myself. I've reread it a couple of times over the years. All I can remember is that Piatigorsky said that he portrayed his real self in *Mr. Blok*."

That, I think, is central to this unique novel. I recognize Blok as a tormented fantasy of Papa, an original anti-hero bursting with ambition, flipping back and forth between exuberant inspiration and waves of sadness verging on despair. My friend Barbara Esstman, an author and editor, said that *Mr. Blok* sounded like "the French Symbolists poets got together to write a novel. Or maybe Kafka and Gogol went drinking together… very dreamlike and surreal… so well-written and the intelligence and artistic sensibility of the author…so astronomical."

Although Blok is a surreal, fictional character, I see many resemblances to Papa. Most important, Blok and Papa both live for their art. Blok, a painter, creates works of art that reach beyond the canvas by physically affecting the atmosphere, such as temperature. Blok says, *"My tropical landscapes will make them perspire and the wintery ones, shiver," Blok laughed.* Blok's "atmospheric" art causes havoc at an exhibition, resulting in one of several lawsuits against him. Thus, Blok's visual art projects senses beyond the canvas, while Papa's music affects moods and emotions.

I hear vintage Papa when Blok, preparing comments for a lecture, declares with humility his dedication to an art that always dangles beyond his reach: *"Ladies and gentlemen, thank you so much for giving me an opportunity to speak about myself and my art, which is, by the way, one and the same thing, for I belong to my art. We are a unit, an indivisible whole; yet I know art is higher than I, and, since it is inaccessible, I have to climb after it. But the faster I climb, the higher it goes, until I must slow my pace and wait for it to descend, to come near me, to let me caress it, to play with it. And then an unbelievable thing happens, ladies and gentlemen — the art actually does lower itself to reach my level, so that I can touch it; but it cannot fool me, for I know it is really I who lower my level. It's I who become weak and impotent and resent the effort. Man knows compromise, but art, never."*

Blok even mentions his reluctance to publish, stating, *"If I were a writer…I would not dare publish a book… No, it is much nicer just to think and let others put it on paper."*

A Russian immigrant feeling like an outsider, Blok has a traumatic childhood, as did Papa, when leaving home bitterly angry at his father. Blok says, *"...I felt the strong arm of Father and heard his words, spoken with incredible hatred. The words which still made my heart and blood burn.*

"Out — get out. Never come back.

"Blok put his fingers in his ears, not wanting to hear, not wanting to remember."

Blok continues to punish himself with memories when speaking to Sober Reality, a figment of his imagination, about his conversion to Christianity: *"And you please don't call me divine," said Blok..."Why not? I think you are divine, no less than the priest who initiated you into Christianity. Remember? When you converted? But perhaps you were too small then and too busy, playing with the lovely little cross you got from your brand-new godfather to remember the priest's face at all. I wonder where the cross and the priest are now? They must have gotten lost."* Sober *reflected melancholically, "I guess we all become losers as time goes by."*

Papa, too, converted to Christianity as a child with his father in pogrom-torn Russia, but he told me that he reconverted to Judaism when he escaped Russia in 1921.

Blok steps in Papa's shadow in numerous other ways. They both had a previous unsuccessful marriage ending in divorce; Blok admits he has no appetite for household chores and domestic life, and says, "I *can't even warm up coffee.*"; their associations, often humorous, take one by surprise, such as when Blok tells Sophia, the doctor he falls in love with, "*To see you here is like smelling a wonderful flower in a slaughterhouse. You are wonderful.*"; Blok twists questions imaginatively, such as, "*What happens to time when it runs away from memory? Does it become never?*"

I hear Papa asking me, "What about the speed of dark?" the title of my memoir, "*The Speed of Dark.*"

Blok, certainly no scientist, makes continual reference to bits of information about biology and far-fetched anecdotes, reminiscent of Papa, such as, *"Is it true that African elephants can stand for centuries on their feet?"* Lying in bed, Blok screams to himself, *"... my thoughts speed like a speeding squid, the sperm whale will catch it and tear it to pieces."* Papa spoke often about sperm whales and giant squids fighting in the depths of the ocean.

Blok did surprise me with his extensive knowledge of little-known subjects. For example, he spoke of many uncommon animals: barbirusa, arapaima, notornis, grison and guanaco, to name a few. Blok also mentioned in passing numerous terms, places, names, tribes and the like that didn't sound like Papa to me, such as threnody, Baha U'Ulah, Art College of Bocquet, Caodaist priest in Indochina, howdah, Havasupai, on and on. I never heard Papa mention such animals or topics or use such sophisticated vocabulary. However, I confirmed each animal and term and place that was foreign to me and found it correct. Where did Papa obtain all this knowledge? Perhaps he picked it up during his extensive travels from friends and admirers, or perhaps in diverse books, although he never mentioned these to me.

Blok's runaway imagination, mixed with humor and absurdity, pervades the novel and is sometimes prophetic for its era. Unwittingly, he predicts pollution of Earth when he says, *"Our stomachs have shrunk, and yet our excrement has increased, polluting all our rivers and lakes, rendering the life of fish impossible and our water undrinkable."* I read recently that a quarter of the planet is experiencing severe water shortages.

Blok also anticipates modern conveniences, some consistent with computers: he speaks of self-driving cars that have television screens behind the driver's seat, protections against collisions and can recognize red and green lights. This fancy new car has innovations even beyond what presently exist. For example, there is a small library with an automatic book reader under the seats that can give the correct interpretation if desired, and emotion regulators. The fantasy flows freely, as it did at home as I grew up.

For me, however, even more meaningful than the surreal imagination and humor when I think of Papa is when Blok reflects on loneliness and his sense of alienation. *"I am walking on nothing," he thought, not searching for the cause of his feeling of emptiness. "Did the fall of my sublime expectation hurt me? Hmmm, sublime is a big word, but expectation can be all shapes and sizes, like those empty streets and empty benches on this empty Square," mused Blok as he entered a side path. He sat on the bench and, looking up at the sky, let his thoughts travel calmly through the spaces crowded with loneliness. He thought of his journeys, of colors, of life and of the brook that rushed by his cabin and yet was always there like the thoughts of his mother. He saw the light breaking through the dark grayish night, not uneven and shy as it does in the country, but with short sudden moves unafraid of the city and the night. The headlights of a truck, weakened by the dawn like the eyes of an owl, did not reach Mr. Blok's tired face. Even the quick bright eyes of a squirrel hardly glanced at him as it hid its shabby tail behind a poplar tree."*

Finally, I felt an eerie connection with Papa filtered through Blok, especially at the end of the novel, when I recalled reading *The First Man* by Albert Camus. The autobiographical novel, found in the wrecked car in which Camus was killed, was published posthumously 34 years later. The story is about Jacques Comery's, Camus' alter-ego, childhood in Algeria, with an underlying theme of searching for his father. In a telling passage, Jacque, 40, stands by the grave of his father, who died at 29, he feels the crumbling of the internal statue he erected of his own identity, realizing that he is the continuation of his father's life. In my case, I was struck by the similarity of the surreal characters that exist in my recent short story collection, *Notes Going Underground*, and Blok. Although I had never read *Mr. Blok*, written by Papa when I was a boy, I created independently literary characters years later that exist, absurdly and surreally, in a transition between being partially alive and partially dead – in a dreamworld, as it were – as if a porous barrier separates the two states resulting in an overlapping period between life and death. Were Blok's surreal, often absurd adventures real or a dream? Blok asks the same question when the novel opens with him in a ditch:

"Mr. Blok thought it was a dream; but he must have been wrong. He walked through the Square one night and arriving at 20th Street, fell into a ditch they were digging for sewer pipes of something."

The story ends with Blok in a ditch again, *"Lying on his back in the mud, soft and warm, with his eyes closed, in the marvelous quietness made him feel almost grateful and glad. How amazingly simple it is to be dead. The transition is so painless, it is hardly perceptible. "Oh, nature is kind," he admired quietly. "Such a short distance from life and such quietness. If people knew, they would never be frightened of death, never – never. Perhaps later I will find a greater difference on this side – the side of death – if there is any. No wonder so many people don't know they are dead."*

How strange, and comforting, to find my mind gravitating to a similar hideout with Papa's.

Whether dead or alive, or awake or dreaming, I believe that you, like me, as Papa writes in the Forward, *"will find Mr. Blok a likable fellow, who will not mind in the slightest being put aside, should he not succeed in holding your attention."*

Joram Piatigorsky
August, 2019

Terry King's excellent biography (*Gregor Piatigorsky: The Life and Career of the Virtuoso Cellist*) tells of Papa's writing *Mr. Blok* and his experience with publishers. Random House and other publishing houses offered a contract to publish the novel, but Papa, for whatever reasons, did not accept, despite the encouragement of Aldous Huxley and Robert Penn Warren to do so.

Among Papa's notes I found, remarkably, his own account of writing Mr. Blok, consistent with King's biography, but adding that Blok represented a deep part of the "real him."

Papa also extends his thoughts of Blok's amazing atmospheric paintings. However, it remains unclear why Papa never published the novel, since apparently the famed author Robert Penn Warren was captivated by it to the extent of sending it to his publisher.

While that mystery may never be solved, I am grateful to Margaret Dimond for transferring the manuscript into a word file, and to Stevan Nikolic, the editor of Adelaide Books, for publishing the book for the world to enjoy. I am also grateful to Barbara Esstman for helpful comments, and Margaret Dimond and Mia Garcia for proofreading and discussing the manuscript with me.

Papa's Account of *Mr. Blok*

I decided to grant myself a sabbatical. This would be my first leave of duty with a long vacation and long desired break. I always dreamed of doing nothing – or something that would amount to nothing – with no obligations, no pressures – no efforts – no demands of oneself – no demands from the others. Particularly from the others. For the first time in my life, I made it possible – I had it on the paper. How wonderful it felt! I was free. I could not believe it. I had never experienced such complete liberation, such joy of being liberated. I wanted to scream – no concerts next week and next month and every month to come – I could do anything I pleased tomorrow and the next month and the next and many more to come – but what?

Although I looked forward to the fact that I had nothing definite in mind of what to do, and the idea of freedom of choice and the lack of obligations thrilled me, I began to give some thoughts to my activity during the time. As always in the past, my unrealistic dreams of going into the jungles began to take hold once again. What would it be – Amazon, Sumatra, or perhaps something even more dangerous and impenetrable? The more of it the better. Of course, I didn't really believe my old dreams would come true. At least I had some taste of Borneo, Sumatra and other wildernesses before, and I really would not mind keeping some of my passioned desires for their true value, which was continuous dreams. Before deciding what to do, I was quite certain I would not use that precious freedom for practicing and preparation for the season to come. I recalled a number of amateur musicians, chess players, golfers, gentleman farmers or whatever people do without knowing much of what they are doing who had in common an envious capacity of true enjoyment of things they did poorly, but with a sense of supreme fulfillment. Hell with professionalism, perfectionism, so challenging and so self-punishing and barely reachable at the end! I had my portion of that, and there is no hope whatsoever of changing it in the future. I had to choose some other activity that would promise total enjoyment, and that would be something I knew very little about. This challenged me, since there were numerous areas in which I was fabulously ignorant, yet a choice had to be made.

I competed with Dr. Koussevitzky, Gregory Ratov and some others for years about whose English had more bizarre pronunciation, grammar and all that goes with it. I don't know who won but judging from the fun and laughter and imitation people made of my English, I must have been ranked pretty high. Soon I decided to write a book in English with no expert help or no translation from Russian, all mine, all for myself. Without further thought, I began at once, even before the sabbatical began. I had no doubt my unexpected decision was a good one. I bought a great number of note pads, pencils, erasers and pens. I sat down without the slightest hesitation and wrote a title of the book – Mr. Blok. The letters were big and the ink thick. Before I knew who Mr. Blok was or what I would make of him, my delight was immense, as if Mr . Blok was the closest thing to my mind and heart.

I knew a number of people by that name, but they all spelled it "ck," but none of them have inspired me for that title. Of course, in Russia I loved the poet Alexander Block, but I knew he had not been a part of me.

Blok, I felt, was no one but I, but not the cellist, not a boy or man known by anyone. Blok was I, the hidden one with all the dreams, violence and love, shame and pride, lonesomeness and unbelonging, an uprooted man with humbleness of a beggar, vanity and passionate desire to belong. I knew there were countless such Bloks uprooted and longing, despite their having names the origin of their country or their occupation. Writing of any one of them would be writing of me, which would make a true autobiography and that much more if lacking facts, dates and other realities. So, I was caught in a fascinating world of fantasy and absurdity that, during the nights I spent writing it, became more truth, more me. All things I would not dare to say of me, I could, totally unsuspected, say of Mr. Blok.

To be unsuspected seemed of importance to me. There was not a word of music, of the country in which he lived or even his age. He was a painter, unaware of his importance, mastery or inventiveness, and he lived in his studio alone. Possessed and passionate in quiet ways, he worked on a formula that would make the art a true reality with all the glory nature provides. The canvas and colors he thought only a poor substitute. He wanted fragrance and temperature, while movements he always could provide with the brush. He never believed his aims would be successful, but nothing could prevent him from striving. A quiet unassuming peaceful man, the morning he first inhaled a magnificent fragrance of roses in his painting it brought him to a state of insanity, soon his studio was filled with an incredible fragrance of trees, grass and flowers. He kept his windows open and he awoke often at night in great anxiety that the fragrance on some older canvasses would be disappearing or flower itself fade. But it never did. Happy and encouraged he began to work on his temperature formula. Succeeding in this and over joyous for the first time in his artistic life, he begged a local gallery to exhibit his works. At first disbelieving, but after visiting Blok's studio, the gallery owner's enthusiasm and astonishment had no bounds. When the day of the exhibit arrived, the art interested people, well prepared by newspaper articles, turned out in great numbers. It was a beautiful summer evening and the exhibition was held in 3 rooms: seascapes, tropical and floral landscapes. The effect it made on people was wonderous as well as disastrous. Because of the warm evening, the windows in the seascape were kept open. Not being far from the ocean, the seagulls and some other birds of the sea, lured by Mr. Blok's sea, flew in numbers through the window into the room causing a disastrous havoc. They pecked the canvas and their shrill noise pierced the air.

Confused and frantic and screaming with droppings caught on their faces and clothes, the people knocked each other over in terror as they tried to escape. As if the unforeseen catastrophe would not be enough, in the other tropical landscape room a lady fainted or dyed of a heat or sunstroke. Confused and totally bewildered, Mr. Blok saw himself running down the street until panting, he reached his studio. He did not move from his empty studio for days and the bare walls did not affect his morale. Strangely he felt it as a relief. There were no visitors except one who handed a summons to appear in the court...

After innumerable traumas, ecstasy, the queerest romances, miseries and triumphal adventures of my *Mr. Blok*, I had to part from him. The bulky manuscript had to be replaced with my bulky cello and with many new and old scores. The life of a cellist had to go on with all its reality and its unreachable dreams. I never quit practicing during the sabbatical, but I did so in a kind of a split personality manner. I really never stopped writing; I did it in trains, in hotels, and in taxis. I developed even a habit to drag some parts of *Mr. Blok* into rehearsals and concerts just in case I would have something to say. The first time the fast-growing manuscript met the eyes of a stranger was in Minneapolis after a concert under the direction of Dimitri Mitropoulos. Along with the Schumann concerto and the premier of my unfortunate, too long and over orchestrated Variations on a theme of Paganini, the only marvelous thing I could recall was Mitropoulos learning it overnight and knowing every note by memory.

I heard many compliments after the performance, but was glad that the only present composer, Mr. Ernst Krenek, though he shook my hand, did not utter a word. After an exceptionally gay and warm party with my colleagues and old friends such as Mitropoulos and Nikolai Graudan, whom I knew since the time we worked together in the Berlin Philharmonic and who now was the first cellist with the Minneapolis Symphony. The next day I had lunch with him and Mr. Robert Penn Warren, the writer and poet for whom I had great admiration. His Italian wife spoke much of music and said that her husband, whom she called "Red," was allergic to music and that she had been at the concert alone. He did not speak much, but when he noticed my manuscript, he asked me what it was. Like a true amateur, I said in my enviable English that I am writing a book.

"A book?" he said surprised. "What is it about?"

"I don't know," I said. "It's about a man I call Mr. Blok. Sort of satire I guess."

He listened, interested. "I take it it's in Russian?" he asked, and when I said it in English, he burst into laughter so unceremoniously and sincere that instead of being offended, I was glad that even unknown, my Mr. Blok had achieved something already.

"You know," he said, "I am teaching English here and so have a lot of reading to do, but this one I have to read. Right now. Do you mind?" He took the folder and disappeared.

Left alone with Mrs. Warren and listening to her speak of her musician relatives and sipping tea, my thoughts wandered to Proust's Dr. Swann and many pages in which he described having tea.

Though impolite in not having given enough attention to the words of the good Mrs. Warren, absorbed in thoughts of Proust because of the tea, I simply could not manage to tear my thoughts away from it. She stood up to look for a composition or photo of her father. Hours must have passed before finally Mr. Warren returned.

"It's the best darned thing I have read in a long time."

Probably seeing me dumbfounded, he had to repeat what he said. Now it was my turn for laughter. I could not stop. Not paying much attention and dead serious, he asked to keep the manuscript with him to make a telephone call to his publishers, Random House. Still dumbfounded, I can't recall what I said, until he spoke to Mr. Haas and Mr. Erskin and said that the manuscript must be sent to them at once. I tore off a few last pages so that I could continue from where I left, thanked my hosts and departed.

Gregor Piatigorsky
1950s?

Forward

You who read best sellers and wear standard size shoes. You who never take unscheduled flights and never share views of the few. You who spit on a chess table and don't eat Snails Provencal. You wasters stuffed with timetables and self-importance — You will never belong to Mr. Blok's admirers. But You who are capable of seeing your own ridiculousness; You, the spirited and the ones undiscouraged by your own futility — You, readers, will find Mr. Blok a likable fellow, who will not mind in the slightest being put aside, should he not succeed in holding your attention.

Chapter I

Mr. Blok thought it was a dream; but he must have been wrong. He walked through the Square one night and, arriving at 20th Street, fell into the ditch they were digging for sewer pipes or something. Under his arm he was carrying a canvas, a portrait of a Negro. But was not really a portrait, as the Negro had never posed for him; and furthermore, Blok had never seen him.

Sitting in the ditch, he was all in mud, a sort of slimy reddish wet dirt. He had hurt himself by falling. He was in great pain. There was no one to help him get out, and in a way, he was pleased to rest there for a while. It was amazing how well he felt there, delighted that the canvas was not damaged. There in the dark he tried to appraise the effect of the painting. Again, he was really delighted. After all sorts of interesting and pleasant thoughts, he decided it was time to get out; but it was not an easy task, as the hole was deep and the sides slippery. Besides, there was pain in his legs, arms, chest, stomach, and, above all, his neck.

He placed the canvas in the corner, near the spot he chose to climb out. There were niches to give a foothold, but when he tried, his foot slipped, and he fell. The mud went into his ears and eyes, and his mouth was filled with clay. Blok coughed it out as he rested, leaning against the wall. "This pestering smell down here can choke a fellow," said Blok to himself and got up to look for the canvas. He tried once more to get out but slipped again and again. Then holding the canvas carefully in his hands and standing on his toes, he let it fly like a kite out of the hole. The fight with the mud exhausted his weak body, and, after clambering out, he could not walk and had to lean against the wall of a building.

As he stood there someone approached him from the dark. It was a giant Negro, who spoke in a low voice. "Mr. Blok," he said, "be not desperate. You are not dead — not even sick. You are just getting old."

Then the Negro snatched the canvas and dragged Blok to the nearest lamp post. "Look at it! Just look at that picture, you wretched bastard! Is that supposed to be me? Mitchel Wrinkly? You certainly don't flatter me. I will not shake your hand and thank you for that portrait," said the Negro angrily and left.

But in a while. he returned and, slipping a book into Mr. Blok's hand, he said, "Mind you, sir, watch the illustrations in that book — the lines — lines and a few circles. Also, a moon and the head of a corpse, but mostly watch the lines, and do not forget to wash your face." There was tenderness in the voice of the Negro, and Mr. Blok sincerely regretted not having made a nicer impression on him. He wanted to run after him, but his legs would not move. "Mitchel Wrinkly? Never heard that name. Never saw him before, and yet he must know me. Didn't he say 'Mr. Blok'? And my canvas! It's gone!"

He began to call for the police, but he soon fainted.

The policemen must have thought he was just a drunkard. Mr. Blok felt it in every question he had to answer at the police station. He disliked the manners of the two cops and the one they addressed "Captain" or sometimes "Chief". Mr. Blok felt him to be the most unrefined being he had ever had the misfortune to meet. The captain obviously was dissatisfied with Mr. Blok's answers and his passive behavior. "So, you are unwilling to tell us the truth, eh? I'm asking again —where did you spend the last two hours before we picked you up?"

"I told you already, officer — in the ditch."

"Nonsense! Now tell me, why do you refuse to admit that your name is Mitchel Wrinkly?"

"Because it isn't. My name is Blok, and besides, I am not a Negro."

"Nobody said that you were a Negro. As a matter of fact, you look to me more like a Jew," said one of the other policemen.

"No racial or religious remarks, please," said Mr. Blok somewhat nervously.

"Hear that, captain," cried the cop. "Only listen to that! Wrinkly is crazy. Just listen to what I found in his book. He is nuts." He chuckled and read: "The piercing cries of ticklish girls, the eyes, the teeth, the glistening eyelids, and the lovely breasts that play with fire, the blood that gleams in surrendered lips, the final gifts…"

"Stop it! Stop! We are not here to discuss the ticklish girls. Wrinkly must be a queer."

"Give me that book, will you?" Mr. Blok screamed. "It belongs to Wrinkly. Now I understand — he gave me the book in exchange for my painting. Give me the book, please."

"No sir, we will keep it as evidence."

"All right then, at least show it to me. I haven't even had a chance to see what it is."

"Okay," said the policeman, and handed him the book. Its title read "THE GRAVEYARD BY THE SEA," by Paul Valery and in smaller letters, "Original text with English rendering and illustrations by Emlen Pope Etting." On the front page was written, in a thick blue pencil, "Mitchel Wrinkly."

"Oh, that's why they think it's me," thought Mr. Blok. "Now it's all clear. Now I will easily explain the misunderstanding to these creatures."

But meanwhile he turned the pages of the book and became so interested in the text and so fascinated by the drawings that he forgot the officers. "No wonder Wrinkly emphasized so dramatically all the circles and lines in the illustrations. He must have known what would stir my imagination."

The book was brutally taken away, and thus his meditations were interrupted.

The cops persuaded him to spend the rest of the night in jail. They treated him kindly. Now Mr. Blok could wash the mud from his face and rest nicely on the bench in the cell which he occupied quite alone, thus enjoying the privacy of which he was so fond.

When in the morning he was called to appear before the magistrate, he felt quite cheerful and in comparatively good shape. The magistrate was very cordial, and his round, red face awoke Mr. Blok's confidence and respect. The magistrate did not bother to ask his name, address, age or religion, but be showed great interest in Blok's profession, and furthermore did not hesitate to express delight at meeting an artist. "If there were more art-minded people, the law would not be needed," he said. Then he went into some details of his own childhood, condemning his parents for not having recognized his true mission in life, despite the fact that he had proved his unusual abilities for art in his early days.

"So now I am just a magistrate," he said sadly. Mr. Blok was too touched to say a word. He stood there, overwhelmed by the eloquence and sincerity of what he heard. The magistrate did not hide his delight at the impression he made, and after a significant pause he reached out his hand and shook Mr. Blok's heartily.

"Mr. Wrinkly, you are free."

"But, Judge, you see, it's a misunderstanding. Mr. Wrinkly is not even an artist. I am..."

"Never mind," said the magistrate. "There is nothing to be ashamed of in being Wrinkly. One day that name will have a different meaning. Don't forget that Van Gogh sold only one picture during his entire lifetime. Goodbye, and good luck. I know I will be proud to have met Mitchel Wrinkly."

"But, Judge, I am not a young man, and besides..."

"Please, my dear friend, if I may call you so. Art is ageless, and as long as the sacred fire burns in your soul, you'll be young forever. Next case."

There were other people waiting, and the magistrate gave them his full attention.

Blok waited. He was miserable. He did not want to leave under a false name, but there was no one to listen to him. He walked slowly out of the building, and only when he was halfway to his studio did he remember that he had left the book at the police station. It was already noon, and Bonnie would be waiting for him.

A strange girl, mused Blok. There she will stand, waiting, with a smile on her fleshy cheeks. It's true...fleshy; she's fleshy all over — except her big white teeth. And they like to dig deep into juicy meat. "A steak, rare, please," he had often heard her order. Hm! Even the apples she paints in such abundance are all meaty — there's no skin on them. I must teach her to paint skin — loose, tight, thick, dry, oily, thin — skin I want to bite or caress, fragrant or revolting skin. Oh, God, but will she ever learn? No! Not if she keeps gazing at me during lessons instead of at the canvas. What does she hope to find! Is it what all lonely young girls hope to find in big cities?

Discovering how little he knew about Bonnie annoyed him. He tried to remember how it was that she first came to him. He wanted to put together all the little things he could think of concerning her life. But the more he thought, the clearer it became that she had always been unnoticed. "It's a shame! Even the police were more sensitive!"

Suddenly he remembered one afternoon when Bonnie said she would pose for him. "What happened to that painting?" It was not finished; only her thighs and her full maiden breasts emerged on the canvas.

He stopped, surprised at his thoughts. "Ridiculous for me to think of her body now. I didn't see it then." But despite his wish to toss away these invading images they kept pounding at his mind, making him walk faster.

As often in the past, Blok's ability to think in the abstract came to his rescue.

He stopped again, saying almost aloud, "I don't know her, as I don't know the street on which I'm walking – and yet I will not lose my direction." He looked up at a building. "I admire this building, and yet I don't know its purpose or its number."

"Numbers, names, as if there were any difference between names and numbers."

In this manner his thoughts came to a taxi driver who once had driven him to the Rue de la General Alphonse Bergerie de Castillon-Boudignon somewhere in Passy or maybe another part of Paris. Poor fellow, how much easier his life would be in New York! After all, Fifth Avenue by no means has less personality; but then, people like to elevate their heroes to immortality. Only they seldom succeed, for only those monuments stay alive which were not built by others...

And he thought again of names and of all the babies who never had a free will to choose their names, their parents, their nurses, or even a convenient color, an agreeable race, or religion, the country of their birth, and later even their profession. All is set for them in advance, all is decided — the chains are ready and handed to them. As long as this state of affairs prevails, there will be no freedom — so reasoned Blok and wondered if that thought were his own, or if he had heard or read it somewhere.

He had often thought of himself as an original thinker but could seldom sustain the pleasure for any length of time, and his thoughts invariably turned out to be someone else's. But the disappointment was never really serious, for Mr. Blok enjoyed the fact that there were other equally developed minds, and so he was not alone in this sorry world.

"If I were a writer," thought Mr. Blok, "I would not dare publish a book. To discover what has already been written, one life would be too short. No, it is much nicer just to think and let others put it on paper."

Mr. Blok reached his studio, but before he put his key to the lock, the door was opened from the inside by Bonnie.

"How did you get in, Bonnie?"

But before she could answer he kissed her violently.

"My darling Bonnie, you are mine, you must be mine. Don't push me away, don't! Kiss me, kiss... I am not your teacher anymore. I am your lover. You hurt me, Bonnie, don't slap me! Put away that bottle! You wouldn't dare throw it! You hear? Darling, darling — you'll never understand. You'll never be a great artist! Oh, I am so tired! I am exhausted. I'm not myself," he whispered.

Bonnie was standing in a corner of the studio. She was frightened and embarrassed. Her hair was in disorder, lipstick was smeared over her cheeks, and her dress was torn. What had happened to that old man? Was he mad? She wanted to run away and never return.

Keeping her eyes fastened on Blok, she was cautiously moving toward the door. On reaching it she noticed that Mr. Blok was sound asleep, and only then did she realize the miserable state he must have been in. She went to the chair and touched his head, and though she did it most delicately, so as not to waken him, some dried mud, like a fine reddish pollen, fell from his hair.

She could not help feeling sorry for her teacher. She was worried and undecided. Should she call a doctor, or run next door to a neighbor and ask for help and advice?

Suddenly she started to undo his shirt and loosen his tie. She tried to take off his jacket, and when this did not wake him, she took off his shoes, then unbuttoned his trousers. She went to a drawer for his pajamas and made the bed. When this was done, she carefully pulled off his trousers. He was naked and looked like a corpse. At this moment there was a knock at the door. Before she could move, a man with a small bag in his hand walked into the room.

"My name is Snok," he said politely. "C. R. Snok. I am working on cybernetics, if you know what I mean."

"Oh yes," answered Bonnie. "I read a perfectly fascinating article on that in *Time Magazine*. Isn't it something about artificial brains or something?"

"Precisely. You see, I am working independently, taking Dr. Norbert Wiener's idea only as a base. At this particular moment I am busy collecting data on creative artists, having in mind the possibilities of replacing their creative efforts with a perfect machine far superior to human talents. That's why I am here - to interview Mr. Blok. Is he at home?"

"Yes. This is he." She indicated the chair. "He is not feeling well, and at the moment you arrived, I was trying to put him to bed. Will you be kind enough to help me put his pajamas on?"

"It will be a pleasure, Madame. Are you Mrs. Blok?"

"No, I am his student."

"Oh, is that so? Perhaps then I can interview you instead of Mr. Blok, especially as he doesn't seem to be in such good shape today."

"Yes, with pleasure. Mr. Blok was quite upset when he came home."

"We must get him to bed before we talk," said Mr. Snok. Bonnie took a blanket from the bed, threw it over Blok's body without looking at him, went to the mirror to arrange her hair, and in almost no time was ready to leave the studio in Mr. Snok's agreeable company.

They walked two blocks to the right, reached the Square, crossed, and entered a bar on 20th Street, opposite the side where ditches were being dug. They chose a nice table in the corner of the half-dark, smoke-filled room.

The conversation was lively and interesting, but after the third drink they switched from the semi-abstract to the very personal. It was a great surprise for Mr. Snok to find himself sitting in a dark booth holding Bonnie's hand. Too unbelievable! Just what had done the trick? Perhaps Bonnie's deep voice, the voice of a boy, not yet quite settled. His self-consciousness disappeared, just as if he had not lived with it for the past 47 years. He was tense when Bonnie spoke and did not try to hide his admiration or control the expression of his eyes, whose buttery quality would have easily shocked an onlooker.

"I will not speak any more — not a word, until you tell me what you have in that little suitcase," said Bonnie with a coy smile.

"My dear little lady, please do continue speaking. You are adorable."

"No, no, I have already said too much, more than I should have, but I do insist on my question."

"All right, I will tell you; but you see, it's not really interesting. In my bag here are just samples of smells and a few gadgets for experiments on reproduction... I mean artificial insemination of cattle, dogs, and so on. It's not really very interesting, as these smells do not differ much from one another, but we are amazed at the extraordinary reaction they cause in male animals."

"How fascinating, Mr. Snok! Please do let me smell!"

"I just don't know how and when to extract this peculiar snake scent; with cows it's so simple! You won't believe it, but cows and bitches not only cooperate wonderfully but even get a certain pleasure out of it. With snakes it's not simple, though with perseverance I hope to succeed. It was a most embarrassing experience, when, after keeping three snakes in a glass box for weeks and weeks, I discovered that all three of them were male. But now I have two females and one male, and I'm sure that this time there'll be no mistake."

"Snakes in that bag?" exclaimed Bonnie. "Quelle horreur!" (She had once been a babysitter in a French speaking family and ever since loved occasionally to speak a few words in French.)

Mr. Snok realized that the atmosphere for flirtation was disappearing, that a certain contact, the desire, and the courage had passed away. Those damned bulls, smells, and snakes had spoiled it all.

"I should never have started to talk about the whole thing," thought Mr. Snok and asked the waiter for his check. Looking at his watch, he remarked that it was late and got up. Mr. Snok picked up his bag, helped Bonnie into her coat, left a tip for the waiter, shook Bonnie's hand coldly, and with a 'Hope to see you sometime,' brusquely left the bar. The waiter, having observed the pair from the beginning was puzzled at such a sudden finish. In a way he felt sorry for her. One could hear it in his voice as he said, "I turned on the radio because I feared that the croaking of the frogs in the gentleman's bag might annoy you."

Bonnie did not like this intrusion and found it tactless. Besides, she was in a bad humor, and ashamed of perhaps having been overheard by the waiter when she spoke intimately of her personal life to Mr. Snok.

"Why must I always announce my virginity?" she thought angrily and walked toward the Square. Then she suddenly re-membered Mr. Blok, but she did not go to see him. It was late and she was tired and hungry and wanted to be alone. That night she slept restlessly, dreaming of mud, powder, and naked men; but none of them looked so ugly, so hairless and white, as Mr. Blok's body.

Chapter II

Great was Mr. Blok's astonishment when he opened his eyes and saw himself naked in the chair. He could not explain a thing, could not remember undressing himself. His mind was blank. He got up slowly and moved toward the mirror that hung on the wall. He stood and looked at himself.

Mr. Blok could never have been accused of narcissism. He was a man of good taste, with a highly developed sense of beauty, and it was always his deep regret that he had not been the one to choose the shape of his own body. He thought the view in the mirror pathetic. It offended his dignity and filled his heart with a deep melancholy.

But Mr. Blok never permitted depressing thoughts and feelings to dominate him for long. On the contrary, he had a helpful remedy for every occasion of that sort. He never ran out of good and reasonable ideas capable of cheering him and restoring his equanimity. After a refreshing shower, he shaved his face, plucked isolated hairs which bad begun to grow long and unwanted in unexpected places, put on his best suit, chose the right tie, and whistling cheerfully, went out to dinner.

He walked toward the Square with the idea of dining at his club but changed his mind. It took him half an hour to find precisely the place he desired. 1t was a nice, quiet, but perhaps too empty restaurant. On many occasions he had heard people say that the food in empty restaurants was never good. Thoughtless people! Absurd! Like parrots they repeat what they hear from other imbeciles. "Take, for example," thought Blok, "my exhibition. A great exhibition, and yet it's empty. Since when are the masses attracted by real quality? I am asking you, you idiots. Isn't root beer consumed a million times more than Chateau Lafite?"

Mr. Blok was pleased with this reasoning and, with a big smile on his face, selected a table. There was not a soul to be seen; no menu on the table, no usual pitcher of water, no waiter, and not even the inevitable cashier. Mr. Blok was hungry, but in anticipation of a good meal he waited patiently. After a while a man came, apparently from the kitchen, holding in one hand a piece of celery and in the other a hard roll.

"I presume you wish to eat, sir," the waiter said politely, and stuck the piece of celery in Mr. Blok's mouth.

"How dare you… you…," he screamed at the waiter with a muffled voice; and the celery fell out of his mouth. The waiter picked it up, put it on the table, and took a seat in a chair next to Mr. Blok.

"I beg you to calm yourself, sir, and listen to me for a few minutes."

At this moment the waiter, taking advantage of Mr. Blok's astonishment and open mouth, tried to force the roll into it, with one hand pulling Mr. Blok's chin slightly downward. This violence on the part of the waiter enraged Mr. Blok still more, so much so that he wanted to strike the offender's face, but the smile and the perfect calm of the waiter were disarming and of such great charm that instead of striking him, Blok merely took the roll out of his mouth, placed it next to the celery on the table, and signaled to the waiter to speak and explain his strange actions.

"You are a gentleman, sir, through and through, a gentleman. And mind you, not in the sense that the English misuse that word. It is an honor, sir, to speak to you."

Mr. Blok was very receptive to kind words like these, and he appreciated them even when they bordered on flattery.

"Yes sir," the waiter continued, "a bum would never listen to me. Why, he would not even try to understand or grasp an action of originality and deep meaning. God knows, it has been proven on many occasions. It would explain also the complete failure of this eating place. I will try to be brief, so as not to take up too much of your valuable time, and yet I must try not to omit some important points. The most suitable start, I believe, will be to ask you certain questions. When was the last time you heard music? I mean not any particular music — just music, any music?"

Mr. Blok tried to remember. "You mean today?"

"No, any day, any time."

"Well," said Mr. Blok, "I believe I heard a radio and before that, let's see. Oh yes, I heard some piano practicing, which came through the wall of a neighbor's apartment."

"All right, I will tell you. You hear music everywhere — in hotels, bars, restaurants, taxis, in the homes of your friends, on trains; it comes through walls, from above and below, from in front and behind — from everywhere. Did anybody ever ask you if you were ready for it, if you were hungry for it? If you care for it at all? Have you any choice? No sir! There is no escape, no safety, to be found from that outrageous intrusion. Your innocent ears, through which They infiltrate music of Their taste, Their choice and volume, are brutally violated, raped: and mind you, sir, you cannot protest — you cannot run away, for nowhere will you be safe from unwanted sounds. Now I beg you, sir, not to misunderstand me. I am in no way a music-hater. The truth is, I love music passionately. Perhaps it is my particular love for it that makes me react with such intensity against the lawful and silent conspiracy to pump indiscriminately whatever they decide to into our ears. I have smashed many radio machines in public places. I have destroyed phonograph records. I have protested and fought for the liberty of such an important and noble member of our body as the ear, but to no avail. Quite to the contrary, I was the victim. I was punished. I lost my friends. My wife divorced me, and once I was arrested and kept in jail. I lost my health and money in that singular fight. I was analyzed by a psychiatrist and treated by other physicians. I tried to break my own resistance by finding charm in the song, "All I Want for Christmas Is My Two Front Teeth." I tried to enjoy it while reading Proust. I tried to concentrate on a symphony while eating apple pie and to follow someone's crooning while filing my income tax. Yes sir, when nothing helped, I decided to take more realistic steps. I had a plan, a magnificent idea: to do to others what they had done to me! That's how I became a waiter, and that's why my way of feeding people is equally logical and lawful."

Mr. Blok was deeply moved; he completely forgot about dinner.

He stood up, shook the waiter's hand and said with great feeling, "It was a privilege to meet you and to listen to you. You are a man of courage." And with the dignity inborn in his bearing, Mr. Blok moved toward the exit.

But after he had taken a few steps, his way was barred by the waiter.

"Oh, no! Please don't leave so soon, Mr. Blok."

"Why, you know me?" Blok exclaimed.

"Of course I do, of course." The waiter spoke fast. "There are many things I would like to talk over with you."

Blok lifted his eyes.

"Yes sir, we all know of you in the Aristocrats of Mind Society. We all admire you very much."

"Hm...curious," mumbled Blok. "Is it a Club?"

"No, not at all," said the waiter, "It's a movement, an evolution of century-old traditions. I'm sure that our Eastern Grand Aris would like to meet you — and confidentially, Mr. Ellis was re-elected for one term."

"Is that so?" said Blok, as the front door opened, and two men entered the restaurant.

Mr. Blok took advantage of this to saunter out. His heart was filled with sympathy for the waiter.

And then he remembered Miss Elsa, the waitress, her tidy little apartment, her silent willingness and gratitude. Perhaps her insignificant looks, her age, or maybe her social standing made her attractive to Mr. Blok. She was so undemanding and passionate. Not many words passed between them, but the understanding was perfect. No matter how irregularly or at what hours he would visit her, there was never a reproach, always a silent agreement in their lust, secretive and satisfying.

Mr. Blok's pace quickened. Then, as he neared the street where she lived, it became still faster, and he began to run.

When he arrived at Miss Elsa's house he was out of breath.

He had to wait and compose himself. It was unseemly for one his age to show so much desire and impatience. He tried to direct his thoughts to something else, something neutral, but his overheated imagination refused to take a safe course. He thought of the sea lion bulls and their refusal to eat during the mating season until they lose their fat and, like wrung-out rags, lie on the rocks by the sea, exhausted and satisfied. This was obviously a wrong trend of thought at that moment, and

Mr. Blok tried to change it towards his art and work; but there was no sincerity in it. He could not get beyond imagining the mixing of colors or the washing of brushes. He was ashamed of his uncontrollable impulses.

"Moral and physical pygmy, that's what I am," he repeated to himself, "and not I alone. We all are, the whole world, with our miserable bias, cowardice, self-pity and hypocrisy. Where are the palaces of Caligula, the passions of Tristan, or Nero's incendiaries? We are diminishing; gone is the grandeur of the past. We have not even retained the vomiting places of antique Rome. Our stomachs have shrunk, and yet our excrement has increased, polluting all our rivers and lakes, rendering the life of fish impossible and our water undrinkable. There are no heroes anymore either. They are not permitted; there is nothing for them to do. All is directed from someone's desk."

When Mr. Blok arrived at this point his thoughts were interrupted by violent hiccups, of which the first four or five were extremely loud and in a high pitch. He explained this occurrence very simply; he was hungry. He did not remember having had any meal at all since, since—oh yes, since before he fell into the ditch.

Mr. Blok turned to the left, and after walking two blocks crossed the Square and entered Mr. Pinkel's drugstore.

"How do you do? How are you, Mr. Blok? I was held up here two times," said Mr. Pinkel proudly.

"Remarkable! Quite extraordinary!" said Mr. Blok, without paying attention.

"Why, you have hiccups, Mr. Blok. I'll give you something that will stop them in a minute."

It did help. Mr. Blok felt greatly relieved. "Do you think, Mr. Pinkel, in the time of, let us say, Julius Caesar, they knew how to stop hiccups?"

"I don't know. I'm not really interested in history, but the stuff I gave you is certainly terrific. It comes, you know, from the army, like the other stuff I have here, a liquid that kills lice, nits and crabs in four minutes. Quite a blessing."

Mr. Blok ordered a cheese sandwich on rye and coffee.

"Did you see Mr. Snok?" Pinkel's policy was to entertain his customers.

"No, I do not know him. Who is he?" asked Mr. Blok.

"Oh, I thought you did. He asked about you the other day. A queer fellow, that Snok. Smart, too, but a little funny sometimes, talks about artificial brains and all sorts of mechanical devices. He has a fancy for keeping strange pets in his house, snakes and frogs. He has screwy ideas about developing in every person a second sex, so everyone can be so to say fifty-fifty — half male, half female. He said one should not have to depend on others and should be perfectly capable of conceiving and bearing a child without help of the opposite sex. Dr. Robin said last week that Snok is crazy."

"What do you think?"

"I am tired of meddling with other people's business. If your Mr. Snok finds pleasure in constructing hermaphrodites, let him. After all, it might be as good as a grapefruit or as bad as — Oh, never mind. Who cares?"

It was not usual for Mr. Blok to address anyone in such a manner, but he disliked gossip and Pinkel's gossipy way.

After eating, he bought some vitamin pills, two cigars, "The Mysterious Poison" by Bob Welldough, two Milky Ways, one Babe Ruth, a magazine and a toothbrush, tidily distributed them in his pockets, and left.

Chapter III

"Please, Mr. Snok, I beg you to come some other time. Don't you see that I am working? You really should have telephoned and asked for an appointment."

"But, Mr. Blok, the druggist told me definitely that I could see you anytime — to just drop in."

"Mr. Pinkel is a fool."

"You see, it is an important matter; my research is vital, not only to you, but also to humanity."

"To me, my work is important. I cannot work and discuss your research at the same time. But what's the use? My day is spoiled already. I guess I'll run around the corner and thank Mr. Pinkel. Huh, Mr. Pinkel, he knows everything — about my time, your research, and your pets. Do you train your little frogs, Mr. Snok?"

"I do sometimes," said Snok with control. He pumped a long breath and settled himself in the only available chair.

"You do?" said Blok.

"Yes, I do, and should it interest you, I am working on oysters, too, though I do not train them. What do you know of oysters?" he shouted, narrowing his eyes.

The sharpness of Snok' s voice shocked Blok, but he said calmly, "Nothing, except I don't eat them during the months which have no R in them."

"I see, I see," said Snok. "Your knowledge must go, so to speak, through your stomach. Very disappointing. Don't you know that an oyster begins its life as a male?"

"Hmm, I presume as yours and mine began."

"Quite true, but what becomes of the oyster after that?"

"I guess it lives," said Blok with a shrug.

"That's right," cried Snok. "Except that the oyster transforms itself into a hermaphrodite and then into a female. We all undergo the same process only it is mental rather than physiological. You understand?"

"No," said Blok.

Narrowing his eyes again Snok said, "So, you don't understand? You who are supposed to express in your art all that the male can understand and the female can feel, as well as all that lies in between?" Mr. Snok went into a very elaborate lecture on sexual transformations and other subjects. But Mr. Blok's never-failing intuition gave him a warning; there would be no end to his dissertation. He must stop him and there was no time to be lost. The only preventative action he could think of was to draw Mr. Snok' s attention to his latest paintings. There were 78 of them, and each and every one had to be placed carefully so as to have the right light, and each was explained in the greatest detail, stroke by stroke, color by color, line by line.

When he was through with them, he prepared to show the canvases of his middle period. Here again, he felt he must make Mr. Snok understand the changes in his style and technique. There were 47 of these. After this was done and the canvases were put back in their places, Mr. Blok got ready to exhibit the very beginning of his artistic development. But to his great surprise and embarrassment, he heard Mr. Snok snoring.

Snok was sleeping soundly in the chair. His tiny head, which grew on the end of an enormously long, thin neck, rested almost on his stomach. Mr. Blok was struck by the idea of painting Mr. Snok. If he would remain long enough in the same position!

Hastily, Mr. Blok put a fresh canvas on the easel, arranged his oils and brushes, and feverishly started to paint. He was so absorbed in his work that he did not notice how the time passed, and only a few finishing strokes were missing when Mr. Snok awoke.

"I guess I fell asleep," he said, rubbing his eyes. "It does not happen to me often," he apologized.

"It does not matter, Mr. Snore. I hope you had a nice rest. Meanwhile, I was painting a little," said Blok, turning the wet side of the canvas against the wall and placing himself in front of it.

It was really unnecessary to hide it, for Mr. Snok would not have looked at it anyway.

Mr. Snok arose and said angrily, "I came here for an important interview with you, the far-reaching significance of which should not be underestimated, even by half-wits. Yet you denied me this interview. I needed important information, but you asked me to leave. Worse yet, you put me to sleep deliberately. I say deliberately because the monotony of your voice and the dullness of your paintings could not have completely escaped your knowledge. My sincere congratulations. You took a part, though in a small way, in retarding the advance of civilization." And, with such unfair accusations, Mr. Snok left.

"The whole future civilization depends upon Mr. Snok," murmured Blok, lifting the wet canvas and fixing it back into the easel. "Imbecile, rooster, no — Snok rhymes better with cock

— hmm, also with Blok," he kept grumbling as he heard a knock at the door. "Who will it be this time?" He shouted, "Come in."

"Oh, it's you," he greeted Bonnie with relief.

"Hi, Teach," said Bonnie, converting her face into two rows of teeth.

"Next time, call me Buddy," said Mr. Blok wryly.

"Why, this is Mr. Snok," she exclaimed, pointing at the portrait.

"An utter failure," she heard him say.

"It's not true," cried Bonnie. "Everything you paint is just wonderful, Mr. Snok and all." Her enthusiasm got lost in his tired face. "Oh, your exhibition will be a great success," she said with exaltation. "You will see, you will remember my prediction."

"Oh God! 'Exhibition' or 'One Man Show'– hard to tell which sounds sillier," said Blok walking away from the easel.

"Mr. Lionshare expects all of your paintings to be delivered to the gallery by Friday," said Bonnie, somewhat injured.

"Awful bother," sighed Blok.

"May I help you, please? There is so much to do." She waited for permission. Blok thanked her frankly. Eager to unload her energy, she swiftly went to work, moving her firm body with great lightness, assembling the paintings according to their size, sorting and leaning them against the wall. Doing this, she spoke incessantly while Mr. Blok eyed her dully.

"Speaking of you the other day, Mr. Snok said that you ought to belong to the Aristocrats of Mind Society. Do you?" Not minding the lack of answer, she twittered, "He is extraordinary, isn't he? And so many sided."

"Must be a learned man," said Blok, looking at his shoes.

"Oh, I am so glad you think so," she said gratefully. "He said that five thousand pederasts had invaded our capitol. Is it true? Mr. Snok doesn't believe, though, that our government is in danger." Apparently, her speech had tired her, for after a deep sigh, she hardly uttered a word until her work was completed.

"Is she naïve or stupid?" wondered Blok after she left the studio. "Oh, I guess just young and trustful. A good girl. Why does she do all this for me? I must do something nice for her." He wanted to think of her the way one wants to repay a long-standing debt. He tried to force back into his mind everything connected with her from the first meeting until today, but his efforts blurred away with persistent elusiveness, bringing him back again and again to her struggles with the same apples. He walked toward the fireplace, and with his foot he pushed an old newspaper under a black, half-burned log, looked at the gray ashes on the tip of his shoe and slowly returned to the easel.

"I must finish the portrait," he thought looking at it. He stepped back a few paces and looked at it again. "Strange, a short while ago I thought it was atrocious," he said aloud. "Bonnie was right – it is good."

In a sudden excitement, he went to the stack of canvases, picked the first one, which was a Siberian landscape, and peered at it scrutinizing. "Brrrr, that snow makes one feel chilly. They will say 'technical devices,' 'Blok's formula' or God knows what." He scratched his ear. "Who cares what they will say. If these atmospheric paintings will not appeal to their minds, they will appeal to their bodies. My tropical landscapes will make them perspire and the wintery ones, shiver." Blok laughed. "It will force them to feel that way." He lifted a small still life of roses from the floor, smelled it, inhaling deeply, and said smiling to himself, "What a sweetness. That will not fail. Perhaps not. What was it Mr. Snok said? Your knowledge goes through your stomach. Hmmmm, strange guy!"

Mr. Blok looked absently away toward the dust-soiled window, on which rain, in the darkness of night, had left smudgy designs. Blok peered through the gray mastodon's body, through a brook with playful and transparent tadpoles, through the delicate branches of a tree, and a woman in a veil until his eyes reached the street where the people hurrying with indifferent lightness along the sidewalks, after hasty meals in drug stores, went back to their monotonous lives.

"Mr. Pinkel, if he were smart, would do like the fellow on the corner of Sixteenth Street – put a sign in front of his drugstore FILL UP FOR A BUCK - DINNERS DELUXE. I'm sure Pinkel could do it for seventy-five cents. I must not forget to speak to him about it," thought Blok, making a note in his little address book.

Then he walked towards his desk, picking up a pile of letters. He turned envelopes in his hand, undecided which to open first. "If people would only mark the envelopes that call for an answer, life would be simpler, and I would not need a desk at all." Suddenly he remembered Rabelais' Gargantua carrying around with him a writing desk weighing more than seven hundred thousand pounds. It made Blok smile. He took a letter from the top of the pile and opened it cheerfully. It was from the "Women's Committee for Promoting Geniuses" inviting him to lecture on his art in Teyton.

"We know," the letter concluded, "that your genius will persevere, and that with our most vigorous support and promotion all your great artistry will shine in glory throughout the century."

Blok accepted the invitation spontaneously, and while he was not quite clear as to the true aims of the committee, he looked forward to the trip and lecture.

"As long as they don't ask me to speak about someone else, it's easy. After all, I'm quite an authority on myself." And with this thought he went to the Frigidaire, drank two glasses of buttermilk, and retired, peaceful and content for the night.

Chapter IV

After a stormy and controversial meeting, the Teyton Women's Committee for Promoting Geniuses had finally agreed to invite Mr. Blok for a lecture on his art. As so often in the past, it was Mrs. Brynow's iron-willed appeal and logical persuasion that made the committee choose Mr. Blok for this engagement. After securing his acceptance, the ladies, who play such an undeniably important part in all cultural matters of the community, were busy arranging Mr. Blok's program during his visit — from his arrival to his departure.

The reception committee was to meet him at the train. Following this, there would be a little breakfast with a few interesting people like Mrs. B. L. Morgan and the recognized connoisseur of modern art, Mrs. H.B. Furgehrson, Jr. (not related in any way to Mrs. H. C. Furgebrson). Arrangements were made for a little sightseeing tour after breakfast, and for dropping into the new post office to greet the postmaster, whose kindness was of great help to the committee.

With the cooperation of Miss Bean, interviews with the *Eagle* and with a reporter and photographer of the *Beacon* were secured following the sightseeing drive. Of course, the arrangements for luncheon at the hotel were of considerable importance — so much so that the luncheon committee, together with the entertainment committee, needed a few meetings to agree upon the menu and the table decorations. Charming Mrs. Bob F. Louis was unanimously elected to make the welcoming speech. Everything was done to make a recording of Mrs. Louis' speech, together with the expected words of thanks from the guest speaker, in order to broadcast them over station ATAY. The spirit of cooperation was admirable.

The youngest (though not the most attractive looking) member of the organization, whose name will not be mentioned here, volunteered to bring Mr. Blok to the party in the lovely new home of Mr. and Mrs. Henry B. Baker. For Mr. Blok's convenience, it was decided to give this reception very early in the afternoon and quite informally. Mr. and Mrs. Baker's generosity was deeply appreciated, and all agreed that their home was just the right place for the occasion.

During one of the meetings, Mrs. Rolsen was bold enough to suggest giving Mr. Blok a little time to prepare himself for the eagerly awaited performance. It was rather cute when Mrs. Froggh said, "Give him some time for a shave, also."

This remark made everyone laugh, with the sole exception of Betty Trum, whose husband's beard was the cause of discussions and all sorts of unpleasant remarks in the community, making Betty detest all conversation dealing with shaving. She simply could not take it casually and now felt rather hurt.

The lecture was expected to be fascinating but tiring for Mr. Blok; therefore, it was important to provide a pitcher of water for the lecturer. This responsibility was entrusted to the ever practical and cheerful Mrs. Samuel Fort Banipompulo.

The fact that on her property there existed a lovely spring assured her election.

Due to the joyful, though rather repetitious, occurrence of Mme. President Matthis' birthday on the day of the lecture, a surprise party was in preparation; and in order to assure complete success they counted not only on Mr. Blok's presence but also on at least one picturesque song from his native country.

It was not a wonder that the attentive ears of the committee heard that Mr. Blok was a native of some foreign country — some said it was Romania, others Hungary — but whatever the country, all indications were that he would deliver a colorful song. Miss Bleak was often acclaimed as one of the most accomplished musicians in town, being particularly proficient in accompanying. Her renditions in solo work and her creative achievements were greatly appreciated also. Mrs. Matthis often said that the performance of her own variations on "Night of Love" will never be forgotten. Miss Bleak was a candidate for the presidency of the Music Division in the Club, and everyone felt that she should be elected; however, future events decided differently and in favor of Mrs. Chonky, but we will speak of that later, or perhaps not at all.

While the whole of Teyton was eagerly awaiting Mr. Blok's arrival and all preparations for his visit were being made, he himself was almost ready for departure. His tuxedo was repaired and was as good as new. A wellstarched white shirt, black evening shoes, vitamin pills, and long underpants, together with everything else needed for a trip, were put in the suitcase – railroad tickets, contract, a few unanswered letters, and naturalization papers were carefully folded and evenly distributed in his pockets. Now it was time to go to the station and he was wondering if Mr. Sonowich from the lecture bureau would come to see him off.

Mr. Blok was a punctual man. He detested those who were incapable of being on time, letting other people wait, and causing not only inconvenience but sometimes even more. He was well aware of his own shortcomings in regard to everyday arrangements, but the penalty was never paid by anyone but himself. There was the great irregularity characteristic of a bachelor's life — there were no meals at regular hours or laundry brought on certain days. His suits were pressed seldom, and he did not see his dentist at pre-arranged intervals. His hair was never cut twice by the same barber, nor were newspapers bought at the same newsstand, and yet he did not do these things purposely. One could go into infinite detail describing all the peculiarities of his life and the absence of some of the most elementary rules and habits that would be the despair of a housekeeper.

Yet Mr. Blok would never let anyone wait for him, and he resented waiting for others. It would be perhaps too mild to call it resentment, for it was really more than that; there was hopelessness and deep melancholy in the meaning of one simple word, "wait."

He had waited once. It was a long time ago, during his adolescence. It was late in the evening when he had come home with a landscape painted for his sister Nina. How did it all start, asked Blok, plunging his thoughts into the still painful past. "It was then that she told me all. I was angry at her for calling me bastard. I hit her."

"I always wanted to tell you why I call you bastard," she said. "Except for Mother, I would have told you a long time ago."

"So tell — speak," I demanded. She told me that I was not born. I screamed and insulted her. With hate, she repeated, "It's true, you were never born. I was born instead — a girl. My father was furious. He had waited and hoped for a son. He wanted an heir to perpetuate something he himself was probably not proud of. But whatever the reason, he brought home, when I was only ten, a bundle of flesh. It was a new-born baby

— dripping and screaming. My father seemed to be pleased, and I saw the worried face of my mother. The mother explained the boy was born to an unfortunate woman in the country who wanted to dispose of it. It was you! Very simple, you see. Already then, looking at you, in the crib I hated you and called you bastard. Do you think father loved you? Stupid." Blok could hear her voice as if she actually stood in front of him.

"Do you remember the broken vase? Well, it was I who broke it deliberately. The stolen money? I took it. The chicken house on the farm. I burned it. Remember? Father's ruined supply of cigars? I ruined them. I loved seeing you spanked. I wanted them to hate you as much as I hated you." She laughed. "I succeeded, but only partly. I wanted to destroy you. I have something in store for you," she whispered. "I made them believe you are going with women already. They think you are quite a kid." She laughed hideously. "Mother still loves you. She can't help it. No one listens to her anyway. I told them you know that I am not really your sister. I also told Father I am pregnant. I really am. The major is married, and he will never acknowledge my pregnancy. I know, for I spoke with him about it. I told Father after you left for school, it was you — that you are the father of the baby." Her words hammered at his head. "Yes, dirty bastard," she screamed. "He is coming home, you hear?"

I hit her again and again. I could not stop, even when Father stood in the door. I could not stop, though I felt the strong arm of Father and heard his words, spoken with incredible hatred. The words which still made my heart and blood burn.

"Out — get out. Never come back."

Blok put his fingers in his ears, not wanting to hear, not wanting to remember.

The night had been cold and dark. A wind was blowing, and the sinister voices of howling dogs came from the distance. He stood and waited. The lights were going out, and yet he knew a voice would soon say, "Come in." It was his home, his family — he belonged there. Bewildered, he waited, he hoped. The wind was biting, but he did not move. With the dawn the pain was gone, and with every step bringing him nearer to the unknown, he began to walk....

"Come in, Mr. Sonowich. It's nice of you to come."

"Nothing at all, Mr. Blok. It's my pleasure — it's nice of you to let me take you to the train. Quite frisky tonight, isn't it? But I like it. Are you ready to go? We don't have too much time, and there are many things to talk over. I kept the taxi waiting. Yes, Mr. Blok, your future manager thinks of everything! The minute I heard from our sales manager that you were being engaged for the lecture in Teyton, I called you right away. Sonowich's lecture bureau is entirely at your service. There is no doubt you have heard of us being the most powerful bureau in the country."

He picked up Mr. Blok's suitcase and, as they walked to the taxi, continued: "We handle the most prominent lecturers in the world — names like Factotum, Kindsneeper, and Milton Power, and many others have had exclusive contracts with us. Speakers like Prince Abbis or Professor Snok belong to our little family, and we hope to have the honor to include you also. But to talk business, I must tell you off hand, that we treat everyone alike and do not play favorites; so, for a mere 50 percent commission every lecturer is looked after with the same consideration and the best of care. We are promoters in the highest sense of the word. By the way, what book of yours was published lately?"

"Mine? I am an artist — painter," said Mr. Blok.

"Oh, of course; you are going to talk in Teyton on Picasso?"

"No, on myself."

"I understand — very interesting. Splendid! We understand each other, I am quite certain."

As they stood on the station platform, Mr. Sonowich said quite suddenly, "Here is the contract. It's standard — you can sign it right away, or if you wish, read it first. But this is not really necessary, as our contracts are, as I said before, all perfectly standard," and he handed Mr. Blok an important-looking document just at the moment the train began to move. Sonowich spoke quickly — there was no time to lose — "You are a wonderful speaker, I'm sure, but if I may give you some advice: the success of a lecturer lies in what happens before and after the performance. Do not forget that women, and women only, are the backbone of our business —the mothers, daughters and grandmothers — they are as kind as they are powerful. Your personality and charm will make them enthusiastic, and as a result they will re-engage you." By this time Sonowich was walking rapidly to keep up with the train. "Please smile at them — smile before the performance as much as you possibly can. Smile during the lecture, and after, praise their spirit and energy; but as I said before, above all, smile — smile as if you had just caught a big fish. That kind of smile will never fail. Goodbye, see you soon!" Sonowich was running by now.

"Is the Professor Snok you spoke of C.R. Snok?" Mr. Blok shouted. But he did not hear the answer.

Chapter V

Mr. Blok carefully folded his coat and settled himself in the reserved space, Lower 7, but after a while had to look for the men's room because of the discomfort caused by his ever-persistent hemorrhoids. God knows, he thought, this illness has no glamor, and it is hard to find real sympathy and understanding among fellow beings. Some people find the mere mention of it offensive, but on the other hand, there are some who make fun of it with their tactless wisecracks. Why, there are brutes who call it "piles" and are shameless enough to advertise in the newspapers all sorts of useless cures. Even physicians do not have the proper respect for it; and though it is an open secret that a great many distinguished people suffered from it — people about whom scores of books have been written and for whom monuments have been erected, geniuses, whose lives, sufferings and joys have been described, interpreted and analyzed in historical works — you will never find a description of it. Like a great conspiracy, everyone in the past agreed to keep it unmentioned, and ignore it. In the future it will also probably be too undignified to speak openly and sympathetically of it. Thus, Mr. Blok sadly mused as he entered, first through the curtain and then through the steel door, the men's room. Knowing how to help himself in such an emergency, he soon felt better, and though he was not a smoker, decided to take a seat near the window and remain, for the time being, in the smoking room.

It is difficult to evaluate people at a first encounter. But in contrast, it is quite permissible to have certain feelings and reactions toward a stranger. This has, by the way, been proven in 19,678 novels and by innumerable happenings in life, when love or hate may occur at first sight. But it is quite under-standable that there could not be a question of love at first sight in the surroundings in which Mr. Blok found himself, for everyone knows that women are not to be found in the men's room of a Pullman.

There was a man smoking a White Owl cigar, accumu-lating saliva with extraordinary rapidity, which made him spit every two or three seconds. His aim was remarkable, for not once did he miss the spittoon which stood near Mr. Blok's feet and comparatively far away from the gentleman. He was not alone. There was a traveling companion with him, a husky fellow wearing a Texan hat. A heavy gold chain with all sorts of good luck pieces hung across his stomach. He smoked a pipe and did not spit at all but laughed often and without ap-parent reason. Mr. Blok thought he could be a cousin, uncle, or a neighbor of Cactus Jack, or perhaps a Congressman or a horse dealer. But after listening to their conversation for a while, a new idea came to Mr. Blok. They are from the South, that's what it is. Of course, they must be Southerners — a rare kind, though — sort of intellectuals. One of them is anyhow, thought Blok. It was easy to arrive at this conclusion for they discussed literature, which is the most pleasant thing to do in a men's room, providing one does not have a book or at least a newspaper to read.

Then he heard one of them say, "Those writers, with their love for Goddamned niggers, those wastrels — wasting their talent and paper. Why they publish that stuff, we'll never understand. They ought to own my plantation for a couple of years, and you can bet your life they would stop kissing those bastards' behinds." At this moment, he spit, missing the spittoon by half an inch. Apologizing, he threw away his cigar and continued.

But Mr. Blok did not want to hear any more and returned to Lower 7. He felt, as on other similar occasions, a stranger in this vast country. Fortunately, these feelings were of short duration.

He opened his suitcase and took out a book. It was *I, Too, Nicodemus* by Curtis Bok. Like all honest people, he started to read from the beginning, which was a preface. But he was too tired to concentrate on it and soon fell asleep with the book on his lap.

Half an hour later, when the conductors on their rounds arrived at Lower 7, something unusual happened — as a matter of fact, something unheard of in the whole history of the honorable, though far from perfect, Pennsylvania Railroad Company. The conductors were so touched by the cherub-like expression of Mr. Blok's sleeping face — so deeply moved by his helpless confidence, like that of a child — that they silently agreed not to disturb his peace with routine formalities. They moved away walking on tiptoe, their faces expressing all the tenderness of a young mother. When they were far enough away, they shook each other's hands, saying that in decades of faithful service, they had never felt so grateful because their hearts had not become hardened by their monotonous profession. When they had collected all the tickets from one end of the train to the other and were seated in an empty drawing room arranging them, they both (thinking of the same thing) jumped from their seats and said in unison, "We will give him this drawing room." With the joy or schoolchildren, they slapped each other on the shoulder and with animation made plans to give him this present.

"But what if he turns out to be one of the company inspectors?" the conductor asked cautiously. He was a Pullman conductor who in 29 years of service had earned respect for his conscientiousness and sense of duty. They decided to wait and see, agreeing on the danger of a too hasty action.

Their first step was to consult the porter. Both conductors were amazed at the information they received. "I think the passenger in Lower 7 is in danger. The two men in the men's room," he said, "have been talking loudly and drinking. They took a violent dislike to the man in Lower 7, and I'm scared of the way they threatened to teach him a lesson for walking out on them when they spoke about colored folks. The one with the cowboy hat said he thinks the man is one of the lawyers whom he saw at the Atlanta lynching case. Yes sir, it's awful the names they called him. They came right to Lower 7 and, while the man was asleep, looked him over and asked me where the bastard was going. They're after him, I'm telling you," concluded the porter, leaving to make beds.

Now the conductors knew that not only were their beautiful impulses to be followed, but far more important, the slogan of the company — "Safety First" — was at stake. There must be no scandal. They had to act and act before it was too late. Calling the porter again, they asked him to make up the bed in the drawing room at once. When that was done, the three of them went to Lower 7. They addressed Mr. Blok; they touched him; they even pinched him slightly — but to no avail.

He was asleep. Not since the time that Bonnie had undressed him had he slept so deeply. Meanwhile, voices coming from the men's room were growing heated, helping the conductors make a final decision. The porter lifted Mr. Blok's legs while the conductors carefully gripped his body, and thus they carried him into the drawing room and placed him on the bed.

In his dream, he heard deafening noises. Shots — from afar — on a late afternoon in one of those streets in Moscow, still wet with the tears from the time of Ruric.

It was the revolution — a hunt, a hunt for Whites and Reds. Oh, what a hunting ground! The mice of yesterday were the tigers of today; the rats were biting and rabbits barking like hyenas.

Now Mr. Blok opened his eyes, and perspiration dripped from his forehead. He looked around but did not know where he was. He did not seem to care, letting his thoughts wander at random. Tomorrow, I have my first lecture. What can I say on my art? I should have brought my paintings; they would speak for themselves. It's silly to talk about oneself. I will start like this: Ladies and gentlemen, thank you so much for giving me an opportunity to speak about myself and my art, which is, by the way, one and the same thing, for I belong to my art. We are a unit, an indivisible whole; yet I know art is higher than I, and, since it is inaccessible, I have to climb after it. But the faster I climb, the higher it goes, until I must slow my pace and wait for it to descend, to come near me, to let me caress it, to play with it. And then an unbelievable thing happens, ladies and gentlemen — the art actually does lower itself to reach my level, so that I can touch it; but it cannot fool me, for I know it is really I who lower my level. It's I who become weak and impotent and resent the effort. Man knows compromise, but art, never.

It is big and demanding and always pure, and it hates to be talked about. If art could speak our language, it would kill me for being here and would destroy all art critics; but it will not punish you, the public, the collectors of art and the listeners, because you are innocent and humble. Art will wait for you until you grow up, for art hates all haste and hurry. It is patient and supreme, like a mountain, and does not need your praise. Yes, ladies and gentlemen — or let's say 'ladies' because I do not see any gentlemen present at this lecture — yes, what I want to say is that art welcomes your immaturity, preferring you to the professionals, for you are ahead of them — I mean one generation ahead of critics. This, mind you, honored ladies, is not my opinion, but Mr. Bernard Shaw's. I merely quote his words. He goes as far as to say, "Should I want to sleep for twenty-five years I should wake up pretty level with contemporary criticism."

But on the other hand, you do not need to fall asleep because you are asleep. You are dormant, although one hears at times of a few alert ones."

And then a thought shot through Mr. Blok's head. What if they should object and demand that I stop? What would I do? Would they be bold enough to stop my lecture? At the idea alone Blok was angered. I know what I would do then. I would ask them if they want a story.... You want a story? A love story, or murder, or perhaps something shocking or scandalous, preferably about people you know, or just something about famous people? No, my dear friends, I would say, I am not speaking for your entertainment. I am not lecturing, either, on any particular subject. This is not my purpose; for that matter, there is no purpose at all.

And I assure you, I am not looking for listeners either.

It would be an unpardonable madness to hope to find one. There are no good listeners anymore. The last ones, whom Joseph Conrad allowed to listen to his "Lord Jim," are all dead.

God bless them! There is a great demand nowadays for listeners. They are needed badly. One flatters them; one promises them all sorts of great things. Politicians promise them prosperity; comedians entertain them. So do musicians, publishers, the radio, the movies, the summer resorts, airways, steamship companies, museums in France, in Spain and Italy; the comic syndicates, dance bands, sport organizations, symphony orchestras and even schools. All want a public — listeners, customers — and all try to lure them.

But alas! Too many false promises have made the listener alert and suspicious. It has become harder to entertain him and almost impossible to hold his attention for any length of time. The worthwhile listener is seldom bored, for he knows what to take, what to absorb, what to eliminate.

The western movies need action; cheap books, a plot; bad composers, thematic material; and poor painters, beautiful views. I warn you, my friends, by refusing to listen to me you condemn yourself; you lower your dignity to that of the average entertainment hunter, and include yourself in the family of all those who want to escape the mental effort for higher pleasures in exchange Bingo games, and comics. Furthermore, by not being listeners, you will compel me to write a book, for one way or another, I must get accumulated and disturbing elements out of my system.

But in whatever state you may be, it seldom affects us artists. Why, I myself derived great inspiration once from an individual who fell asleep sitting in a chair while looking at a few of my pictures. Pray do not be offended by my calling you dormant — there is no offense meant — for it is a joy to watch the soothing effect art is capable of making.

No, my dear ladies, one does not have to be an inferior artist to put you to sleep. A critic also should never react in this manner to artists' efforts, for those noble men are not looking for pleasure — their own or anyone else's; and furthermore, they are not paid for such silent manifestations.

Oh, after that they will never want to interrupt me again. They will realize how easily they could have excluded themselves from the true elite and the society of connoisseurs.

Mr. Blok was delighted with the clarity of his ideas and the flow of his speech. There was, as at all previous moments of satisfaction, a big smile on his face.

But at that moment, a tremendous jerk of the train, followed by some still stronger, brought the train to a rough stop with an ugly noise. It knocked Mr. Blok to the floor, and in this manner, he was brought back to reality.

Chapter VI

In a perpetual blur, the wintry landscape passed before Mr. Blok's eyes, with trees in their naked dignity rising from the frozen round. In great monotony, the colors changed from gray to darker gray as the bus raced along the depressing straightness of the highway.

But Blok did not mind the route his bus had chanced to take, nor the bare fields and dead cornstalks which raced by as the bus rattled on. Perhaps there was a certain similarity of his mood to the barren country he passed through that prompted his alliance with it, or just a feeling of lesser annoyance to find his surroundings gloomy.

"Queer fish," he had overheard a lady saying, pointing to him after the lecture in Teyton, while another added, "a stuporous stultifier" or something similar. And yet they almost made me believe in the success of my lecture. They were all so sweet to my face... "You must, you simply must come to us again," Blok heard their words in his head.

He hated to think about his lecture, receptions, sightseeing rides, the post office, or the president's birthday party, but above all he felt bitter against Sonowich's advice to smile....

I certainly followed his instructions, I almost smiled myself to death — and he remembered the long receiving line after the lecture when he stood sandwiched between intro-ducing ladies who not once omitted the middle letter of the 475 names they presented to him. They tried to plant these names deep into his memory, repeating and spelling each one until they saw a reassuring smile on his face. This smile never left until after several hours, exhausted and green with fatigue, he saw it in the mirror of his room, and only when he forced the grin from his face did he recognize himself.

The bus, filled to capacity with shaking and jolted citizens, stopped at Middlesex Junction, which was a food market, drug-store and post office. That wondrous phenomenon, the bus driver, pressed a button, and the door automatically opened to let out a few creatures who in their innocence made their homes in Middlesex Junction.

The bus driver announced a ten-minute stop, and Mr. Blok went out with the others. It was windy and cold, and the hard-frozen dust hit at the bus while pieces of frozen dirt rolled into the doorway of the store.

Blok found himself in a drugstore with a stove burning coal in the center. He stuffed his pockets with Kleenex tissues and bought several newspapers. Passing around the stove, he overheard two boys praising Hopalong Cassidy and one de-fending the Lone Ranger, until all three were disagreeably inter-rupted by a bass voice singing of an enchanted evening through a loudspeaker installed above the door of the men's room.

Behind the counter stood a man with a baby face, sucking the butt of a cigar that looked like a nipple. The man had an expression as if he were about to ask a question, but as Blok passed the counter twice, he only followed him with his cu-rious and sleepy eyes.

Back in the bus again, Blok settled himself in his seat at the window and glanced through the newspaper. Turning the page and brushing his neighbor with the paper, Blok apologized. He folded the paper more carefully, blew his nose in a Kleenex, made a small ball of it, and after disposing of it under the seat, was ready to go on with his reading.

But there was not much in it to hold his attention, and as he considered drawing Mrs. Bleek of Teyton by memory, his eyes fell on a headline which made him jump.

"Aren't you feeling well?" angrily muttered the lady who sat next to him. "You knocked off my hat, and my doughnut fell on the floor." He heard her from below as she searched for the lost articles.

"Sorry, tremendously sorry," said Blok, trying not to step on her hand or the doughnut.

She got up and with a sigh of relief planted her hat back where it belonged and said something about homemade doughnuts and pies, but Blok was too absorbed in reading to listen. His hands began to tremble slightly as his eyes ran over the lines. He read them again and again with increased excitement. Throwing one newspaper on the floor, he unfolded the other, went feverishly through the pages and, pointing with his thumb to a column, said loudly, "Here it is again! Those stuffed gophers. Look at it, please," and placing the paper on the lady's lap, he began to run through the pages of a third newspaper. There the headline, in still bigger type, seemed to enrage him further. Blok was in a fury, as only a kind man can be, and he so wanted to cry for help rather than call for vengeance.

"Look here!" he said to the lady with the hat who peered at the headlines:

"SENSATIONAL EXHIBITION ORDERED CLOSED"

"LADIES PROSTRATE AT TROPICAL LANDSCAPES EXHIBIT"

"ARTIST PAINTS UGLY PORTRAIT - SUED FOR A MILLION DOLLARS".

It continued: "Mr. C. R. Snok, according to his attorney, Mr. K. S. Kospick, was lured into the studio of the well-known artist Blok, who, deliberately and maliciously put him to sleep and, taking advantage of his helplessness, kidnapped him on canvas, later to put it on the market for sale."

Not finishing the article, the lady offered Mr. Blok a doughnut, collected her packages, and left the bus at the next stop. I will never see her again thought Blok — never, never – and wiped the perspiration from his face.

Upon Blok's arrival home, the janitor handed him several messages. "Very important," he said looking worriedly at Blok. "There were people asking for you. They came at all hours of the day and night."

Blok hurried up into his studio. He found many messages and letters under his door, but he hardly glanced at them.

He was irritated and tired from the trip, but as he began to unpack his suitcase, there was a knock at the door and soon after a short and extremely thin man entered.

"My name is Kospick. K as in Holofernes, 0 as in Justice, S as in Crime, hah, hah, hah," he laughed noisily and then very abruptly, "Your name is Blok?"

"How do you do, sir."

He cleared his throat. "My client, Mr. C. R. Snok, has empowered me as his attorney to make a settlement of the matter about which you already know. I mean — before the case goes to court."

"I know, I know! I read the ridiculous charges," said Blok with impatience. "Your client would have liked me to make him as pretty as Madame de Poitiers, no doubt."

"Please," reprimanded Kospick, "jokes aside."

"Vanitas vanitatum," said Blok.

"Please speak English," objected Kospick. "A million-dollar suit is not a joke, and unless you agree to burn the disfigured portrait publicly, make proper apologies, and offer your body for scientific research — after death of course — we quite justly will proceed with our charges." He looked at Blok's worried face, paused and continued somewhat tersely, "I know, sir, you will agree the deal is only fair. Please sign this agreement. It will settle the matter legally. Here it is." He handed a paper to Mr. Blok.

"Splendid, you want only my corpse, the cremation of only one picture, a few nice words, and my signature. It seems almost too modest." He then took a pen and without reading the paper wrote with quick strokes on the bottom:

> There was an old fellow named Snok
>
> Whose features resembled a cock
>
> Blok had a plan…
>
> To make him a man…
>
> Yet It's Snok who wants Blok in the dock.
>
> Sincerely yours,
>
> Hortense Pumpernickel

"That's fine," said Mr. Kospick, taking the paper. "Peaceful settlement like this is the only reasonable thing to do. By destroying the portrait, you will not destroy the fame it brought you. It was a joy to know you." And folding the paper carefully, shaking Blok's hand in a most amiable manner, he left the studio.

"A drenched game-cock," muttered Blok as he turned to answer the ringing telephone. "Hello, hello — yes, it's Blok speaking. Who? I can't hear. Hello…." He dropped the receiver and went to his desk. He saw an envelope with a Honduran stamp on it. He opened it and read: "Dear Mr. Blok: Your son Stephan is on his way to you. Hoping you find him in excellent health, Sincerely yours, L. P. B. W. Cheezis, Sr." That was all. Blok read it twice, put it in his pocket, took it out again, and read once more. "Strange," thought Blok, puzzled. Slowly he walked out into the street to refresh himself.

The moment he started toward the Square, he was approached by two men. "You are Mr. Blok, aren't you?"

"I am," said Blok startled.

"We are deputies of the Aristocrats of Mind Society. It's an important matter."

"Perhaps it is," said Blok with irritation, "but I am busy. I have an appointment. Perhaps I can see you some other time."

"No, sir, it cannot wait. You have to come with us. It is an order."

"Order? Let me alone. What do you want from me?" screamed Blok hoarsely.

"Calm yourself; it is in your own interest. The Grand Aris gave orders to bring you to Mr. Mlauzinski."

"Who is Aris ?"

"He is the Grand Apostle of the Aristocrats of Mind Society. It's too bad you don't know it," the big man said with a sad and resigned voice.

"It will be very unfortunate for you and for us should you refuse to come with us," said the short man with a quiver in his voice.

"I am sorry, gentlemen, I don't want to hurt anybody, and if I can be of some help… well… I will go with you."

There was great joy on the faces of the two men. But the exaggeration with which they shook his hand made him almost regret his consent. The big man's hand was flabby and wet and just strong enough to lift Mr. Blok's arm in the air, let it fall, and then lift it again an unnecessary number of times.

During this procedure, he introduced himself, stuttering, "Mr. Ondra. Very happy. Thanks. Ondra is my name."

The handshake of the other, whose name was Miller, was firm and strong. It snapped Blok's hand with the grip of a snare.

"Oh, you hurt me," cried Blok.

"Very sorry," said Miller and, as if having difficulty in losing his grip, still held his hand. Not until Mr. Ondra reprimanded him – "The Aris forbids you to shake hands." – did he let Mr. Blok's hand free. The three men walked toward the Square, crossed, went two blocks to the right, and soon stopped at the Professional Building. "Here you are," said Mr. Ondra. "Mr. Mlauzinski will not keep you long. We will wait for you right here."

Mr. Blok stood before an oversized desk, speaking to Mr. Mlauzinski, his attorney. "Your case needs study and long preparation," said Mlauzinski, shifting his wet cigar to the opposite corner of his mouth. His bulging eyes and the timbre of his voice were revolting. "You see, Mr. Blok, you should not have written on the settlement document, but never mind… all depends not only on the existing laws but also on the interpretation of such. Here, and only here, we must find the weakness in their case. There is no doubt they will try to base their argument on Article 87 of the Criminal Code as amended in the state of Ohio, but be quiet and leave it all to me. Let me worry. The Aristocrats of Mind Society have paid me a little retainer — to grease the wheels a bit — of $1400.00. Or course, a million-dollar suit will run pretty high as the case progresses. Never mind — the main thing is to beat them! Mlauzinski knows how to do that! You just leave it to me. Yes sir, one has to know one's business, and, of course, have connections. Connections, so to speak, are like a live bridge for crossing a stormy river. Do you know my dear friend, Judge Thigh? No? A great man! Too bad that those cowardly rascals, those envious bloodhounds and hypocrites, made him appear to be involved in the slot machine business so that he had to resign from the bench. Before an important case, it was he who once told me Napoleon's axiom: 'To win a battle, one needs only three things –money, money and money.' Ha! Ha! Ha!" He almost choked himself, his cigar fell out of his mouth; and his rippling stomach made cigar ashes roll to the floor.

Mr. Blok was tired. He had had no breakfast and was in an irritable mood, but above all he resented standing so long and listening to Mlauzinski, angry not to have been offered a seat. He was startled when he heard Mr. Mlauzinski yelling, "Can't you hear me? What's the matter with you? I said your share of the retainer can wait until tomorrow — I mean for your convenience —preferably in cash, if you don't mind."

"Of course, of course," said Blok, absent-mindedly.

"Tomorrow, or perhaps a little later. In a few days, if I have time and money. Everything came so suddenly — I mean the lawsuits and other things. There was also a letter this morning. It turned out to be about my son. I never realized I had one. It's all so confusing. But I will not take your time up anymore. You have been most kind. I really appreciate your sincere interest. I do hope to see you in a comparatively short time or perhaps even sooner — it all depends. I am sure you understand." He shook Mr. Mlauzinski's hand and left the office saying, "I also have only one chair in my studio."

As soon as the two men saw Mr. Blok come, they rushed to him, asking anxiously if Mr. Mlauzinski had accepted the case. "He did," said Blok gloomily.

"How wonderful. Now we must hurry. Mr. Ellis is waiting for us."

"I am rather tired. As you know, I just arrived this morning. Could we perhaps arrange something for another day?" Both men seemed to be shocked at the idea of the postponement. "You can't do that," said Mr. Ondra, as he took Mr. Blok by the arm and started to walk. Blok did not resist.

"What is the Aristocrats of Mind Society?" he asked feebly.

"Our Society is the movement of noble thoughts that in name of beauty places itself above accepted rules. It seeks the truth from wherever it comes," said Mr. Miller with great persuasion.

"But who decides what is the beautiful truth?" asked Blok.

"We do," said Miller.

Mr. Ondra explained, "You see, the truth is so highly subjective that all our efforts for objectivity had to be abandoned. In our offices are the statistics of one million one-handed, half-nosed, one-footed, eyeless, mouthless, cheekless, stomachless, and toothless as well as assless combatants who, after losing their accessories in various wars, holy and otherwise, became quite subjective in their thoughts and feelings."

"The Great Aris will not be pleased with the wording and style you have chosen to describe our aims and principles," remarked Mr. Miller as they entered the Aristocrats of Mind Society Building.

Chapter VII

Mr. Blok and the two men walked through the long corridor and, without knocking on the door, entered an extraordinarily large hall which was quite bare, with no curtains on the windows or carpets on the floor. They crossed the hall, at the end of which was found another door. Mr. Ondra sniffed the air and looking at Blok asked," Smell something?"

Blok also sniffed and said, "I smell coffee; I think it's Brazilian."

"For heaven's sake" said Ondra, "Don't mention this to the Great Aris; he despises Brazilian coffee and drinks only Turkish." He whispered confidentially, "I'll tell you something. Mr. Ellis once had an Egyptian mistress who is now the widow of a Turkish prince, and she sends him her inherited allotment of the precious royal coffee. You will never believe, sir, that the color on that black coffee is white. To cook it right takes, I believe, over seventy-five minutes," he said, sniffing again admiringly. As he was about to knock on the door it was opened suddenly from the inside, and they saw a tall man who said bad-humoredly, "Ondra, you ought to know by now that cases like that of Mr. Blok do not belong to this entrance. But it does not matter now. Will you come in, please?"

This time Blok walked in first. "My name is Blok," he said. "Never mind, never mind," Ellis repeated absently.

The room was small and cozy, with strangely mixed furnishings of a business office and a boudoir, and fresh flowers on small tables and pink covers on soft chairs. Mr. Ellis gave the impression of being a combination of disciplinarian, executive, politician and poet, or a lady's fashion designer. His bushy eyebrows fascinated Mr. Blok, making him forget to look above them at Ellis' graying hair, or below at his yellowishbrown eyes, or his well-formed, womanish mouth and his unhealthy teeth. "I will be frank with you," he said, moving his eyebrows: "We were strongly in favor of electing you as an honorable member of our Society, having in mind one day to see you in the Chair as Aris Superior of the West. Well, as I say, we all had a high esteem for you as an artist and as a man. Having in mind the coming General Assembly, we were preparing the ground for your election and were rejoicing over the possibility of having you with us. Just then we received the unfortunate information of your having abandoned your own child. At first we were skeptical at the news, but the lamentable facts were against you."

Blok sat in the chair and listened in bewilderment as Ellis continued. "I promised you to be frank, so I will lay all the cards before you. We have a letter, dated and properly signed in our possession. If you wish, I will read it to you."

Taking an envelope from a chest of drawers, he cleared his throat and said, "It's addressed to our Civil Tribunal, and signed by the Great Aris of Honduras, Mr. Cheezis, who is also the new chairman of the Committee for Anti-Honduran Activities."

Then he read:

"Dear Fellow Aristocrats:

I regret that I cannot give my consent to bestowing upon Mr. Blok the honorary membership of our Society, as you desired. After a thorough investigation, there is no doubt in our minds that the said Mr. Blok is the father of an illegitimate child. Please allow me to state his case briefly. About twenty years ago, a lady by the name of Miss Natalia Ivanowva Kropushnikowa emigrated to our country. She had a two-year-old son with her, whose father, she admitted, was a certain Mr. Blok. She was never able to locate him and died heartbroken and in poverty.

Her boy, however, whom we call Stepan, grew big and strong, and at the age of ten had already become a fine bonebreaker. At that age, cracking the neckbone of an adult sheep took him no more than a minute. Now he can master a fair-sized bull barehanded. However, his intellectual development proceeded rather slowly, and he needs good schooling. He showed interest in the United States and knows of the George Washington Bridge and the death of Senator Bilbo. Therefore, I am seriously urging all fellow Aristocrats to help bring the boy to his father, whose repentant conscience (let us hope) will make a human being out of a scoundrel.

Sincerely,
The Grand Aris of Honduras
L. P. B. W. Cheezis."

As if to soften the effect of these embarrassingly harsh words, Ellis said, "We nicknamed Mr. Cheezis 'the lump in the throat.'" But no one smiled, and Blok did not speak. After a short pause Ellis asked, "Did you do it deliberately? Didn't you love her and your child?" Then, very sharply: "When did you first start making love to women?" When Blok did not answer promptly, he shot at him: "When? With whom? Where? Does the word 'Funzapoppin' mean anything to you?"

And when Blok said, "No, nothing at all," Ellis came close to him and said with great feeling.

"Please tell us. All of us made mistakes in our youth, but upon reaching maturity we face those mistakes courageously. Your resistance will hurt us deeply." Blok's eyes wandered from Ondra to Ellis, to the desk and along the walls, returned to the desk and rested on a little frame inside of which he read the letters in silver and gold: "The one who knows the secret does not speak; the one who speaks does not know the secret." It was signed "Lao-Tse."

"There it is! There is written the answer!" cried Blok agitatedly, pointing to the frame.

Ellis shrugged his shoulders and said warmly, "Please don't be upset. The truth is we do believe in you strongly. We admire you as much as we disapprove of Mr. Snok's action against you." He stood up and pronounced solemnly, "With all our power, we will defend you. We will protect you and fight for you, and as the charges against you accumulate, we will double our efforts." He tapped Blok in a friendly manner on the shoulder and continued, "From now on, we will take complete charge and responsibility for your safety. You will not be alone."

At this point he ordered Ondra to bring some papers, and as Ondra handed him a neat folder with documents, Ellis exclaimed, "There they are, those brazen rascals. You see these?" He showed Blok a paper. "It's from the lawyer of the two women claiming damages for the sun stroke at your exhibition." And then, "Ha, look at these here, the charges of the professional escort," and he read a sequence from it. "… the fine Knize Gabardine suit (double-breasted) was completely

ruined by sea gull droppings at the Atmospheric Exhibit…"
Mr. Ellis moved his eyebrow vigorously and said, "There are of
course, many other charges, some of which are of a grave and
menacing character, but with nothing are we concerned more
keenly than with your bastardy case."

Now he spoke softly and confidentially. "I promised to
be frank. There is a suspicion of a dangerous plot threatening
you." Almost whispering, he went on. "Even the case of your
paternity has some fishy loopholes. Our Executive Chairman,
Mr. Van Horn, who personally went to Honduras to investi-
gate, wired this morning that there was never known a person
named Kropushnikowa."

"I assure you that I was never the father of any bone-
breaking boy in Honduras or anywhere else."

"Rest assured, I believe you. At the same time, I want you
to realize the danger in which you now find yourself. They are
after your atmospheric formula and will stop at no lengths
to get it. Don't forget the General Freezing Company has a
mighty hand. Your life is in danger! Your life is now our cause!
The best and most reliable people have been assigned by the
Society to guard and protect it. They are already in your studio
waiting for you, and I know you will love them. And now, we
will have some coffee."

Mr. Ellis pulled on a string, and Mr. Blok saw a gracefully
shaped container descend smoothly from the ceiling and place
itself on a little table. The aroma of the coffee was exquisite,
but Mr. Blok's thoughts were too pressing and anxious to allow
him to fully enjoy the drink. Mr. Ellis must have noticed this,
for after a few sips of coffee he said, "Now go home — bless
you!"

Blok walked wearily from the building. His heart was
throbbing as if it wanted to break itself loose and fly away to

lands where feelings are not punished with guilt, where joy is delightful and memory short, where no one is expected to be grateful and where the heart is not ruled by the head. Oh, wonderful youth! What sweet reveries. Why must one be defeated by the bothersome facts of the day, so sober and cruel? And my child — how absurd. I almost wish it were mine. Kropushnikowa... Natalia... Nata... Natashinka... hmmmmm! Why Funsapoppin?

Chapter VIII

It was decided — it had to be big or nothing. Therefore, with the cooperation of all leading writers and poets, the most extraordinary appeal was sent to numerous individuals with an invitation to the Preassembly Conference. The wording and the style of the appeals varied as greatly as the persons to whom they were addressed. Even the paper on which they were written varied in quality and size: some were written by hand, others in the form of a poem; some printed and some typewritten. A summons was sent to three of Mr. Blok's oldest and best friends, Abka Perk, Alexander, and Blum.

After several months of hard, though pleasant work, all the invitations were ready for mailing, and all concerned proudly congratulated themselves upon their honorable and gratifying effort.

Considering the importance of Mr. Blok's impending trial, the greatest care was taken in choosing those who should be present to witness and judge for themselves, for the best interests of humanity's spiritual progress and general justice toward the intellect were at stake. Therefore, the invitations were sent, to name just a few, to: masseurs and managers, sculptors, philanthropists and magicians, janitors and bridge experts, priests, bankers and engravers, shirt manufacturers and clarinetists, music critics, printers, upholsterers and chess players, nurses, teachers and postmasters, surgeons, brokers and prize-fighters, dentists, trainers and corsetieres, druggists, telephone operators, a great many chairmen and a few presidents, curators, one apiarist, undertakers, and above all, two thaumaturgists. The telegrams were sent to ten lexicographers and two ichthyologists, to one orchestra conductor and a few entomologists and astrologers. For no apparent reason, Alcoholics Anonymous and the Presbyterians were omitted. The poem sent to a pedicurist was so effective that it was decided to make several copies, one of each to be sent to a bartender, a philosopher, and the supervisor of a corrugated box company. It went as follows:

"The man of spirit is accused;

He is the victim of our time.

His tender feelings are abused

By those whose souls are worth a dime."

Two physicians, a nurse, two bodyguards, and one lawyer were assigned to watch over Mr. Blok, and one young but extremely capable psychiatrist was completely at his disposal, sharing with him the same room and bed. With the exception of Mr. Blok, all were active members of the Aristocrats of Mind Society. Though Mr. Blok himself was deeply interested in the noble aims of the society, he did not entirely approve of it. He based his objection on the existence of differences in the interpretation of the word "aristocrat."

Its history was too full of pirates, brigands, rapists, and arsonists. Such were the founders of that exquisite clan, which by growing in size and power grew in ferocity and brutality. They defended their high position with all the means available — and these were not noble deeds, self-sacrifices, or heroic acts.

The sword and poison were their proud tradition. On the other hand, there were other interpretations, and some of them were based on scholarly facts and centuries-long research and were presented in such a scientific, specialized, scholarly, and detailed manner that Mr. Blok had to admit his information on the matter was inadequate.

The busiest and most unpleasant hour of the day was Mr. Blok' s awakening in the morning. He profoundly disliked a crowd — any crowd — and the crowded condition in his own studio became unbearable to him. He felt bitterly abused — far more by his roommates than by all the trials and accusations.

Never before had he allowed anyone to spend a night there. In defending his privacy and freedom, he was a fanatic, a miser, and a bachelor. For this he was ready to sacrifice all. He felt disgust at every contact with the hairy breast or legs of the psychiatrist during the night, and in the morning, he invariably found himself completely uncovered, all the covers having been pulled to the side of that apostle of mental hygiene. Besides his inconvenience in bed, there were other obstacles to his comfort, one of which was when, in the middle of the night, he had to walk on the stomach of one bodyguard and the spine of at least one physician to reach his bathroom. But the worst of all was listening to the whispering passing between the lawyer and the nurse. Oh, how relieved would Mr. Blok be when the nurse decided in favor of the lawyer! But would she? This was the tormenting question! The physicians were less disturbing, though Mr. Blok was very much amazed at the persistence with which they, in turn with the nurse, took his pulse and fed him vitamin pills. The bodyguard named Fritz was a peanut fiend, and the moment he discovered, through the physicians' statements, all the riches and blessings for health to be found in them, he doubled and tripled the amount he had consumed in the past. As a result, no one could help hearing him crack and chew that blessed food, and the floor was covered with their shells.

In contrast to the mornings, evenings were sometimes pleasant and instructive. The recollections of the guard Alphonse of his life in Macassar, for instance, were of great interest. He was a man of determination and passion and, though he was born in Kalamazoo, he was a man of considerable imagination and courage. "It was a fine life there on the border of the jungles, folks," he used to say. "I had a nice hut to live in and a pretty girl to sleep and to eat with. There was a nice river, too, and many fine crocodiles sunning themselves lazily on the soft yellow bank. It would have been a cinch to start a crocodile farm there; you would have to do only one thing — jump on the back of one of them, providing his skin was of commercial value, and squeeze out his eyes with your two thumbs. The first thing the beast does the moment you are on his back is to rush into the water, but the moment he is blinded he stops dead and is yours. A fine and easy living — profitable, too, I am telling you — a cinch."

Mr. Blok could listen to such interesting stories for hours, but they were usually interrupted by the physicians who were habitual debaters. It was hard for them to agree on any subject — not even on the incurability of the common cold. But on those rare occasions when they did agree and stopped arguing, their faces beamed with happiness and it made the nurse cry.

Every morning Mr. Mlauzinski and his associate brought mail, official papers to sign, the new summons from the court, complaints, police reports, and tax examinations.

Some of the charges brought against him were incomprehensible even to the lawyers, like the fire in the cellar caused by one of Blok's tropical landscapes. Bonnie's charges for attempted rape he thought outrageous. It filled his heart with great disillusion and pain.

One other case brought against Mr. Blok also gave him considerable depression. He had a small house in the country, poetically situated and surrounded by dense forest. He loved the place, and its wilderness made him feel alone in an unknown, mysterious, and beautiful land. At night, there were many strange noises from the forest, sometimes faint ones, and at other times, terrifying and crashing ones coming from the porch or one of the windows. Blok loved those dark nights and the eerie life in the woods.

He loved to listen, trying to distinguish one animal from another by their sounds. There were raccoons, skunks, foxes, woodchucks, and many others. Raccoons were the most daring, coming not only quite near the house but at times into the house itself. By leaving the kitchen door open, one could be certain of a raccoon's visit during the night. Sometimes these guests caused havoc, leaving the kitchen in a formidable mess. Mr. Blok never made plans to punish these altogether peaceful and sympathetic animals, not really holding them responsible for their crimes, which could be prevented by simply locking the kitchen door.

Mr. Blok's handyman, whose steady job was in a funeral establishment, did not share his patron's sympathy for raccoons and regarded their visits very gravely, almost as a personal offense. There was something cunning in the handyman's face, and Mr. Blok at times found his behavior suspicious because of his frequent consultations, held in a most mysterious manner, with Marshall the butcher.

They were after something — but what? One morning Mr. Blok knew the answer. He found, in the doorway of the kitchen, a raccoon, its paw held in the iron grip of an ugly trap.

The animal was old and not pretty, but that did not make Mr. Blok feel any better. He was upset by its desperate struggle and suffering and could not hold back the tears which ran down his face.

A veterinary was called immediately, and the animal was placed in his care. The fee for its room and board and all other expenses were paid in advance. Mr. Blok visited the raccoon regularly and was present at the amputation of the animal's paw. He did all he could to ease its suffering and spare its life. The operation was performed by a famous surgeon from Canada, and the anesthetic was given by a specialist from Nevada; but alas, nothing helped, and the raccoon died. A big marble stone, wonderfully sculptured and with an inscription on it, was erected over its grave. It read: "Here rests in peace an old raccoon. He will not be forgotten soon."

Of all the many cases brought against Mr. Blok, none, he felt, were as unfair as this one. That is why Mr. Blok was angry when Mr. Mlauzinski exclaimed, "Formidable! What versatility — trapper, country gentleman, artist, and lecturer," and then added: "Do you like big game hunting?"

Mr. Blok refused to attend to business that afternoon, but Mr. Mlauzinski would not leave until Mr. Blok put his signature on the "not guilty" plea for trapping animals out of hunting season and keeping them without license or special permission from the game warden.

Mornings were occupied with lawyers and official papers, and afternoons were entirely taken up with reading newspapers. He gave up reading books, finding enough intellectual stimulus in his own surroundings. To seek information from books was reasonable, he thought, but the best thinking was at firsthand, and the thought derived from books was secondhand — already woven and digested by someone else. Lately, he liked to read newspapers. He found there information, humor, tragedy, and above all, the truth — yes, the truth in every newspaper, everywhere. He knew, of course, how to look for it. The truth, he thought, is a tricky thing; it is elusive and broad-minded and reserved for the elite exclusively — for the masters of fantasy and tolerance. That is why so few can find it. His favorite method, which he thought should be applied by beginners, was the system of creating truth, because without the method there would be almost insurmountable difficulties in finding it.

Perusing a newspaper in front of him, he was puzzled by an item which can serve as a typical example of the news Mr. Blok enjoyed reading.

"The case grew out of the dismissal of Archibald H. from his post as superintendent of the apartment house, and the building owner, Mary M. L., told the State Labor Relations Board that she was afraid to keep him on the job because she understood he had once drowned a black cat by sliding it down a coal chute with a brick tied to its neck into a garbage can half full of water.

"Keith L., member of the S.L.R.B., commented that the cat may have deserved oblivion if it was anything like the homeless species which disturb mortal slumber and make night hideous with their caterwaulings.

"The superintendent, denying any felinocidal tendencies, said he had merely opened the front door of the apartment one night and let out the black cat, which had a habit of spending the night in the hallway, to the annoyance of the tenants. He added that he really loved cats; in fact, he kept one of his own that jumped on his knee when he whistled. The Reverend W.T.K., chairman of the Board, took no part in the discussion of cats but joined with Mr. L. in an order that the superintendent be reinstated, and that the owner stop violating laws of the union."

Did the superintendent lose his job because he hated cats or because his employer hated unions? When he was about ready to take the superintendent's part, he changed his mind, imagining the cat jumping into his lap and being trained to do so by his whistling. He hated people who whistled and had never met anyone worthwhile who had that deplorable habit.

Some whistle in the dark, out of fear to appear unconcerned and to frighten away all imaginable enemies; some whistle from pure boredom; and some to annoy others. Of course, there are also those who simply brag by showing that they know the tune; and some whistle because they are badly brought up — in their natural stupidity they never think they're disturbing anyone with it. Mr. Blok had much less contempt for professional whistlers, for it is their way of making a living, and he placed them in the category with harmonica players, acrobats, orchestra conductors and other entertainers. On the other hand, Mr. Blok disliked the idea of making the man lose his job only because he, Mr. Blok, disliked amateur whistlers.

The lady owner of the building, he imagined, was a frustrated woman who would not even keep a cat as a mild substitute for a husband — she was a stingy and unsympathetic woman. Considering that the superintendent's only shortcoming was his habit of whistling, and imagining that the spinster could not possibly be allergic to that in any important degree, she should not only have kept him in his job but eventually elevated him to more intimate relations — at first to a gin rummy game, leading later — who knows — maybe to marriage. As tolerant as Mr. Blok was toward bachelors, he disapproved of spinsters. Every woman should marry at least once, even to an older man, as it is a well-known fact that only thirty per cent of all men reaching the age of seventy are impotent. This thought filled Blok's heart with joy, and his satisfaction with this favorable outlook made him dismiss the superintendent, the owner, and the cat altogether, in order to concentrate on more important and personal matters.

But Blok found it dangerous to wander in his own mind and to attempt to penetrate the dark mystery of his libido, with its thousand senses and nine hearts — the libido with its greedy and frightened eyes that feeds on its own blood and soul, the brainless monster who does not know good from evil. Mr. Blok was a courageous man and not afraid of the discomfort of exploring such territories. He did not worry about returning to sobriety without new discoveries from those journeys. But what did sometimes distress him was the cataloging of these discoveries, putting them into neat mental compartments under the proper classification. They had to be put in order, and chronological order at that, always start from the beginning. But how to get back to the beginning? To walk backwards? Yes, walk backwards, baby, he said jokingly to himself. It's a little show, and besides I am not a crab.... Crab? Who spoke lately of crabs? Oh! It was Pinkel. Poor Pinkel — I wonder if there have been any more holdups in his drugstore — and on this point he parted from the libido and turned his thoughts to the myriad chores of daily life.

Chapter IX

"How is Mr. Blok?" asked Mr. Van Horn as soon as the guard Alphonse entered his office.

"Oh, he is pretty jumpy, sort of depressed. Last night he said that he was sick and tired of us all."

"Hmmm, did he?"

"The nurse was very hurt."

"Was she?"

"Yes, she cried. She also complained of our spying on her at bedtime and when she dresses in the morning, but I swear I never even peeped at her, I swear."

"Never mind," said Van Horn. "Did any strangers come to see him?"

"A few, but we brushed them off."

"Good work, fine. We must keep everyone away from him including his friends. It is very important for his own safety," said Van Horn. "So, you say he is sick and tired, eh? Well, I can't blame the poor man. He certainly is crowded over there in the studio."

"But I do enjoy living there," said Alphonse and added, "How long do you think it will last?"

"It depends, perhaps a few weeks more. There are still new charges coming in, but we are not sleeping either." Saying this,

Van Horn handed him an envelope. "Please hurry and take it to Mr. Blok as soon as possible. This message, I know, will give him great pleasure."

"Of course, I will," said Alphonse, ready to go. "Mr. Blok is a wonderful man." He took the letter and left.

When he reached 17ᵗʰ Street, he remembered a bowling alley around the corner and decided to drop in there for a minute or two. He was sure Max was bowling there like crazy.

Sure thing. "You rascal," he hollered, tapping a red-headed man on the shoulder. "I knew I would find you here, Maxie."

"Jesus, glad to see you," reacted Max rolling up his cuffs. "Have a round with me?"

"Sure, just a short one."

"Okey doke," said Max.

After several rounds, they drank a couple bottles of beer and, chatting pleasantly, settled for a game of pinochle. "I always have a deck handy in my pocket," said Max and started to deal.

Alphonse had an unlucky day, and though Max treated him to liverwurst sandwiches and some more beer, after several losing hours he could not regain his good mood again. Parting with his pal he said, "Next time it will be me who'll give you a shave," and his voice sounded sour. On the street again, he suddenly remembered the message. He felt for the envelope in his pocket and looked at his watch. "My goodness, I'm cooked," he said and began to run. He arrived at the studio panting and unable to speak. His irritation frightened everyone in the room, but as soon as they saw Blok smile as he read the message, they also began to smile. "They are here. My old friends have arrived," cried Blok joyfully. "What time is it now?"

"Six-thirty," said the nurse.

"They expect me at 8:00. I got permission to stay with them as late as I wish. Mr. Ondra will accompany me there," said Blok, galloping gayly into the bathroom. "Don't keep a birdie in the cage, tra la la, tra la la. He'll never sing when in a rage, tru tru tru, tru tru tru," they heard him sing as he prepared himself and waited for Ondra.

Alexander, the pianist, Abka Perk and Blum, his old friends and former roommates, celebrated the long-awaited reunion. They warmed themselves with various drinks in anticipation of Blok's arrival. The short, bald-headed Alexander came from Luxemburg; Abka from Glasgow; and the most practical of all, Blum, from Harbin. He had curly hair and laughing black eyes. Before the German swastika had dispersed old friends in all directions, he had been a medical student in Berlin.

There he was quick to get his doctor's degree and marry a woman he did not really like. After performing several very successful abortions on her, he specialized in this field, earning much money and many honors for himself.

All three rushed to answer the knock at the door. "Greetings, gentlemen," said Van Horn, looking at the disappointed faces. They had seen him only once, when he and a few others of the Society had met them at the airport and had brought them to this lovely apartment. "Your cooperation is deeply appreciated by our society," he said, walking into the room.

"Where is Mr. Blok?"1 asked Mr. Abka.

"He will be here presently. We thought it would be more convenient to get all of the information regarding his character when he is not present," Van Horn stated gravely.

"Your friend is in a great predicament, and any information you can give will be of valuable help to him and to the Committee in his defense."

"What did he do?" asked Blum.

"He wouldn't hurt a fly," said Alexander.

"It's true, quite true," said Van Horn. "This is the reason for our being here." He looked at his watch and, apologizing for not mentioning the details of all of the charges and suits against Blok, proposed to go straight to the core of the meeting. Making himself comfortable in the chair, he said, "Let's proceed. I understand you all were together in Germany. Did Mr. Blok already then show great promise as an artist?"

"I should say so. His suprapsychic paintings created a furor," said Alexander. "You remember?" He looked at Abka and Blum.

"It's true he acquired quite a reputation," said Blum.

"His phenomenal gift of drawing anything just by the description of it helped to solve several crimes. He was well paid for that work, but he refused to call it art. Already, at that time he worked hard on his atmospheric formula," said Alexander.

"This is nothing," interrupted Abka, with a strange giggle. "I could speak of the old boy the whole night."

"Why do you laugh?" asked Van Horn.

"Oh, I just remember playing a practical joke on him, pretending to walk in my sleep and scaring the poor fellow almost to death. He presented me later with a remarkable portrait called "The Somnambulist" — really extraordinary. In whatever light you would look at it, the moony night would reflect itself around the painting." And he repeated again, "Extraordinary!"

"What happened to the painting? We never heard of it," said the two other friends. "Where is it now?"

"Well," said Abka with great feeling, "I had to abandon it with many of my other belongings in Germany, and the last I heard of it was that it was declared as degenerate art and burned. In their hasty blindness, the experts on degeneracy failed to see the greatness of this work. I cherished that portrait dearly and was glad to run across an account of the ceremony of the cremation given by an eyewitness, a German poet. I translated the verses for my students in Glasgow and brought the original cutting for Blok as a souvenir of his wonderous creation." Taking a piece of paper from his wallet, he asked, "May I read it to you?" All waited silently as he began.

"The high greedy flames of the pyre lit up the
distorted faces of the celebrating mob.
Let darkness march into denser darkness,
cried their leader.
Let us free ourselves from the immortals,
let us see whether our flames will fail to devour them.
Devour them, echoed the mob.
Their roaring encircled the globe
While art works only crackled in the fire.
Drag that degenerate sleepwalker,
get him, shrieked a woman.
He is bloodless and sad, waiting so long over
there in the corner. Heil! Heil! Heil!
He looks like someone in the bible.
The fire's hissing angry tongues fell upon the
somnambulist and then — Oh God!
All sank into silence under the shadow of the
starless night.
Even the smoke betrayed the fire, and hid its
formless black wings.
In terrible fear, the crowd lifted their heads
and saw a vision of a human face, white as the bark of

the birch trees, painfully smothering in the dark flames,
yet smiling.

It was fleeting.

The flames licked with new fury toward the hangmen
who, bent and mute, staggered to safer places.

Places where nothing will break the victorious pace,

Nor silence the songs of praise for a great master race."

"It's very impressive," said Van Horn, after a long silence. "May I have a copy of the poem for our society? I would also like to know the name of the poet." He wrote the name down and, thanking Abka for the poem, declared that his society seeks such people as the poet for its membership.

"I hope the news of the destruction of the painting will not upset Blok. He used to be so sensitive," said Alexander with great concern.

"We were sometimes rough on him," said Blum.

"We certainly were," agreed Abka.

After they offered Mr. Van Horn some Nicolashka (which is nothing but vodka with a slice of lemon and sugar) and helped themselves to some more, Alexander said, "There was not sufficient courage in the shy chap to start a romance and acquire a girlfriend, as we all had, and in addition, he did not possess enough cynicism to accept the services of a prostitute. But if you remember, we had a plan — we thought it was a brilliant idea — and we swore to succeed. There was an acquaintance of ours — you remember her, the red-haired, middle-aged woman who walked the upper part of Kurfuestendam in the afternoon from six on. What was her name?"

"Greta! Good old Greta! Of course. Well, we were all her clients, and we all valued her highly. Her appearance was agreeable, her character admirable, and her little apartment, charming. Nothing cheap or in bad taste — quite to the contrary — there was simplicity and warmth, a choice of books on the shelf, the piano, as well as a few excellent prints on the wall, the discreet colors of the carpet in the living room matching the curtains. But above all, her bedroom was a triumph of cleanliness and calm respectability. There were no pink covers, no perfumed air, and nothing to reflect her profession. In short, she was a woman of taste and distinction and yet a low-priced prostitute available to all.

"It was Blum's idea to consult her and to secure her cooperation. She understood Blok's problem perfectly and was touched by our concern and interest in a friend. It was decided to arrange a tea in her flat and to invite Blok and a few friends. All financial arrangements were made as to her time and efforts."

"I remember that damned expensive business!" exclaimed Abka.

Alexander, looking at Van Horn, continued: "It was my mission to speak to Blok of the charming young widow who would be delighted if I brought him along to tea. The invitation was accepted with pleasure. The party was lovely, and Blok was charmed with everything. Greta played her part admirably — she was discreetly coquettish. He hummed pleasantly, one of the Schubert songs, and she was near him. We all left one by one, leaving him alone with her.

"No one saw Blok for a week, and we were worried about what had happened. It was decided to send Abka as ambassador. Now, please, Abka, tell us the end of the story."

"No, no, you must continue, especially since it seems that you took the whole thing more to heart than anyone else."

"All right, I will. Abka's report was devastating. Blok never left her apartment. He was madly in love with her and had only one idea — to marry her. He had lost all sense of self-control, all logic and even shame. The poor woman was desperate; her passionate and jealous lover would not leave her alone for a minute. She begged our ambassador to take him away — she had had enough of him, of us, of everything. Yet she refused to tell Blok the truth. She must have been somehow touched by his passionate and naïve affection — after all, she was a woman. But who could stand his constant whining, declarations of love, and ridiculous baby talk? In addition, to all the difficulties she had with him, she complained about not earning enough money and neglecting her clients. There was no way to receive them, and she was in danger of losing them all.

"I remember that we decided to pay her more. Even though our financial resources were in not too healthy condition, she had to be compensated. Three weeks after the decision was made to tell Blok the truth, with heavy heart I climbed up the stairs to Greta's apartment. Never had I hated anything more than this ungrateful mission. I rang the bell, but for a long time there was no answer. Finally, the door opened, and I saw him. What a picture!! He had not shaved for days, his hair stood up high in fantastic disorder, the pale face was like that of a drunkard or madman."

"Oh, it's you," he said. "Come in."

"How are you, my boy?" I greeted him with a false gaiety.

"Come in," he repeated.

"Where is Greta?" I asked casually.

"She?" There was a long pause, then he said slowly and sort of absent-mindedly: "I am not a Catholic, so she will not marry me. She is like a little child and is under the influence of her numerous relatives. They will never permit her to marry a Jew. Those disgusting uncles, cousins, brothers, and brothers-in-law of hers — you will never believe how many there are.

I was surprised when I opened the door for you that it was not one of her uncles again. They don't even want to see or to speak with me; they won't come in, and sometimes they slam the door and run away. Disgusting family!" He was profoundly puzzled and very sad.

"Yes," I said, "some people are funny that way, and you would never be able to fight so many relatives. Where is she now?"

"She went to see her cousin Albert at six this afternoon; then her brother-in-law is supposed to arrive from Hamburg, and she will spend the evening with him at her uncle's; and so it has gone now for the past six days."

"All right, old chap," I said to him warmly. "You just have no experience with women, that's all. Write her a note — right now! I will tell you what to say — my God, I know them!"

"I will, I will. Just wait until I get a piece of paper."

"Then I dictated, and he wrote; it was a masterpiece of. determination and manliness, ending with: "I—or they." He was in tears when we left Greta's apartment. So ended Blok's first passion, and so began his manhood. It was bitter, yet sweet. Let us never spoil the great illusion with which he may still live today."

"Pst! Pst! Blok is coming. There he is — all alive in the flesh and blood."

"Hello!" they all screamed and ran towards Blok, shaking his hands, patting his shoulders, kissing his cheeks, and embracing him heartily. "By jove, old chap!" Each showed affection in noisy excitement. "My goodness," said one, "you certainly do not look any younger!" And another: "Your face was never puffed up like this sort of swollen, like — and that stomach!"

"Good life, good food," remarked another; and then another, "What have you done to yourself?" After many other similar remarks, though of course, all said with affection, Blok smiled shyly and said, "You look at me like that mob looked at the dead dog, each saying how badly the dog smelled and how ugly he was — until they heard a voice say 'Look people, at his beautiful teeth.' They turned their heads and saw Mahomet."

"Good! Good! Wonderfully said! Our Blok has not changed after all."

Nikolashka was served in large quantities and with great joy the friends sat close to each other and spoke of the old days. After they had all the desired information about each other's lives and future plans, Abka asked Alexander the whereabouts of his former professor, Herr Berthold.

"That son-of-a-bitch," said Alexander. "Do you remember him? The musicologist who wrote volumes on the origin of music with that truly Teutonic grundlichkeit."

"I think I heard that name," they heard Van Horn say, who since Blok's arrival had sat quietly close to Mr. Ondra.

"It was he, I think, who supervised the music to be played during the procession to the gas chambers of people of inferior races, marked with crosses on their foreheads. He loved to watch the impression his concerts made on that walking death, enjoying the stern earnestness with which they paid their last tribute to great German art. I believe that, after being completely cleared by all the courts and the denazification authorities, he is very successful now and is organizing fine programs in England and elsewhere," remarked Van Horn.

"There is a great renaissance of the Deutsche kultur now," said Alexander. "So great is their influence that the whole of Paris has become experts on German art."

"Prosit! Bravo!" cried Blum. "The art, and the art alone, is important and above all vulgar politics and prejudices. Besides, those inspired artists really were never aware of doing anything wrong. How could they?" he cried sarcastically. "Since when are they supposed to have ordinary brains? Or for that matter, brains at all? Their minds have been preoccupied with the high message of art, and they simply could not follow the orders of the leaders and the acts of the mob. Would they have been forced to witness all the crimes and murders committed, I am sure they would be very sad! It would reflect unfavorably on their art and make them lose some of their natural vigor of sturm and drang.

"No, my friends, those great artists have never heard of wrong done to the innocent. And yet, there are people today who speak against them. Of course, they are only a minority — a few ringleaders who want to preserve their happy hunting ground for themselves. Envious colleagues, that's all, and the protests coming from those whose relatives were annihilated and burned alive in various camps should not be taken too seriously, either, for they are not thinking objectively. But let's forget all the nightmares — there is no use of abusing anyone. The war is over, and Ilsa Koch is alive."

"He is right," several voices cried. "Let's have a drink and speak of something else." Everyone got up to fill their glasses while Mr. Van Horn took Ondra aside and spoke very softly. "I must leave now. The legal advisors are waiting for me." He shook his head gravely, "Very alarming. Some of the cases took a pretty bad turn. I hope the courts will be willing to postpone the trials. We are not quite ready for them. We have a great responsibility on our hands. Take good care of Mr. Blok. Don't let any stranger approach him and bring him safely home. He's in a poor state — and needs a little distraction. Let him be happy with his friends." Soon after this, he shook everyone's hand and departed.

The friends drank more Nikolashka and also acquainted Ondra with the drink. He liked it and consumed great quantities of it. At first it made him gay, but soon he showed fatigue and began to speak incongruously about the hairy horns of the rhinoceros and of Gorgeous George. He then fell asleep. To the tune of his snores and whistles on the sofa, the conversation continued, taking a rather frivolous course.

They spoke of the Blue Monkey and other establishments, which for them had been homes but for others just whore-houses. These souvenirs failed to please Mr. Blok as he watched them drink and listened to their laughter.

"It is good to find something that has been lost, but with things thrown away, it is like looking at yesterday's garbage," Blok thought. He had a splitting headache. "Wrinkly was right, I am getting old," thought Blok sadly, getting up from his chair.

He walked into the hallway and listened to the loud voices, and with drooped shoulders, he walked away.

Almost automatically, Mr. Blok took the direction toward his studio. His thoughts were still with his friends and the laughter seemed to stir the stillness of the night and deaden his steps. "I am walking on nothing," he thought, not searching for the cause of his feeling of emptiness. "Did the fall of my sublime expectation hurt me? Hmmm, sublime is a big word, but expectation can be all shapes and sizes, like those empty streets and empty benches on this empty Square," mused Blok as he entered a side path. He sat on the bench and, looking up at the sky, let his thoughts travel calmly through the spaces crowded with loneliness.

He thought of his journeys, of colors, of life and of the brook that rushed by his cabin and yet was always there like the thoughts of his mother. He saw the light breaking through the dark grayish night, not uneven and shy as it does in the country, but with short sudden moves unafraid of the city and the night. The headlights of a truck, weakened by the dawn like the eyes of an owl, did not reach Mr. Blok's tired face. Even the quick bright eyes of a squirrel hardly glanced at him as it hid its shabby tail behind a poplar tree.

"This is a beautiful morning," reflected Mr. Blok, watching the early risers passing by. "Free… free." As if bit by a sudden sobriety, he sprang to his feet. Ondra — Abka — Van Horn, Blum, his protectors at the studio, and the trials — in the chaos of anxiety all went through his mind. "I will not return," he thought. "This is the time to escape. Escape — yes! Run away from them all, from the whole dreadful reality, but where? Where?" he demanded of himself, walking fast around the Square. He slowed down. "Where to go? Ondra spoke of Gorgeous George. I have never seen wrestling. No, no — fool! It's too early in the morning." He turned sharply into 19th Street. I will never return to the studio, never. Snok, Mlauzinski, peanuts, nurse, never again! But where to go?! Steam bath? It's not far," he remembered. Somewhat relieved at having made a decision, he looked forward to the quiet of the steam bath. There he would find peace, with his mind closed and his pores open.

Chapter X

"'Hello, hello, Mr. Blok," the husky attendant greeted him. "I have not had the pleasure of seeing you for quite a while. You're sort of early today. Funny, just yesterday I spoke to the inspector about you. I was lucky enough to remember your address."

"My address? What for? Who is the inspector?"

"Oh, don't you know? Don't you read the newspapers, Mr. Blok?"

"Oh, of course I do," said Mr. Blok. "Perhaps lately I've been too occupied, though."

"Ha, ha, that's interesting. You are perhaps the only patron of ours who doesn't know what happened lately."

"What is it?" asked Mr. Blok anxiously.

"You remember that little guy who used to come here every Tuesday and Friday afternoon?"

"Hmm… who was it?"

"That oldish-looking, peaceful fellow with funny spots on his ass. By jeepers, you still don't remember? I'm really surprised. It's the guy with athlete's foot — who hardly speaks any human language."

"Oh, of course," said Mr. Blok. "Now I know."

"Jesus, when I think of having scrubbed his bumpy body, I get the shivers. Dog bite my flesh if the guy didn't give me the jitters."

Meanwhile, Mr. Blok undressed, put his clothes in the locker, and with the towel draped around his middle made ready to step into the steam room. He asked the attendant, "So what makes you so scared?"

"Sure, sure, I haven't told you. That miserable fellow came here for the first time about two years ago and with a kind of lisp asked in a queer jargon for special treatment. I told him he would get all the works he wanted, and so ever since I have pepped him up good to his complete satisfaction, though I was never crazy about working on him. By gosh, to rub him was like scaling a fish, and those bumpy spots on his loose surface made me think of handling something dead. The chap was fussy, too — not like other gents. Take for example — after an honest tryout you did not like the works, and that was all there was to it. Some like it hard on the back; some want work on the joints; others, smooth neckwringing. Even with ticklish personalities you always know where you are. But Jesus, that guy would always take me by surprise. One day I had to pull his stomach for circulation, or gently rub his elbows. Another day I would have to beat evenly and firmly on one bumpy spot only, until I felt like an automatic drumbeater with a switch on and would sweat like a polar bear in a parlor. The guy never really knew what he wanted, but I can't blame him for that because it was all the physicians' fault. Not feeling good, he went from one doctor to another, not omitting one in the city. He paid good American money for the visits and medicine, but there was no improvement. His teeth were pulled out, and he ate no eggs. He gave up smoking and swallowed vitamins. For two weeks he had to eat raw spinach and drink soya bean milk, and then he had to eat meat and walk two hours a day. By jeepers, it would take me hours to tell you of their ways to fix up a guy's jalopy. No wonder he became a kind of nutty personality."

"It's very interesting," said Mr. Blok. "I would like to hear more about his ailments sometime, but right now I think I am ready for the steam room. I'll see you later," he concluded, and serenely walked away.

"Okay, sir," said the masseur, "but I bet you won't need steam to sweat after you bear the end of this story."

Mr. Blok felt relieved after he left him. He was conscious of how ridiculous people look standing naked and conversing on unimportant matters. There was no excuse for that! And just as he entered the steam room he thought of an earthquake in Tokyo and the shock people had when they saw the nude, frightened author of "He Died Bravely" running out of his room, straight into the lobby and out into the street, screaming hysterically and speaking incoherently.

Mr. Blok smiled, imagined the scene and remembered the charming lady who had witnessed and described it so colorfully. Ready to settle himself on a slab and with a smile still on his face, he looked forward with great anticipation to being completely alone. But at that moment, the attendant entered and excitedly said "For heaven's sake, don't sit on that! Not on that bench!" he repeated. "We have not removed it yet. That is where he used to sweat. Jesus, you had better get out of here before the inspector closes up the whole damn place."

Mr. Blok was highly annoyed and told the attendant to mind his own business or to tell him what this was all about.

"Gosh, Mr. Blok, it's not my fault if you don't want to listen to me. Let's get out of here to the locker room and I'll tell you." Mr. Blok followed him reluctantly.

In the locker room, the man looked straight in his eyes and whispered: "He was a leper. How do you like that? Leper. Yes, sir — an authentic, a real, a true, an honest-to-goodness leper. His missus was a leper, too. She was the original one, so they say, but they discovered it only before she died. By Jeepers! They examined the chap, and that was that. Now the missus is dead, and he is being deported. Yes, sir, they say it's not very catching and that the Goddamned thing does not penetrate the other guy's system easily. But Jesus, I am telling you…" He was speaking of a physician's examinations and other things he himself had gone through, but Mr. Blok did not listen. He put his clothes on feverishly and left the place.

Panting and out of breath, he reached the Square. As he started to cross, he heard a booming voice behind him calling, "Oh, there, mister." Blok turned and saw a man waving a tie in his hand. "Here, mister," he said, handing a tie to Mr. Blok. "You lost it running across the street. You must have tied it around your neck mighty loosely," he added and, receiving Mr. Blok's thanks, departed.

Mr. Blok, wiping his wet face with the tie, saw a park guard walking toward him. Mr. Blok wanted to run. His heart was pounding. "What does he want? Is he the inspector? They're looking for me. They want to lock me up! I'm a public danger, a leper. Sure, I'm a pest, an outcast." Almost in tears, he stood and waited for the guard.

"Good afternoon," the guard greeted him. "Is there anything I can do for you, sir?"

"No, thanks, I'm just looking at this tie a gentleman gave me."

"I see. It's a pretty nice one," said the guard. "My wife gave me one exactly like this for Christmas, but I wear it only on Sundays or when we have company."

Mr. Blok listened to him and tried to look casual and unobtrusive. He felt grateful that the guard did not suspect him of anything. The pleasant voice of the man even encouraged him to conversation.

"Well," said Mr. Blok complacently, "it's not safe living in our good old city anymore. First there were pigeons infecting people with this virus, then the troubles with garbage removal, then the slums and rats, and our drinking water is no good. Now there are a lot of people running around with leprosy, touching kids playing in the Square, eating in restaurants and patronizing public baths and pools."

"What you said about the pigeons and water might be quite true, sir, but about the kids playing in the Square with people afflicted with leprosy is a malicious lie spread by some defeated politician. We guard children's health and safety, and we wouldn't permit any of those lepers to touch them," he continued eagerly. "The other day there was a fellow completely minus his nose who started to get friendly with a baby, but I was there in a jiffy and personally told him to leave the infant alone. He raised hell and told me that he was the father, that he would complain about me and that I would be fired, but I'm not afraid, sir, and I know my duty. And besides, it's not his business to have babies. I have had some myself, and I know how they like to play with their dad's nose. The inspector told me the other day that I acted quite right and that we should never take any chances."

"You said inspector? What inspector?" asked Mr. Blok casually.

"The health inspector of our district. Quite a man," said the guard admiringly. "And believe me, sir, he would never let anyone run around with leprosy. Not in our district," he proudly concluded and walked away, leaving Mr. Blok standing alone with his gloomy and bothersome thoughts.

He was afraid to visit a physician for an examination, and he dreaded finding the inspector in his studio. No, he could not return there. He would not anyhow. What should he do?

He wanted to know all about leprosy. The disease was not painful, he had heard. It creeps slowly and spreads almost unnoticed until it is too late. Too late, he repeated bitterly. He was possessed by fear and felt helpless—alone—doomed. He was rooted to the spot, without being able to make any decision. I must pray like Elisha prayed for the Syrian leper to make his flesh grow new again. Oh, where is Elisha? Even the deserted Square, or the oncoming rain, falling in fine lines, wetting his hair and face, did not make him change his position. But perhaps this was the right and reasonable thing to do; he had to wait and adjust himself to a new and threatening situation, to calm his feverish imagination. "I am a ridiculous fool — a coward — an ignoramus. That's what I am," he blamed himself bitterly. He was shivering with cold, and the water dripped from his face. He began to walk aimlessly around the Square, and gloomy thoughts about a leper's death began to form in his mind. He murmured the lines to himself:

> The crumbling ribs in stagnant water
> Did not frighten the ailing fish.
> The dry curvy fingers tense;
> They trembled a little and made bubbles.
> The elbows and knees were dry as matches
> And only sores were wet.
> Eyes were wet too,
> Looking up to lofty skies
> and watching birds soar and play
> Above his troubled head.
> The blanched feet at last caressed,
> Deeper sinking in the mud.

A requiem for him who lives

Long remote from people

And praise for death among the fish.

"What birds...so lovingly?" he wondered. "There are almost as many vicious species among them as among humans. Take the colorful parrots of the Andes who kill the sheep by plucking through their thick wool coats until the liver is reached and eaten, leaving the sheep to bleed slowly to death. Brrr...brrr."

With these morbid thoughts persistently hounding him, Mr. Blok moved aimlessly through the crowded streets. The rain had stopped. His wet clothes clung to his body. He found himself at the railroad station without being aware of what had brought him here. "Why did I come here? They would not know the time schedule to Abyssinia or other remote and safe places. Stupid, of course not." He bought a newspaper and went into the lunchroom. After he drank two cups of coffee, he noticed a man looking at him. "I must not be recognized and fund," he thought, completely covering his face with the newspaper.

His eyes fell on an article: "TWIN SONS UNDER SPELL OF MYSTIC, Los Angeles Seer Blamed as Texas Cowboy Is Found Staring into River. A worried mother, notified that a 'Cowboy' identified as her son had been arrested while staring moodily into New York City's East River, said today the youth and his twin brother had been 'under the influence' of a California mystic for months. The mother said her identical twin sons had been working with a mind reader in Los Angeles for several months. She said the boys had 'been scared stiff' of the mystic but had refused to confide in anyone.

The tearful mother said she had heard that a former assistant of the mind reader had committed suicide by jumping off the Golden Gate Bridge in San Francisco. She said her son was in Amarillo two weeks ago to visit his family and buy a resplendent cowboy outfit. However, a man who identified himself as the mystic's manager appeared in 'a big Cadillac' and drove him away immediately without even a chance to take his new cowboy togs with him. 'Mother, I can't talk,' she quoted him as saying. 'You've got to remember you have another twin mixed up in this thing.' She said she understood the boys had been living in the Great Northern Hotel in New York City but had checked out about a week ago. 'I hope they keep my son in that hospital until we have a chance to get things straightened out and find out where my other son is.'"

"The seers of California have always been dangerous. It is fortunate that there are as few of them as there are lepers in this country," he thought. This brought back his extreme anxiety. He paid for the coffee and rushed back into the street. It was raining again, much harder, but it did not distract Blok's thought that he must do something. He started to run. Perhaps Pinkel could help. Pharmacists sometimes do. Running many blocks at a furious pace, he flung himself completely drenched into Pinkel's drug store.

"Mr. Blok, Mr. Blok, you are shivering!" cried Pinkel. "You're not well. Please sit down. You're trembling all over." Holding him with both hands, Pinkel helped him into a chair.

Mr. Blok, breathing heavily, looked steadily at Pinkel and said, "Call a specialist, please, it's confidential — an authority on leprosy, someone you know, and please, a physician, only, not the Inspector of Health. He must not know. I'll explain later. Do you hear? He must not know. Please take me away from here." The last words were hardly audible.

"I will, of course. Please calm yourself. I'll help you to my apartment next door. Come, sit here for a while. It's nice and warm here. The doctor will come in a minute." And he left the room.

Mr. Blok's eyes glowed in the dimly lit room. His heart was beating rapidly, and his burning thoughts of fear and danger were maddening. With lightness he moved to the door and listened to the soft voices coming from the hallway.

"We will handle him gently," said one voice.

"But, Inspector?" he recognized Pinkel's voice.

"Don't worry," the first voice said. "We have rounded them all up, and the public places are safe and clean now."

Then came another man's voice: "As a physician," he said gravely, "my duty is to examine the patient, and I insist that the examination should precede all other actions. Besides, I know the man and ... pst ... pst ... he may hear us."

"Where is the man?" asked the first voice.

"Right there in that room," whispered Pinkel.

Mr. Blok opened the window with the skill of a prowler and, noiselessly climbing through it, found himself on a small terrace from which he slid into a small court surrounded by the high walls of neighboring buildings. He stood looking and listening in the dark. The walls, gray and ugly, were closing in on him with menacing slowness from all sides. He was trapped. He tried to move. He wanted to run, to escape, but his leg was chained to a brick wall. "I am a racoon," he said to himself. "No, no., I am Dante approaching hell."

The wall of one building became the shoulder of a huge mountain with strange rays showing the way into an inferno. Almost relieved, he moved toward it, his weary body willingly obeying the command of an omnipotent and mysterious master. There was something evil in the ghastly, still air that choked Mr. Blok's throat. He walked forward, groping in the dark, until he reached a wall. As he stood there, he heard a rustle quite near, coming from inside the wall and then more perceptibly from behind. When he turned, he heard a scratchy and dull sound behind him. He turned his head again toward the wall, which stood cold and mute before him. The silence returned, but when he reached out to feel the stones, something warm and wet licked his hand. It did not frighten him, and he did not draw his hand away. Ha drew nearer, and now he could feel coarse wool and the massive body of an animal — a huge dog, which stood on its hind legs and placed its paws on Mr. Blok's breast and tried to reach his face with its tongue.

It was then that he perceived the smell of' alcohol on the dog's steamy breath — a sickening smell of strong alcohol. There was something revolting in the way it pressed its body ever tighter against Mr. Blok, letting its drunken, moist tongue lap over his face. There was no sound as Mr. Blok, filled with fear and disgust, stood benumbed in an unholy and mute embrace. His eyes, now used to the dark, were too close to define the contours of his monstrous partner, which pressed him with increased force against the wall. Its odorous and acid saliva blinded Blok's eyes, and its paws penetrated deep into his chest. The pain was nauseating, and he could not endure it any longer. At first he tried timidly to push it away — to indicate gently a desire to free himself, but the animal only increased its pressure. Mr. Blok pushed it away from him more resolutely. He bent one knee and tried to hit the animal's stomach with it at the same time he pushed the dog with his right hand, but sharp bristles went into his hand and made it bleed and burn. "It's not a dog," thought Mr. Blok in terror. His antagonism angered the animal and stopped its amorous attempts. The beast tore Mr. Blok's jacket and bit into his elbow, then it gurgled and spit a spray-like liquid in his face and, with a sudden strong jolt, threw Mr. Blok on the ground. It walked away, growling and spitting, and did not once turn its ugly head as it went along the wall and disappeared through a narrow gate.

Mr. Blok tried to get up but after several attempts could only bring himself to a sitting position and lean his back against the wall.

He was ready for a supreme effort to direct his thoughts to safety when he saw flashlights beaming from the window. "They are searching for me ... the inspector, he's after me. Run — hurry — run." Nervously Mr. Blok got up and, following the path of the animal, walked warily along the wall, and disappeared through the gate.

It was a narrow back street, dark, dirty and deserted, with garbage cans filled to the top on both sides. Mr. Blok turned to the left, then two blocks to the right past the Ionic Shop. He crossed the street and, just before reaching the Square, stopped at a lamppost and looked at his right hand. The palm was red and inflamed, and stuck into the top of the forefinger were two black quills. The larger one had white spots in the middle and fine reddish hair growing on top. Mr. Blok gently pulled it out and placed it carefully in his pocket. He started on the other, which was thin, moist, slippery, and deep in his flesh. The slightest contact with it only burrowed it deeper and caused great pain. Observing it closer, he noticed that it trembled like something alive trying to free itself, but in its blindness and despair, it was going the wrong way. "What is it?" thought Mr. Blok. "Queer thing. Look how it moves. It wiggles. Funny."

His eyes fell on his trousers and jacket, which were damp and covered with peculiar pieces of wool and dark reddish hairs, a few of which were long and thick. "A bloodthirsty harlot," thought Mr. Blok with disgust, "a freak, or an ape, or a porcupine. Whoever will know? Who? I know! I know! It was an incarnation of Abraxas. That's right," he thought triumphantly. "Every mystic would think so. Abraxas, the demon of magic who unites the divine and the diabolical. Hmmm. Divine. What's divine in that beast. What?"

Passing the Square and entering 20th Street, Mr. Blok calmed himself sufficiently to make apologies for his fears. But on the other hand, he said in his own defense," who can blame a person suspected of being a leper and being hunted for deportation?

"Where do they send them? Do they wear uniforms? I hate uniforms! Where will I spend the night?"

He thought of the waitress, and this filled his heart with anxiety. "What if she contracted my leprosy, if I am infected! Poor Elsa. Oh God, I kissed her, slept with her. I ruined her life, and that of the psychiatrist who shared my bed with me! Of course, we did not kiss. That is good; he may have a chance! I will warn them!" The inspector cannot possibly know about Elsa. I'll write and warm them.

And then he thought of the happy time when he had wanted to see Gorgeous George, and it seemed unbelievable that it was today. "Now I'm a fugitive, a roofless vagabond, and perhaps a leper. One day is a long time," reflected Mr. Blok nostalgically. At this moment, lifting his eyes to a brightly lit movie marquee, he read: "The Family Honeymoon." Taking some change from his pocket, he bought a forty-cent ticket and entered the theater.

The young lady cashier distastefully brushed away a queer looking quill that she noticed among Mr. Blok's nickels and dimes.

Blok followed the usherette's flashlight down the aisle. She pointed to an empty seat in the middle of a crowded row.

"I don't want to disturb anyone," said Blok, but the usherette disappeared. Apologizing, he climbed over feet until he reached his chair.

"I shouldn't have come to this congregation," said Blok inwardly. He felt an unpleasant nearness of strangers whose features be could not distinguish. The images and voices on the screen came only vaguely to his attention, but as his eyes became accustomed to the dark, he glimpsed at the man to his right. The man's arm rested negligently on Blok's elbow. Blok wanted to draw his arm away. The man's folded overcoat moved slightly on his knees as his hand began to feel its way stealthily toward Blok.

The man's nervous face did not once turn from the screen, but Blok knew that his mind was not concentrated on it. He touched Blok lightly pressing against his shoulder. Blok wanted to shrink, to fold himself inside his own body. He moved away, almost leaning upon the neighbor to his left. But the man's hand followed him always, attaching itself with intimate familiarity. Now Blok felt the man's leg touch him with feathery lightness, subtle and fine, as though seeking further contact with insecure hope. "What's he doing this for," thought Blok in fear and disgust. The man took his lack of resistance for encouragement for he pressed Blok's arm more daringly now.

Suddenly, for a long second, he remained motionless, as if listening to something, and with reassurance started anew. Carefully shoving over his coat on part of Blok's lap, be stopped once more and listened, never once turning his head. Blok's temples throbbed, and his legs shook as he turned towards his molester and saw a hideous smile on his face.

"Let me go," Blok heard his own voice rasp. And trying to free himself from the stranger's hands that grasped at him, he pushed the coat to the floor and rushed from his seat up the aisle and quickly out into the street. The lady cashier smiled at him as he heard a voice behind him call to the doorman, "Did you just see a man run out of here? Get him, you hear. He is a pansy. Outrageous."

Blok ran down 18th Street and, sharply turning to the right, found himself in a dark narrow street. He pressed himself flat to a building and stood there for a long time until his tired heart became only an echo of its recent wild beating against its own walls. With downcast eyes, he began to walk along the empty streets, his mind in a turmoil of gloomy agitation. He turned to the right and stood before the door of a bar. "There must be a telephone here. I must find a reliable doctor," he thought. "There must be a woman skin specialist in this city. A woman will not deceive as Pinkel did, that swine. He certainly didn't lose a minute in doing it."

Blok entered the bar. "Good evening," said the bartender. "What'll it be?"

"Oh, anything. Something not strong."

"Italian Vermouth, sir?"

"Very good," agreed Blok. "May I use the telephone?"

"Sure, right over there."

Blok went toward the booth. He looked through the classified pages under P: Buttke, B. F.; Daich, R. Joseph; Fisherman, Chaim; Kooper; Sophie, Dermatologist. His finger stopped, "Ah, that's the one." He wrote the address on a scrap of paper and returned to the bar.

"From midnight on, we get quite a crowd here," said the barman.

"What time is it now?"

"Almost 11 :30."

"Thanks," said Blok and tasted the vermouth.

"It looks as if you have just had an accident," said the man, adding apologetically. "It's not my business, but before people start coming in — I mean if you would like to stay."

"No, no, I am leaving. I have no time," said Blok.

At this moment, the door opened, and a man entered. "Oh, here you are. What a surprise," he said, coming toward Blok. "I almost felt I would find you." Mr. Blok recognized his neighbor from the movie.

"Carl," said the barman, "you know you mustn't come here without an escort."

"But this gentleman here invited me," said Carl, pointing at Blok. "Isn't it so?" and he showed his obscene smile.

"I don't know him," Blok said with a trembling voice. "Check, please," and took out a dollar bill.

"Hah, hah, hah," laughed Carl. "He doesn't know me, he doesn't know me," he repeated sarcastically. "You see, Joe," he turned to the barman, "we weren't properly introduced in the movies — you know what I mean," and he laughed again. "I should have had him arrested," he added, "if he didn't appeal to me so well, hmmmm, Schatzi."

"Please, please, boys, not here," said Joe. "There is a booth for you." He pointed. Blok was too indignant to speak.

"Whiskey sour, please, " ordered Carl and asked Blok, "What will you have?" Blok started toward the door. "Oh, no, you won't run out on me again," cried Carl. "Joe, stop him. He's got a lot of dough." Both held Blok firmly by his arms and brought him back to the bar.

"Do you have a charge account here, yes?" screamed Joe. "Well, you can't run away without paying."

"I have paid," grunted Blok.

"Did he?"

"No," said Carl.

"How much do you want?" asked Blok.

"It all depends," said Joe vaguely. Blok put a ten-dollar bill on the counter, but as he began to move to the exit, he was held back again.

"Let me go," cried Blok, trying to tear himself free.

"Schatzie," whispered Carl clutching Blok's arm. "I don't want your money, you little bashful turtle dove." Blok pushed him away.

"Don't get fresh with Carl," warned Joe playing with the ten-dollar bill.

"Don't touch me," rasped Blok in extreme anger. "Don't you see who I am? Take a good look at me."

"You look cute. Just right to me," pouted Carl.

"Very cute," Joe seconded.

"Did you ever see a leper?" Blok asked calmly.

"A leper?"

"Yes," said Blok.

"We are not in Abyssinia," said Joe.

"It's true," said Blok, "but there are some in this city, and one is standing right in front of you now."

"He is not kidding," said Carl.

"Jesus, he looks like one," said the bartender, peering at Blok. "He is rotten all over."

"Joe, tell him to get the hell out of here. I'm scared," squealed Carl.

"Get out," barked Joe. He turned to Carl. "We'd better get some disinfectant or something."

"Pssstt, get out of here." Both men were extremely agitated, while Blok, tired and apathetic, slowly moved out of the bar, murmuring to himself. I am a leper, and everyone can see it.

A leper! Leper! Leper!

Chapter XI

They laughed and talked and, as Mathilda was putting on her hat, getting ready to leave, when the doorbell rang.

"Who could that be? It is so late — almost one o'clock." Sophie opened the door. There was a man standing there.

"Is this Doctor Sophie Kooper?" he asked shyly. "I am so terribly sorry. I know it is late; my intrusion is inexcusable. I am... please forgive me." His begging eyes, his hesitation in speaking, and his state of despair did not move them very much.

"What do you want, sir?" asked Sophie, but not waiting for an answer, concluded, "If you are a patient, please call me tomorrow at the office."

"Oh, please, doctor, it is so urgent. My name is Blok. I need your help. It is a rare, a strange case. I realize that I should not have disturbed you so late at night, but that quill is alive — and then the other thing — it won't take long. Please, doctor, I will be ever so grateful."

Sophie looked at Mathilda and then made a sign to Blok to enter the apartment. "Please sit down, Mr... Mr... I am sorry, what was the name?"

"Blok, madame," he said, and sat in the chair. The two ladies went into the other room. "Shall I stay here?" asked Mathilda. "He is rather strange. Are you afraid?"

"Not at all," said Sophie. "As a matter of fact, I have pity for him. His eyes are so sad. I am sure he is not a common man. In any case, I will find out what bothers him and try to help him."

"All right, darling. Then I will say good night." She kissed Sophie on the cheek and, promising to call her tomorrow, left.

"Well, Mr. Blok, what can I do for you?"

"It is a quill," said Blok, getting up. "There was another, a bigger one, but this one moves. Do you see how it moves? It tries to get out all by itself. Do you see it, doctor?"

Sophie looked at the spot indicated and said, "Your hand is trembling. I will get the splinter out. Please wait a minute." She came back with tweezers, and soon the quill was out. "Why do you say it moves?"

"It does, doctor, it does."

Sophie placed it on a white piece of paper and, after studying it carefully, mumbled to herself: "It does not move. Where did you get it?"

"I really don't know. There was a strange animal in Pinkel's courtyard, but really, it's nothing. I am afraid… you see, my state of nerves… it was caused by… It's rather unusual—I mean for this part of the country. There was a man and his wife – you have probably read that in the papers—they were afflicted with leprosy, and as I used to visit the same steam bath — I mean rather a Russian Turkish bath – they think I may have contracted it. I am so scared."

"Mr. Blok, why don't you go home and rest and call me tomorrow at the office? I know a fine psychiatrist."

"Oh, no!" said Blok. "It is not imaginary. The proof of it is that they are after me — I mean the inspector of the Department of Health. It was daring of me, I know, to call on you so late at night. I know you would not deliver me to them. A woman is much kinder in such matters."

"Thank you, Mr. Blok," said Sophie smiling. "What do you want me to do?"

"Please examine me. Please!"

"But not tonight. Please come tomorrow to the office. I am sure you have nothing. You have to calm yourself. You know, Hanson's disease is really not very catching."

"Thank you. I am really most grateful to you. But I don't know how I can possibly wait until tomorrow. I don't dare to go home. The inspector is surely waiting for me in my studio. You see, I have no place to go, and besides, maybe I am a great danger to the public. Oh, please do examine me — now! Shall I undress?"

"Please don't," said the doctor sharply. "You will have to consult a specialist anyhow — I know nothing about leprosy."

"Doctor, they are supposed to have bumpy places. The attendant in my steam bath told me about it. I am almost certain you could see it easily — I mean, if I have it."

"Nonsense. Good night, Mr. Blok. Tomorrow we will have a consultation in the office," she said dryly.

"All right," said Blok dejectedly. He looked pathetic and shriveled. She looked at him disdainfully. It was revolting to see a man like this, but at the same time, there was something so helpless and naive in the way his big eyes begged that she could not bring herself to put him out.

He must have felt the sudden change in her attitude, for he calmed himself sufficiently to speak with greater dignity. "I am very sorry. It is a shame. I hope you will forgive me."

As he made ready to leave, she asked him: "Who are you, Mr. Blok?"

"Hmmm—a ridiculous man."

"No, really. What do you do? I mean, what is your profession?"

"I am an artist."

"Oh," she said. "I have seen some of your work. My friend, the lady you saw here, has a portrait of a pink woman by you. She simply loves it. It's wonderful. Let's introduce ourselves to each other now," she said, smiling and reaching her hand toward Blok.

But Blok started back. "Oh, no, you should not touch me — not before we know... Oh, please do examine me now! Or let me stay here until morning. I do not dare be seen. I will not disturb you. I will not touch a thing, and if I am infected, I will deliver myself to the right authorities and leave for some island. But please let me get emotionally prepared for it. If one is ready inside, nothing can really hurt on the surface. Please, just imagine that a stray dog had run into your place, perhaps a little dirty and not pretty, but not really bad. Wouldn't you assign a little bare corner to him?"

"It is somewhat unusual," she said indeterminately. "Please wait, I will see if there are enough sheets and pillows."

"No, please don't look for them. I will not use anything. My father was a Spartan, and we all used to sleep on the bare floor. It was not an effort. You are so kind."

"You must rest. It is late. Good-night."

The next morning Blok found a note: "Hope your night was not too uncomfortable. Be in my office at 11:30 for the examination. Dr. S. Kooper."

"Mathilda dear, hello. Yes, it's, Sophie. I am in the office. Listen, I haven't much time. I just want to tell you about the patient. Do you know who he is? He is Byron, Seneka, poet and hero. Yes, him, him—with the big eyes and the torn jacket. He is at home. He stayed there. You don't believe me? No? Do you know who he is? No? And yet he has given you so much pleasure."

"Me? Pleasure?"

"He painted your 'Pink Woman'. Yes, it's he — Blok. Please, I don't want anyone to know about it. Later I will tell you why. I will call you tomorrow."

Sophie was agitated, tired and nervous. Before her on her desk were several open books, and pamphlets that she busily leafed through. There were "Medieval Leprosy;" treatises on modern leprosy in particular localities by Danielssen and Boeck; the dermatological works of Habra and Jonathan Hutchinson; G. W. McCoy's *Leprosyn;* and Tice's *Practice of Medicine.* She repeated absentmindedly: "Lepra, Arabum, Elephantiasis Grae-corum, nodular, anaesthetic, mixed, Arabum, Abum, bum, Blok, home, Lepra, Le-pra, Blok, foi gra. Stupid! Stupid!

"I will call Dr. Wilson. Will it be nodular? Or mixed? Nonsense; he is well. The incubation sometimes takes two years. Ridiculous. Dark red, coppery patches, symmetrical, on the face or feet or body."

At two o'clock she returned to her apartment. Blok greeted his hostess with a nuance of affection. It was really hardly perceptible and yet enough to make Sophie notice it with a certain displeasure. Her attitude was very professional and to the point. "Why didn't you come to my office?"

"I was afraid they would catch me on the way," he said embarrassed. She agreed to examine him right then. He was to occupy the maid's room. The necessary dishes, towels and laundry were placed on the table, and he was told politely and firmly to take complete care of his room, of his laundry, and the washing of his dishes. A small bathroom was at his disposal, which he had to keep equally clean and in order.

After all arrangements were made, she was ready for the examination. Blok felt shy end asked if she could examine different parts of his body separately. "Have I to be nude?"

She shrugged her shoulders and said, "It's not essential".

While he was taking his shoes and socks off, she put rubber gloves on her hands. He stood in his bare feet with the rest of his clothes on when she began to examine his face and head. She touched his cheeks very delicately, then went over his forehead and slid down to his neck. His skin froze in agreeable tenseness, making him close his eyes and hold his breath. He opened his eyes, and she asked him to lower his head. With her rubber fingers, she parted his hair carefully, stopping occasionally on one spot, touching the scalp with the point of her finger. It made him think of his mother before she washed his hair on Saturday nights. It was like the interruption of a sweet dream when he heard Sophie remark, "You have a lot of dandruff in your hair." She asked him to sit down and show her his feet. Since childhood he despised that part of his body, and with the years, his feelings towards them only solidified. How often he had said to himself, gazing at his crooked toes, "A sample of degeneration; look how crowded they are, suffocating and not letting air come into their stupid existence."

Sophie went carefully but quickly over his feet, separating his toes and making him lift each foot to look at his soles. This done, she said rather dryly, "You ought to take care of your feet; you have ringworms. I will give you some medicine."

The examination of the whole of Mr. Blok's body was completed at 4:35, and patient and doctor were both very tired.

Before Sophie retired to her room, she announced cheerfully: "So far, so good. Not a trace of the disease is visible. Of course, there must be some laboratory work done, but I would not worry; there is very little probability."

Blok did not worry any more. This was the astonishing thing. During the entire morning, the anxiety of yesterday had not once taken possession of his imagination. As a matter of fact, he was in no need of suppressing his fears and panic because his thoughts took a different turn. Something else had gotten hold of him but was not yet strong enough to define. And yet, he was conscious of the sudden change in his reactions. He was as astonished as he was pleased and yet sad at the same time. There was a subtle loveliness replacing the frightening mountain that had been ready to crush him.

Mr. Blok, cleaning his jacket, tried to remember the portrait of a "Woman in Pink". Was it a portrait, or the same as with Mitchell Wrinkly? He could not remember a woman in pink. Most women wear pink underwear—God knows why. But he would not paint a woman in underwear, pink or any other color. Blok was sitting in the chair, meditating agreeably, when Sophie knocked at his door and brought him some milk, American cheese, bread and two slices of cold tongue for dinner. On the tray there were also two big apples that looked so beautiful and shiny that he thought it would be profanity and a barbaric offense to eat them.

He heard the doorbell ring, and eating his dinner, he unintentionally overheard a conversation.

"Sophie dear, I hope you realize how unfair you are. After all, really, this mysteriousness is ridiculous. Haven't I told you all and trusted you completely? I never had secrets from you. I even faithfully described to you my journey with Kratki, didn't I?"

Sophie laughed long and so heartily that Mathilda, forgetting all her reproaches, had to join her. "Oh, Mathilda, I will never believe… It's too funny," and she started laughing again. "It cannot be true — it's too revolting for words." Sophie calmed herself a little and asked: "Is it really true? Did he actually stick his huge tongue into your mouth so unexpectedly that it made you… " She began to laugh again.

"Stop it! Stop it! After all, it is not that funny," said Mathilda. "It is rather sad and vulgar."

"I know; I am sorry, but please do tell me, did it really make you vomit all over him in the taxi?" This made Mathilda very angry, and from his room Mr. Blok heard no voices or laughter anymore.

"I had better close the doors," said Mathilda, "so that your guest, prisoner, patient or lover does not hear us. If you don't want me to know of your relations with Mr. Blok, I will not intrude into your intimate life anymore, though it is a pity. I was never more curious."

"There is nothing, really nothing extraordinary I can tell you about him," said Sophie, "except that he suffers from an extreme skin irritation, is nervous and lonely, and, like so many Europeans, is afraid of hospitals. He is rather helpless." As soon as she finished the phrase, the doorbell rang.

"It is Kratki," said Mathilda, hurrying across the room to open the door.

"How do you do, learned lady?" He greeted her with an agreeable smile. "It was so kind and charitable of you to ask me to come. A man of my age is very appreciative." With the deportment of a gentleman of the world, he kissed the ladies' hands. Taking a place in a chair close to Mathilda, he said, "On the corner of 19th Street today, I ran straight into Professor Snok's arms. We had a good time together, sitting and gossiping in a bar. By the way, he sends you his regards."

"He is a busybody," said Mathilda. "No one knows what he is really doing in life — except suing people."

"Though you may be right about the lawsuits, he was very perturbed, speaking of some artist whom he is suing."

"An artist?" asked Sophie. "Who?"

"Oh, you wouldn't know. Tell me, did you ever hear of the Aristocrats of Mind Society?"

"No," said Mathilda. "Why?"

"Oh, just because I understand Snok is worried about their interference in his case," said Kratki. After a short pause, he looked at Mathilda and asked, "You really think our substances will never mix?" There was a long and embarrassing pause, after which Mathilda turned toward Sophie and explained casually, "Our friend believes in 'subito' effects." And to Kratki, "Is it true?"

But Kratki did not answer while continuing to play with his tie and sitting sullenly. The atmosphere grew heavy, and the conversation dull. Sophie felt relieved when her guests left the apartment together. Friends are sometimes like dishes that require washing after contact with them, thought Sophie, emptying the ashtrays.

Chapter XII

Each time Sophie returned from the office Blok's feelings of joy were so overpowering that he was tempted to run to the door like a dog greeting its master. His longing for Sophie during her absence was growing. At first Blok attributed his feelings to the loneliness of his semi-confined existence and to his lack of activity, but soon he knew better.

He wished the laboratories would keep analyzing his specimens forever; their verdict either way would not be welcome, for it would force him to leave. There was really no doubt that Blok was free of the disease, and yet the precaution they now took were more elaborate than they were in the first days of their meeting.

Sophie was conscientious and meticulous in the thoroughness with which she supervised all examinations. The reports from the laboratories were checked and re-checked, only to repeat the process anew. Sophie was reserved towards Blok, but whatever she said or did was of singular significance and meaning to him. The mere mention of his name and the sound of her voice made his heart beat faster. He was aware of the strange situation in which he found himself, and it made him feel uneasy and guilty. Yet never before had he tasted with more naturalness the sweetness of safety and comfort.

Blok was not really displeased with his inactivity; and during many leisure hours of browsing through past events, he had the pleasure of imagining himself all sorts of personages he had met in his reading. He caught himself once laughing at the thought that he was Oblomoff. What a fabulous giant of laziness! How could Goncharov create such a character?

"What does it matter?" thought Blok. "It only proves that even laziness can be inspiring, and that doing absolutely nothing can be a great art; it all depends on how and why." Blok thought of laziness in general and of all the great services it brought to humanity. Were it not for laziness, people would still travel by mules.

One afternoon, Sophie returned home unusually late, and called Blok "Congratulations - you are completely well and a free man. You understand? There are no impediments to your freedom and happiness." But Blok was silent, gazing with grave serious. "Are you not pleased? We will celebrate your escape from the dreadful anxiety."

He still did not react. "Mr. Blok," said Sophie, with a note of perplexity, "Can't you understand? You are well — completely well. You are free to do as you please and to go wherever you want." But Blok only stood there, silently, looking shyly at Sophie. "What is wrong with you?"

"I will — oh, ... of course, if you wish. ..." he said softly with a sort of vague submission. "Of course, I will go, if you want me to go." And he added timidly, "In a way it is almost — I mean the news — in a way it shocked me. It will compel... force... me. Do you want me to go?"

"You are a strange man. The first impression I had of you was of an overly-anxious person with a very acute imagination and many fears — I mean concerning your health — and yet it does not seem that you feel relieved now."

"You are right. I am not so certain. Maybe it's you, dear doctor, who had the wrong impression."

"Whatever it is," said Sophie, "don't you feel like celebrating?"

"Of course, I do, I will be delighted. There is nothing I would rather do. But is it safe?"

"What do you mean? Of course. Even your persecutor the Inspector of Health now knows from my report that there is no taint of a disease in you," laughed Sophie.

"Oh, it's wonderful, but there are other things that I haven't mentioned to you," said Blok. You see, I left some people in my studio. They must still be waiting for me."

"What people?"

"Oh, you wouldn't know them."

"You're really strange." She smiled lightly.

"I don't know them very well myself, but it's certain they mean well. It's only that I couldn't stand any more protection."

"Protection? From what?"

"Oh, it's all so complicated. Bothersome ... hard to explain," he said with sudden desperation. "I swear I'm innocent. And yet they're after me. All of them." He came nearer to Sophie.

"I won't let them crowd me. Be they protectors or accusers, I don't want to hear their stories, I refuse to share my bed with them and hear them cracking peanuts."

Gazing at Sophie's puzzled face, he continued, "It's a plot conceived and executed by maniacs. The best proof of it is that nobody was ever frozen or burned to death by my atmospheric pictures before that damned exhibition. How can they explain that?"

"I remember reading in the papers of some trouble you had, but I thought it was all over."

"All over? Mlauzinski should hear that!"

"Who is Mlauzinski?"

"He is my lawyer who doesn't even have time to enumerate all the law-suits they are bringing against me. It's certainly a bulky list already — files of it!"

"You're sure it's not a persecution mania?"

"Once before you wanted to recommend a psychiatrist," said Blok. "No, I assure you, I don't suffer from illusions."

"I don't really mean it," said Sophie, and after a short pause she added, "I know so little about you."

"And yet you did not act like a stranger. I gave you so much trouble. I wish I could express my ... that I did not deserve."

"I'm glad I was able to be of service to you."

"But now it's all over — I can't ask you to do more for me."

"What bothers you? Who are all those people who wish to harm you? It's not out of curiosity that I am asking." She looked at him warmly. "I feel there is a confusion I thought perhaps we could try to clarify together."

"You are so wonderful," said Blok.

Once seated, she said, "You said you refused to share your bed with someone."

"Oh, that was the young psychiatrist."

"Psychiatrist?"

"Yes, he is employed by the Aristocrats of Mind Society, as they all are – bodyguards, physicians, nurse."

"Whom do they guard? Why? What is the Aristocrats of Mind Society?" cried Sophie bewildered.

"They are really, I think, fine people. It is a worldwide organization, very broad-minded and efficient. They are trying to help me. They believe I am in grave danger. My life itself... Oh, I wish they had made it clear to me."

"But if they are so wonderful, why do you resent them?"

"I couldn't stand living with all of them in my studio," he said. "It became unbearable. I was imprisoned in my own home. I ran away, and I will not return. Not now. Oh please, please — let me stay here a little longer." Blok spoke with passion, assuring her of his innocence and pleading for her understanding. "Behind that," he pointed toward the door, "All evil is waiting for me." And with tears in his eyes, "I fear my enemies, and I don't understand my supposed friends."

Sophie, listening attentively and impressed, wanted to say something warm to comfort him. She got up from the sofa. "Of course, you can stay here until everything is settled. I am certain the Society will help you with these legal matters. Only don't you think one must notify them? They may need you. When will the first case be tried?"

"I think it is Snok's," Blok uttered nervously. But the Society will attempt to postpone it because they are not quite ready. But they have many legal advisors, and they are holding conferences daily. It is their life. They will not need me. Not until I am prepared to face them again."

"Of course, as you wish."

"I am so grateful," Blok looked deeply into her eyes and pressed her hand with great emotion.

"I feel we will know each other," said Sophie slightly embarrassed.

As he stood close to her, he wished to hold her hand forever. The doorbell rang. Hesitatingly, and as if unwilling, Sophie freed her hand and went slowly to the door.

"Sophie darling," Blok heard Mathilda's voice. "Do we disturb you? These are my friends," and he heard men's voices.

"Come in, please."

Blok felt like leaving the room or insulting the intruders as they entered the living room. "So pleased to see you again," Mathilda said as she recognized Blok. "Hope you are feeling better." Mathilda introduced Mr. Shopklang, a young American composer, and as Shopklang offered his perspiring hand, Kratki moved aside suddenly as if he were ill-at-ease. But as abruptly, he returned and, staring at Blok with his small yellowish eyes, said "God! Can it be possible? After all these years. Do you remember?"

"I remember only too well!" said Blok with hostility, his face turning white.

Fixing a stare at Mr. Kratki's prosperous features, Mr. Blok felt an old and painful wound reopen. "What is he doing here?" He tried to control his growing anger. "I must not show my feelings," he said to himself, turning to Shopklang.

"I understand you also did not escape being labelled." Looking around as if to challenge the audience, he added: "We artists are carefully numbered, sorted and knighted, but not according to our deeds, genre, convictions, values or the services we render. Not at all. We are classified and titled according to the papers we carry in our pockets. Sometimes they are birth certificates, sometimes mere newspaper reviews, or checks with which we are paid for our services. Of course, the first move in classification starts with the birth certificate — it's clear and simple; Romanian painter, American composer, etc., but later on, as the career progresses there will be "the great Rumanian painter, and soon — if that title should, for some reason, not stick — there is a great assortment of others, always pointing to the excellency of the bearer."

He sat down, avoiding Kratki' s steady gaze.

"Your objection to titles," said Kratki, "only indicates your belief in the American way of life."

"Indeed, I am proud to be an American," said Blok hotly, and looking at Shopklang, he asked, "What did you compose?"

"Oh," said the young man, "what's the use for us Americans to compose? No one would perform it anyhow. To have that privilege one must come from France, Germany, or Russia."

"Hm," murmured Blok and repeated the question, "What did you compose?"

"I wrote a violin sonata and five songs."

"What else?"

"What else? Isn't that already something?"

"Well, something, perhaps, but hardly enough to be a composer," said Blok. "It is like having a haberdashery with one shirt and a pair of socks on the shelf."

"Mr. Blok," whispered Sophie reproachfully. But Blok knew that nothing would keep him from talking.

"I am sorry. One is not personal in these matters. We so-called intelligentsia must speak — no, act." And then abruptly, he added, "What are you for, the past or the future? I am asking you and answering you at the same time. You all say it's the future you are concerned with. Is that right?"

"It all depends," mumbled Shopklang, hardly audible.

"We all are for the future, right? But then, why do we support those mausoleums of art, the museums, antique shops, and ancient societies. Why? Do we want to discourage all those whose creative genius would resemble those of the past? Perhaps someone would paint like Vermeer or compose like Mozart, if they never knew of their existence. Why in the name of the future don't we lock the crop of the old every hundred years in vaults? And hide them from the eyes and ears of the young? Don't laugh, Mr. Kratki!"

"Human emotions undergo evolutions, and there must be a change of expression," remarked Sophie reproachfully.

"It's true," agreed Blok, feeling that Sophie had taken Kratki's side against him. "But there is a limit to all forms, and they are almost exhausted now. We are desperately looking for ever new ways of expression. We go back to the jungles and man eaters in a search for originality, and we crawl into deeper holes.

New, new, everyone demands from us, as though we were inventors and scientists."

"Love always was modern — as it is new and modern today. I can't bear to see all those good people wander in the jungles and creep into dark holes for inspiration," said Kratki with sarcasm. "It's too sad!"

His remark angered Blok. Sophie offered drinks but no one seemed to be thirsty. Mathilda looked at her watch, and soon after the guests left the apartment. Just before passing through the door Kratki took Blok aside. "Are you really against Anthropophagi?" Then he left.

"I hate him," said Blok to Sophie, when they were left alone.

"You are unduly severe on people," said Sophie.

"No, I'm not — not where Kratki is concerned." Blok's violent reaction was rather unexpected.

"So, you knew Kratki?"

"Of course, how could one forget him? One must die to forget him. Like Luba and her mother died. They forgot him." he said. "I am sorry. I shouldn't have started, but on the other hand, perhaps I shall — I mean — considering his relation to Mathilda."

"Please do speak," said Sophie.

"As I said, Luba — I mean the girl I intended to marry and who later married Mr. Kratki instead — was a very lovable person before she married. You understand, it was a long time ago. I..." Blok did not know how to begin. He was confused and reluctant to speak.

"Please, tell me everything from the beginning." There was hope in her voice, as if she were trying to convince herself that the forthcoming story would not be as bad as expected.

"I will, certainly," said Blok. "You see, Luba's parents were extremely wealthy. Her mother was a sophisticated and shrewd woman who completely dominated her insignificant husband.

They wanted their only child, from the time she was just a little girl, to understand the power of money and the beauty of possession. Poor Luba herself told me how they would take her into the vaults of a bank and show her bonds and stocks heaped in a big pile. 'It belongs to you, sweetie,' they would say — 'all yours, and a lot more to come after we die. You are a rich little girl, and you must be smart and not let anyone take it away from you. They will try hard, darling, because they would all like to have it.' Then they would lead her to another safety deposit box and show her many glistening things — diamond necklaces and ruby rings and golden cases and pearls. Always fondling her, they would put rings on her little fingers and let her touch all the wonderful things and play with them."

"Why are you telling me about people I don't know?" asked Sophie impatiently. "You wanted to tell me something about Mr. Kratki."

"Yes, indeed; I thought you would be interested. I love to think of Luba before the time she met him. She was so lovely! But when she reached the age of seventeen her mother had a lovely surprise for her — a self-made man in his thirties and already a successful businessman. He knew what he wanted and knew how to cast aside all that was in his way. He certainly did not have much trouble getting me out of his way."

"Oh, now I understand your resentment," said Sophie.

"No, you don't," said Blok, annoyed by her remark.

"Do you want to get even?"

"No, I don't! I don't believe in vengeance, and besides, he does not exist for me anymore."

"All right, then please go on. What happened after he married Luba? ''

"He gained importance and influence in the world of finance and industry and was regarded as a respectable family

man. He zealously guarded this reputation by paying gener-
ously for the discretion of those who took part in his shady
and clandestine life."

"Is it a variation on Dr. Jekyll and Mr. Hyde?" interrupted
Sophie irritatingly.

"Perhaps," said Blok and continued. "She hated him, but
she was not skillful in hiding her fear of him. He was hurt and
allowed his aggravation to grow into hatred. Realizing how urgent was her desire to escape from her life with him, and how
sensitive and delicate she was, he played on her weaknesses and
contrived all sorts of fiendish device, driving her to the point
of submission and finally into a mental institution.

"It goes without saying that he succeeded. She gave herself
up only too willingly to the powers which promised freedom.
Now she was safe in their hands, and her occasional resistance
was not of much concern."

"But was she really sick?" asked Sophie.

"No, not really. She was driven to it," said Blok getting up.
"Mr. Kratki succeeded, but the wanderings of a mean mind are
unpredictable, and there is always something missing, even in
a perfect crime — some little detail, some link. There are too
many impulses to cope with, too many imponderables." Blok
took a breath and spoke quickly.

"One day Luba's mother entered his room to get information about her daughter, but Kratki did not listen to her
questions. He looked at her luxurious dressing gown, noting
something he had failed to see in all the past years — the way
she placed her legs, the sound of her voice, and her promising
eyes. He saw her well-formed breasts showing through the silk
or her gown. Shall I leave you at this outrageous striptease?"
asked Blok, smiling for the first time. But Sophie was silent.
"You will guess that her passion soon tired Kratki, and their

relations became so abusive that he decided to terminate their ignoble pact. But it was not an easy task, for she clung to him with the ferocity of an at-last-awakened passion. In her lust, which was not now shared, she was as dangerous as she was desperate. She had no pride left. She begged and threatened. Even more revolting were her attempts to seduce him anew." Blok imitated her with a grimace. "'Don't you like your little mommy anymore?' she would say coquettishly. She became a nuisance, a whore, a miserable scavenger, and repulsive to him. She had no ears, no feelings for, anything but him. Her husband, miserable and alone, was left to view the disintegration of his family."

Sophie sat silently, her face expressionless, as Blok said in a matter-of-fact tone, "There is a short epilogue to this tale. When he definitely abandoned, her, she hanged herself in the kitchen, and when Luba heard of all this, she entered the ranks of the incurables. But our dear Mr. Kratki was free and wealthy, and after the death of his wife he became the happy fiancé of another attractive and equally wealthy woman."

Sophie got up from her chair. "Is it the truth?"

Blok felt sorry for himself and the whole world. Pacing the room, he punished himself by calling himself a gossipy fellow, a gnat, a mosquito. Sophie went to the couch again. "So, this is the truth," she said in a halt-voice. They both felt the heavy silence. Sophie looked at Mr. Blok on the chair, his head resting on his arm, "You must have loved Luba very much." He heard her remark, as if addressing someone else not present and suddenly looking at him, "You never married after this, I suppose?"

"Hmm, eh… a formality… I mean actually — yes, but really — I don't think so."

"How long were you married?"

"It seemed to me very long," said Blok, playing with his curly eyebrow. "There should be new systems invented of measuring time, with many different calendars and watches to live by, according to the age and temperament of each person."

"It sounds complicated," said Sophie.

"Yes and no," said Blok, going through all his pockets. "Oh, here is my pencil. Can I have a piece of paper? It is rather simple…I'll show you what I call a fair system built on the principles of… "

But Sophie said, "Some other time." And then, "Who was the woman?"

"Hm… she still is. I mean, we are divorced. God bless that day! Asmodeus should have prevented that marriage in the first place, but I guess he lost interest in weddings a long time ago."

"Did you love her?" asked Sophie.

"I loved the day of divorce." Mr. Blok smiled, remembering embracing strangers on that day and distributing his possessions among them.

"Why did you marry her?" asked Sophie somewhat impassioned. "Why?"

"I wish to know myself," he said. "I was young and silly, and my vocabulary was so poor."

"You could not talk yourself out of it?" Sophie smiled.

"Perhaps," said Blok. "She spoke so beautifully. I mean the first time we met I was fascinated like a savage in front of the unknown. She said so many words that sounded so strange to me, and I listened to them as though I understood what she said. She was deceived. I was too cowardly or too flattered to admit my ignorance and to confess that only one of her words out of a hundred reached my brain."

"Yes, how can I admit it," he said fervently and stood up. "A fool, so much I knew — that she proposed, and I accepted.

It was too late to back down, and there was no cause. She was superior to ordinary people. In all matters of culture, but above all in her usage of English she was a unique phenomenon. Her father was a scholar, and so was her entire family, and it was my former wife's passion since her early days, instead of dolls, to play with words. She loved them, adding to her already incredible collection ever new words and expressions. She was greedy for them and skillful in using them. In the first grades of school, her language was already too formidable for the teachers to cope with, leaving them embarrassed and mute before the child."

"It is most unusual," remarked Sophie.

"Indeed, I used to write down and learn by heart whole sentences. I studied them staying awake sometimes entire nights. Whatever she said apparently always made sense. I begged her to say simple things like 'good morning,' 'how do you feel,' or 'lovely day' to no avail. She spoke in circumlocutions or quotations from learned books.

"At times in despair, I would lose patience and call her a walking encyclopedia, and she would cry, and I could only guess her complaints. She would call me names, presumably offending. The names of died-out devils or fossils or modern pimps. I guessed always the meanings of words by her facial expression and the tone of her voice, always feeling my own inferiority. But even her face and her voice would sometimes mislead me, making me act contrary to what was expected.

"My life became a nightmare, and so consequently did hers. We tried to understand each other, tried to find a common language, only to give up at last. Even the milkman stopped deliveries in extreme irritation, and the laundress and the maid refused to deal with her. There had to come an ending climax and final break, and so one day when she entered my studio and spoke solemnly – 'of our 'crystal ball in which murky depths all supercilious ties already glowed faintly into the dawning century,' and when she went on that 'one should always be conscious of the fact that the supposition of the existence would lead to suggest approximately prognosticated experience, but which was in principle always arbitrary and...,'. I could not stand it anymore and threw my best frame at her and painted her face with the pale blue and green oils that were fresh on my brushes."

Mr. Blok continued. "She sued me for divorce, the usual cruelty, of course, but there still is justice... I was always sincere in my desire to understand her, and I proved the point by showing the judge many sheets of paper filled with phrases and words spoken by her in our daily communications. I wrote down my own interpretations of them and gave my sources and the names of respectable dictionaries. I tried to make clear to the judge my honest intention and handed him all I had written. He read it and granted the divorce on grounds of cruelty to me. I expressed my readiness to take the guilt, but the judge was very firm. The verdict stood. It was a queer misunderstanding, and she probably still lives with the belief in my intellectual deficiency and mental cruelty."

"It makes a nice story except that it does not make one laugh or cry or, as you see, even smile," Sophie remarked with vexation.

It touched Blok disagreeably and harshly. "I did not intend to impress you. Besides, marriage stories are seldom amusing."

"You may change that rule," said Sophie softly, and only then Blok noticed her sadness. But he was not touched, for he knew many shades of that feeling, whole palettes of it... pure sadness, and the solid, permanent, and quickly changeable sadness of art... the sadness of the clown, the sadness of death... the sadness after the end of joy... or of tormented expectations... nocturnal sadness and the sadness of unknown origin... of the limitlessness of time, ache of the stomach, or lack of funds... but Sophie's sadness was that of the aggravation of a woman.

"You are really married only to art..."

"Never had such drastic relations with it."

"I thought art was your whole life."

"Yes, I live on it, as the termite lives on wood."

"They are destructive."

"Sometimes I am too. I throw away my bad pictures and sell the good ones — which often amounts to the same thing."

"What do you mean?"

"Those who buy them, hang them! Good joke, isn't it?"

"Please tell me what has real meaning in your life?"

"Love! I love love, and I always love. I am always in love with something — with things I paint, with women, with Nature, and with art; but I am an artist, and as such, I am ambitious. All artists are. It's a pity — ambition does not bring joy; it is tormenting. I fall in love easily and often, sometimes with only a part of a thing. Oh, sometimes single parts are so complete." He smiled. "Once I fell in love with the scroll of a Guarneri violin. What a beautiful thing it was! But I did not admire the rest of it and did not want to listen to the sound. I loved the scroll only! I painted it to replace the head of a woman that did not match the beauty of the rest of her body. I was in love with the hands of one person and with the eyes of another, with a branch of one tree and the trunk of another. I was in love with ruins in Greece, with a new chair, and with old people as much as I loved blue and red, a voice, hair, or a beautiful thought. I fell in love with a watch, with fur, with a pair of shoes, with a moon, and with a strongly built chess table. I also wanted to fall in love with myself, if only for a day, for a minute or an hour, but I had to give it up and satisfy myself with being only pleased with myself occasionally." He looked deep into Sophie's eyes. "Permanently and passionately I loved only God, art and my mother — but now... now... I think I love you, also."

There was a silence, then Sophie asked, "Any particular part?" But there was no real sarcasm in her voice — only in the words behind which she hid her feelings. Blok threw himself' at her feet.

"All of you, darling — all, all." He kissed her hands. "All of you..."

The doorbell rang sharply. With a start he got to his feet.

"I think it's Pinkel, delivering my order," said Sophie in confusion, leaving to open the door.

"It's a stab in the back — that damnable Pinkel," thought Blok bitterly. "Will that stolen, that precious moment ever return again?" he asked himself, tears in his eyes.

Chapter XIII

"Sophie shouldn't have left," he thought. "I hate being here alone. Without her, this place becomes a hideout and a prison. I can't stand it. I will get claustrophobia. I must go out, even for a few hours, since I can't sleep anyway." Blok looked at the easel and canvases Sophie had given him before she left to visit her relatives in the country for the weekend. "Always relatives," reflected Blok, remembering some painful events in this connection in the past. Sophie didn't want to see them. "Obligations! They forced her — stupid. Also, I was stupid to lie to her. Now she thinks I am an expert cook. I, who can't even warm up coffee. Oh, those apples and buttermilk, nothing but buttermilk. Hmmm, isn't there a restaurant on 18th or 17th Street that is open all night?" He smelled the air, and his tongue licked his lips, as if a hot dish had been placed before him. He got up with decision — "I will go there."

Suddenly he heard a noise. It was as if someone had shuffled in his bare feet on the floor, and then something creaked and scraped. This time it came from a different direction. "It's too loud for a mouse," thought Blok. He listened with tension. "Someone must be in the kitchen." No, no! Didn't he hear light steps passing his room? Something fell, he thought in Sophie's room. It's not Sophie. She will not return until late tomorrow night.

There was silence again. Blok stepped to the door and, with his hand on the doorknob, hesitated. Then he opened it and walked on his toes into the corridor. There was a light in Sophie's dressing room. He moved quietly toward it. Looking through the door that stood half ajar, he saw a small skinny man bent over a chest of drawers, whose content he was placing in a gray canvas bag. He appeared to be quite unconcerned, very absorbed and slow. His hand shook a little as he lifted each object to his face and examined it carefully before putting it either in the bag or back into the drawer. There was something very peaceful and natural about him and the whole procedure.

He was unaware of all feelings of danger, and that lessened Mr. Blok's alertness. The man stood and half turned, exposing the left side of his face where instead of an ear, Blok noted an elongated incision. "Just like the ears of a Marabou stork," he caught himself saying. There was no doubt Blok clearly heard his own voice. The man remained completely undisturbed. Blok coughed, the way people do to draw attention, but this did not have any effect, either. Not having any definite plan but no longer biding his presence, Blok entered the room. The prowler, his back toward Mr. Blok, now walked over to the cupboard, but changing his mind, suddenly turned and stood before Mr. Blok. His watery eyes expressed surprise rather than fear, and only his pointed yellowish-white beard quivered a little. At a complete loss, the two men stood frozen, staring at one another, not knowing what to say or do. He is a thief, I must call the police, urged Blok's reason as he approached the man.

"Drop this," he pointed to the bag. The man looked at him and his leathery cheeks tightened, but Blok saw that they remained wrinkled and white.

"Drop that bag," he ordered again, though this time somewhat less menacingly. The man put the bag on the floor carefully as though handling his own precious belongings. While doing this, he never took his old eyes off Blok.

"I do not hear very well." Blok heard his nasal voice. "I thought there was no one at home," he explained, and the point of his beard vibrated with every word.

"Evidently, evidently," said Blok. The whole body of the prowler seemed like a big question mark that would burst open any moment.

"And what now?"

"Yes, and what now," Blok also demanded of himself. There was silence. It helped Mr. Blok come to a decision. "Leave this place at once, get out, please." He forced the words from his mouth and motioned his hands towards the door. But the man only pointed to the other side of his head where he had a normal ear.

"I can't hear very well. Sorry, you must speak a little louder."

"I say," screamed Blok into his incision, "you must get out of here."

"Oh yes, yes," nodded the man quite happily. "Of course, now I have heard you perfectly, of course, I am leaving. No harm done. It's understandable, my apology," he said and started towards the door. Blok hustled into the corridor to switch the light on, but at this moment, the prowler was seized by a coughing spell so violent it seemed to choke him. Mr. Blok dashed for water, but when he came back with it, the man had recovered, and wiping his eyes and mouth, he said, "No thanks, I never drink water. It only irritates my throat." After a short pause, he added, "I get these spells only after nervous tension." The color in his face began to retreat from purple-red to his normal color.

"Would you like some buttermilk?" asked Blok.

"No. It tastes like milk of magnesia," he retorted with a grimace.

"You seem to suddenly hear very well," said Blok, ashamed of catching the man in a lie.

"Yes, sometimes I do," said the prowler quietly and, quickly changing his tone, added, "You don't suspect me of pretending?"

"No, not really," muttered Blok insincerely.

"That's fine," said the man. "I wonder what time it is now?"

"It is almost 2:00."

"I just thought," said the prowler, "that I didn't have my dinner yet. There is a fine oyster bar only a short way from here. Delicious, too. Oh boy!" His mouth watered.

"You say it is nearby?"

"No distance whatsoever," assured the man quickly and advanced ready to go.

"Wait, just a minute," said Mr. Blok putting his hat and coat on. "I should never have done this," thought Blok following the man through the deserted streets.

Entering the restaurant, Blok saw two men at the counter and chose a small table at the window. "I used to be a dishwasher here during the war," said the prowler. "Just rinsed them once in a while. A fine job it was — no one ever complained. You know during wartime it would be considered unpatriotic. Dozens of people ate practically with the same forks and spoons." The man giggled softly. Blok enjoyed his vegetable soup immensely and, save for the involuntary slurp of the man eating his oyster stew, there was a silence until the plates were empty.

"What Is your name?" asked Blok.

"If you don't mind, I'm incognito."

"There is a piece of oyster stuck in your beard," said Blok.

"Thanks." He took it off with his polka-dotted handkerchief, and said, "My dad would be crazy about a man like you. He used to say, 'Look here, little rascal, I will teach you a lesson they don't learn in schools. There are people,' he would say, 'who would push you down, but there are also people, though a lot fewer, who want to pull you up. The first one will offer you ease and a lot of fun, but the other, will offer you toil, work and pain. They are awfully demanding, but good. Stick to them and run away from the others.'"

"Did you?" asked Blok.

"No."

"Why?"

"Because at one time I did the pushing and pulling of others. Quite a fellow," he caressed his beard. "They all resented and waited until I weakened. Then they crushed me. They certainly did hit me from above and below."

Blok would have listened more attentively to the man, had he not noticed strange carryings on of the two men at the counter. They tried not to draw Blok's attention by stopping their whispering whenever they caught Blok' s eye on them. One of the men went to the telephone booth and, scanning Blok's table, spoke to someone excitedly over the phone. Returning to the counter, he said quite audibly, "All is set," and again quickly glanced at Blok.

"Anything wrong?" the prowler asked.

"The two men over there seem to be interested in us," said Blok.

"Must be a couple of dicks," the prowler said with a quick look, and in a half voice, "no one else is interested in me. Let's scram." But the moment they were ready to leave, the two men barred their way. "Don't hurry, boys," one of them said, showing his badge. One minute later, a uniformed policeman entered.

"Take him," they pointed at the prowler. "Also, this guy, just for the company." The police car waited for them outside.

At the station, the prowler was locked up right away while Mr. Blok underwent a rain of questions. "Working together, eh?"

"I'm always working alone," said Blok.

"Alone, eh? Don't like singing birds? Just met an old acquaintance for a peaceful meal? Now talk, and talk fast," they urged.

"Listen, gentlemen," said Blok, "it is the second time in the last few months that I have been questioned at the police station. The first time they thought I was Wrinkly and thought I was drunk. Perfectly ridiculous! Well, they apologized and left me alone."

"Did they?" One officer smiled.

"I am telling the truth. My name is Blok, and if you wish, I'll show you my identification at home."

"Where is your home, if I may ask?"

"Hmmm, right now I'm visiting a. friend, I mean temporarily."

"You are? But never mind your address. Is there any decent citizen in town who will identify you?"

"Dozens of them."

"Who are they?"

Blok hesitated for a long moment, then said, "Call the Aristocrats of Mind Society. Ask for Mr. Ellis or Mr. Ondra. There is always someone in the building."

The policeman went out but returned soon and offered Mr. Blok a cigarette. "Thanks, don't smoke."

"We're sorry to keep you waiting, Mr. Blok. It won't be long. They said someone would be here in a minute." In a few minutes, the door was flung open, and Mr. Ellis and Mr. Ondra rushed in. They embraced Mr. Blok heartily. "Oh, how glad we are to find you again. Why did you do that? Why didn't you return?" They also shook the hands of the officers, thanking them for finding Mr. Blok. "We are grateful to you. Grateful beyond words," they said and shook hands again.

Before leaving the station, Mr. Blok got permission to see the prowler in the jail. "Is there anything I can do for you?" asked Blok.

"Yes," said the man tugging at his beard. "Don't mention to them how we met." Blok promised.

"Is that all?"

"If you can spare a few dollars…" Blok uncrumpled a five-dollar bill and gave it to him.

"Thanks," said the prowler, "I knew my old man would be crazy about you."

"Very kind of him," muttered Mr. Blok.

"There is something else I would like you to do, a very big favor. I had a lousy deal in a drug store and got stuck with an oil painting. I got rid of everything from the job except the oil painting. That darned thing, painted by a longhaired swine, Blok is his name. Maybe you could get rid of it for me. I keep it in… " foreseeing a coming coughing attack, he forced the words out while grabbing for air. Blok stood speechless, looking behind the bars.

"Mr. Blok, Mr. Blok," he heard Ellis and Ondra calling.

"If you will help me," continued the man coughing.

"I am coming," Blok answered the call. And, with his heart filled with sadness, he left the jail.

"We worried so much about you," said Mr. Ellis as the three men walked from the station. "At first we thought you had been kidnapped by the General Freezing Company. The next day, Mr. Pinkel telephoned. But when I came to Pinkel's apartment as an authority of the Health Department and learned that you were suspected of spreading leprosy, what a shock it was to me! Then, you disappeared again. Oh, why did you do that?" asked Mr. Ellis with great feeling. "You don't seem to listen," said Mr. Ellis with a nuance of reproach. But Blok was thinking of the prowler, Pinkel, and the painting.

"What?"

"Nothing." said Mr. Ellis. "You must rest. Then we will have some coffee and lot of talk. I think the news I have for you will please you very much." Mr. Blok followed the two men passively into the Aristocrats of Mind Building. He refused to rest and insisted on hearing the news while the coffee was being made. Mr. Ellis began to speak at once.

"We were very pleased indeed with the success of our committee for your defense," said Ellis agreeably. "Through the intervention of our legal advisors, poets and artists, the Game Warden and the Justice of the Peace dropped their charges against you for trapping a raccoon out of season. Through the efforts of our best speakers and humanitarians, the Guild for Abstaining from Cruelty to Animals made you an honorary life member of the organization. Isn't it wonderful? But that's not all. Thanks to the well worked out plans of the twenty-two psychiatrists, all attached to the Society, Bonnie not only dropped her charges of attempt at rape but begged for forgiveness."

"Did she, did she?" cried Blok emotionally.

"Yes, poor child," continued Ellis with a saddened face. "She expects to be a mother, but Mr. Snok refused to recognize this."

"How dare he? It's criminal!" Blok sprang to his feet. "I pronounce herewith solemnly to adopt the child and to help Bonnie to the best of my ability."

The two men, deeply touched, also got up and said, "You are a wonderful man."

But the words did not lessen Mr. Blok's anger. "That mean super-modern apparatus," he cursed Mr. Snok, pacing the room.

The gentlemen waited until he calmed himself, and after Mr. Blok was back in his chair, Mr. Ondra said pacifyingly, "Believe us, dear friend, Mr. Snok paid for his deed. Our most valuable team of philosophers argued him to admit that the tool with which the crime is committed is always removed from the guilty party."

"What do you mean?" asked Blok puzzled.

"Mr. Snok was castrated," said Ellis. "Don't be upset, please. He is much calmer and happier now, and judging from what our surgeons say, he is more active mentally than ever."

"In that case," said Blok, "let's hope that it won't be necessary to remove his brain one day." Blok really regretted having said this. Not knowing how to smooth the remark, he made it still more awkward, muttering shyly, "Nature never is guilty. Hmmm, he probably will gain weight now."

"The whole incident was very painful indeed," said Mr. Ellis. "And I assure that during the entire existence of our Society, we have urged only three men to be castrated."

"Better than that," Mr. Ondra interrupted, "all three of them were homosexuals."

"Now, my dear friend, really good news," announced Mr. Ellis. "We were able to locate the true father of Stepan. It was very amusing. His father is also named Blok, but mind you, Block with 'ck'." Both men laughed heartily. Mr. Blok also tried to smile, but not succeeding, he remarked, "It is morning already."

"My goodness, we shouldn't have kept you up so, how shall I say, early," and both of them chuckled.

They accompanied Mr. Blok to a large room, in the middle of which Blok recognized the oddly shaped bed. "We hope you will rest comfortably, at least for a few days, until the remaining cases are settled, we hope favorably. By the way, the

Aris of Honduras – you remember I read his letter to you, Mr. Cheezis? – feels very badly having believed you guilty."

"It's nice of him'! said Blok, stifling a yawn. "What will Sophie think not finding me in the apartment upon her return?" he wondered.

"We will let you sleep. Only a little more news of Bonnie. You remember the waiter? He told us you would. He said he fed you by hand. Well, I'm not sure whether you know that he heads our Anthrophosophic Department. You are probably acquainted with Dr. Steiner's teachings, of which…" Mr. Ondra touched Mr. Ellis' arm. "He's asleep," he whispered. On tiptoes, they left the room. "Poor Mr. Blok, he is so exhausted. I will send the nurse to undress him," said Ondra.

It must have been late afternoon when Blok opened his eyes. It took him sometime to recall the recent occurrences. He found his underwear and his suit neatly folded. "Who could have undressed me?" wondered Blok. He stretched, rubbed his eyes, coughed a few times, got up, and crossed the room in search of the bathroom. When he reached the middle of the room, there was a knock on the door, and before he could utter a word, in they marched, in single file. The first was Alphonse, the guard. Caught so completely unexpectedly in the middle of the room, Blok ran first in one direction toward the bathroom, then changing his mind, ran to the bed in great embarrassment and covered his nakedness. The next to enter was the young psychiatrist followed by the nurse and his other companions at the studio. Their joy was great at seeing Blok again while Blok's feelings were mixed.

"You look fine," one of them said. And another, "We were certainly worried about your welfare. You must never, never do such a thing again." And one of the bodyguards, grinning, offered him peanuts. "The same set-up," said the psychiatrist.

"I would like to go to the bathroom," said Blok.

"But of course, by all means." They all peered at him.

"Could you look out of the window just for a minute?"

"Sure," they agreed, except Alphonse, following his instructions, rushed to the door.

Ten minutes later, Blok, well combed and dressed, walked out of the bathroom. He looked concerned and worried. "There is some urgent business I would like to discuss with Mr. Ellis."

"Of course," said the physician. "He is waiting for you in the office." Alphonse accompanied him.

"You look so rested," greeted Ellis. "Were you pleased to see all your friends?"

"Why must they guard me? I understand I am to remain here for a few days."

"We simply have to take those precautions. You don't seem to realize it's all for your own good."

"I must notify some friends who are expecting me."

"Whom?" asked Ellis. "Abka Perk has to go back to Glasgow, Blum is in Havana and Alexander in Mexico waiting for an immigration visa."

"Hmmm, are they?" said Blok. "But it is not they whom I want to know I am delayed."

"May I know who it is?"

"Can't I have any privacy?"

"As you wish, Mr. Blok, but I repeat it is for your own good."

Blok weighed the possible indiscretion of giving Sophie's address. "She will be terribly worried and even angry, he thought. I had better let her know." He wrote the name and address on a slip of paper.

"Oh, is this the physician who gave a report of your examination?"

"Yes, it is."

"That dunderhead Miller lost the paper and thereby lost his job. Couldn't even remember the name of the doctor. Anything more we can do for you?"

"Perhaps I could see Bonnie."

"It' s easy. She wants very much to see you."

"Where can I see her privately?"

"Right here, of course, any time." A few hours later, Bonnie's arrival was announced, and Blok hurried to the reception room. The moment she entered, he greeted her affectionately. "Come in, dear, sit here and tell me all about yourself."

"I've wanted to see you for a long time," she said.

"How is your work coming along? I hope you haven't neglected it."

"I did. I was too upset. I hope you are not angry with me. I shouldn't have let him influence me to sue you."

"Who?"

"Mr. Snok."

"What bothers you, Bonnie? Please tell me."

"I don't know, I really don't know how to tell it," said Bonnie.

Go ahead, just tell it and be simple," Blok said.

"It is rather disagreeable; I don't know if I should. Please, please, try to understand."

Blok took Bonnie's hand and patted it in a fatherly manner.

"Do you think Mr. Snok is a pansy?" asked Bonnie shyly.

"Why do you ask that?"

"Oh, just like that. He said he was, but… "

"But what?"

"You see, it is… I sort of think… I am not sure… that that is the truth."

"Why?"

"Mr. Snok is going to be the father of my child," she murmured.

151

Instinctively Mr. Blok looked at her belly, and not knowing what to say, he considered patting her stomach. But finding this improper, he changed his mind and said, "He did not do it by way of a scientific experiment?"

"Oh, no," said Bonnie seriously. "All his experiments are done with snakes, frogs, and cattle. Mr. Snok said it was accidental in so far as I belong to the receptive species, or rather I represent rich soil that hardly needs fertilizing, or something like that. Oh, Mr. Blok, it is so difficult to understand him. At times he admits he cannot cope with all the problems which confront him."

"I see. The professor likes to give problems to others to solve."

"Yes, it is true, he really does. Though he helped me understand certain puzzling matters, like pinching, for example."

"Hmmm., pinching?" asked Blok.

"Yes," said Bonnie. "You see, my father never gave me a spanking in the ordinary way fathers spank. He pinched me instead, and ever since, well, I don't know how to say it. Since the day I left home, I kind of missed it. Mr. Snok explained my feelings and gave me some Freud to read, and then one evening, when he was sure I was cured of my peculiarity, I mean to prove I was cured, he pinched me exactly the same way. Oh Mr. Blok," said Bonnie sobbing, "how can I be helped?

Gently stroking Bonnie's head, Mr. Blok did not answer. He wanted to comfort her and to say something tender and warm, but he was afraid of further upsetting her. So, he said, "I knew a girl whose most sensitive spot was just under her ear. But I think she is married now and has children. The spot caused her a great deal of worry when she was very young. I remember I advised her never to mention or expose it to anyone — to hide it." Then looking steadily at Bonnie, "Will Mr. Snok marry you?"

"No," said Bonnie drying her eyes. "He loves Mr. Shopklang and is very happy with him. He is a young composer. Mr. Snok said Shopklang will be frightfully angry. He is very jealous."

"Look here, Bonnie," said Blok impatiently. "Mr. Shopklang can never become a mother."

"Mr. Snok says a male sea horse can."

"Perhaps, but I find Snok's behavior ridiculous and distasteful. And furthermore, his versatility is in no way a contribution to humanity. I am sure you must realize that."

"And yet," said Bonnie defensively, "it will be a contribution. My child will be an asset to humanity."

"I know it will be an adorable baby. I would like to have it for my very own, to adopt it and to be of help and comfort to both of you. There is another person," said Blok, thinking of Sophie, "who would understand you and just love your child."

"I want you to be the godfather. My baby's godfather. You are so good, Mr. Blok. I thank you for wanting to adopt my baby. I knew you would. But it won't be necessary. I must tell you something, something I know will give you pleasure. I met a man. You know him. We have become very good friends. He knows all about me and is willing to adopt the baby. He is much younger. Oh, I hope you don't mind."

"Who is he?"

"He is the waiter, do you remember? He told me you would. He said he fed you by hand."

"He quit his job because the proprietor had a television set installed in the restaurant, but he is very busy with anthroposophy. He got me interested in it too. It's such a distraction."

Blok kissed her on both cheeks and said goodbye after she had promised to return very soon to see him. Blok then went to his quarters.

The next few days were spent with the same monotony that he spent at the studio previously, only now the room was much larger, and he did not have to climb over anyone to get to the bathroom.

Also, the fact that the young psychiatrist agreed to sleep on the floor, Blok considered a big improvement. Blok's nerves, as before, became very shaky, although his tension lessened somewhat after Mlauzinski informed him of the willingness of the two sun-struck ladies to drop their charges against him, provided he was willing to paint their portraits. Blok agreed. "Fine, I will paint them as hysterical crabs."

"Don't do it," said one of the physicians. "Remember the portrait of Snok?"

Snok's case also took a more favorable turn since after his castration he seemed to have mellowed greatly. However, the committee for his defense was quite concerned over the activities of the General Freezing Company, whose agents would stop at no lengths to obtain Blok's formula. The committee's position, that Blok's formula was not useful for commercial purposes, went unheeded by the Freezing Company, until finally they were able to convince them that Mr. Blok possessed no magic secret formula. On the contrary, just like all great art, his art was persuasive. After a ten-hour session, the outstanding spokesman for the Society made the point once and for all that great art can never be manufactured. To try to heat one hundred thousand apartments and to keep them cool at the same level would be impossible merely by hanging hot or cold landscapes.

Furthermore, if the psychological effects were so great as to accomplish this, Mr. Blok would have to live until he was at least four hundred years of age.

The great news was broken to Mr. Blok at a moment when he was filled with great melancholy and longing for Sophie.

He was in despair at his lack of freedom. The President of the Company himself, together with Mr. Ellis, rushed into Mr. Blok's quarters.

"Long live the great art and the artist," he sang in a sonorous basso. All of Blok's roommates perked up their ears as they watched the president shake Mr. Blok' s hand.

"We all are friends," said he, "and as proof of my admiration, I would like to commission you to paint two portraits of my dogs or anything else you would like to paint. Just name your fee, and whatever that amount, you shall have added to it two Frigidaire's of our own make and one super-extra SZY deep and shallow freezer."

By now, realizing what had happened, everyone in the room, with the sole exception of Mr. Blok, shouted "Hooray" and sang "FOR HE'S A JOLLY GOOD FELLOW." Mr. Ellis beamed with joy. "Now you are almost out of danger, and you can go wherever you please. The few remaining cases, I am sure, we will be able to handle with ease."

The President clapped his hands and boomed, "We have been saved a huge sum of money by this wonderful man who prevented us from engaging in this foolish and ignorant deal. But we feel so magnanimous tonight that we will not even fire some of our chemists who almost got us into a fiasco." With these words still ringing and with great enthusiasm, he turned to Ondra, who had just come in and who stood quietly at Blok's side, and kissed him vigorously on both cheeks. Realizing that he kissed the wrong man, he reached out for Blok, but meanwhile having lost his fervor, he only shook Blok's hand.

Chapter XIV

"Darling, it's so good to see you again," said Mathilda, greeting and embracing Sophie.

"You look wonderful, Mathilda dear, sunburned and young. How was your journey? How is your beau? Did you like Mexico?"

"Oh darling, everything is just perfect — so exciting.

"By the way," Mathilda said, "Kratki thinks our substances are mixing splendidly now. But the big news is — we are going to be married soon."

"Wonderful," congratulated Sophie, kissing Mathilda's cheeks. Mathilda said, "To tell you the truth, I have something in mind — perhaps it's silly — but it would be such fun if... if..." Mathilda hesitated and then asked suddenly, "How is Mr. Blok?"

"Mr. Blok?" repeated Sophie with seeming indifference. "I don't know. I have not seen him much."

"What? I thought he lives here," said Mathilda, and then, "Oh, please, please tell me, aren't you very close?"

"Close? Hm... I would rather hear about Mexico. How did you like it there?"

"You will never change," said Mathilda reproachfully. "You are always guarding your precious privacy. All right, just as you wish. Mexico is fascinating only I almost suffocated driving out to see the Mayan pyramids, the road was so dusty. It was beastly enough to kill all interest for me forever in ancient history and archeology."

Sophie laughed. "Is that all the impression you had of Mexico?"

"No. Kratki insisted on seeing a bullfight, but at the time there was only one corrida on a Sunday afternoon — sort of a charity affair, and not a big festival with a famous torero. We saw three bulls slaughtered and one horse killed in a not too elegant manner, but the fourth or fifth bull was a real thrill. To start with, he was a huge and ferocious animal. He had been in the arena hardly a minute when he gored a fellow — a sort of helper, or someone they call 'monkey', though I assure you, dear Sophie, he was a man, and a not too happy one being dragged by the bull's horns. But the real thrill. though, was when all of a sudden, a young lad of fifteen or maybe sixteen, an enthusiastic amateur, jumped from his place in the stand into the arena and, armed with a piece of red cloth and a dagger, ran straight towards the bull. The bull dominated the arena completely at that moment, being the undisputed superior there. He was ferocious and bloodthirsty and made everyone seek safety behind the barrier until no one was left in the arena."

"How exciting!" said Sophie.

"Yes, it really was," continued Mathilda. "Everyone was screaming 'Espontanio! Espontanio!' when they saw the lad running with incredible speed and determination toward the angry beast. Probably even the bull was astonished to see such a strange challenger, for he just snorted in disgust and did not charge. We held our breath in fear when the boy reached the animal and came almost in front of his long, widely-spread horns. The boy made a few fancy maneuvers with the cloth, and when the bull charged, he turned his small body gracefully, making the bull miss his flesh by half an inch. The bull turned his ferocious body clumsily and charged again, but the lad escaped, and this time in a still more elegant way, ending up by leaning on the ground with one knee, holding the red rag in the air. I wish I knew all the professional names of his movements, but everyone, without exception, said that the boy was terrific and that if he remains alive, he will be another Manolete."

"But Mathilda, how did it finish? What happened to the boy?"

"Oh," said Mathilda, "he just had time to jump over the barrier and got there only with the help of the 'monkey'. The torero was either wounded or killed by the bull — I really don't know, for I just saw him being carried out of the arena. There was so much blood that I began to feel sick and asked Kratki to take me home. Poor dear, he wanted so much to stay. He thinks bull fights are fascinating and, from an artistic point of view, far superior to boxing matches."

"So, you had quite a time together," said Sophie, "though, to be frank, I did not expect your relations with Kratki to take such a serious turn. Judging from your past attitude toward him, I never had the impression that you were really in love with him. I am sorry to tell you, but never since the day I met Kratki have I had great admiration for him, neither for his person nor for his achievements."

"You don't understand, " said Mathilda with exaltation. "I am happy, incredibly happy! He is so cute. It's really wonderful when a man of maturity and noble dignity is capable of being cute! Do you know what I mean?"

"Of course, I know," said Sophie. "It is what Heine meant when he proclaimed that those who do not behave in accordance with their age are fools."

"That is unkind of you, Sophie. What makes you dislike Kratki?"

"I don't," said Sophie thoughtfully, "but people do dislike things they don't know, though often when they know, they dislike them still more."

"You are talking nonsense," said Mathilda nervously. "The more I know Kratki, the more I like him. No one can help liking him, of course, providing one takes the trouble to know him. I love him! I cannot live without him! Not a minute — not a day. I would die — perish — without him!"

Not looking at Mathilda's agitated face, Sophie murmured:

"Apropos your inability to live even for one day without Kratki, a rooster died yesterday who lived for twenty days without his head. The owner of the bird assured everyone that the fowl lived for this twenty-day period in complete contentment from the minute it was beheaded."

"Please don't try to be funny," exclaimed Mathilda, "because you are not!" Sophie handed her the *New York Times*, pointed to the column on the first page and said, "Here, read it."

There it was — all about the headless rooster whose name was Lazarus. After glancing at the article Mathilda said that the whole thing was hideous. "Imagine how horrified Mrs. Green was when she had him beheaded and took him home to clean and saw him stand up and strut about trying to crow. Awful!" Then putting the newspaper aside, Mathilda remarked with a nuance of reproach, "Though my happiness leaves you indifferent and my choice does not meet your approval, it happens that Kratki also strongly disapproves of your behavior with Mr. Blok." But just as Sophie was about to suggest that Mr. Kratki mind his own affairs, she heard the front door open and saw Mr. Blok stealthily walk toward his room.

"It's he?" whispered Mathilda.

"Yes," nodded Sophie. They did not speak, both having an expression on their faces as though they expected something unusual to happen. They listened and looked in the direction Mr. Blok had disappeared. Soon they heard something fall with a big noise, followed almost immediately by the sound of glass breaking, and after a few minutes of silence, Mr. Blok entered the room, greeted them politely and, after apologizing for the disturbance, explained shyly: "I was very much intrigued by the declaration of Dr. John L. Lindquist, professor of surgery at Northwestern University, that man would be better off walking like a horse, and so I tried to verify that expert opinion — I mean the theory." Noticing the ladies' astonishment, Blok, smiling and hesitating, continued. "Dr. Lindquist assures us that the human anatomy is patterned after and has evolved from that of four-legged animals, and that much of the human body, while essentially sound for quadrupeds, is inadequate for an erect position. Don't you think there is something to that? If we walked on all fours, the way we are supposed to, the lower back, the feet, and lower abdomen would not be so affected by strenuous labor." Then suddenly, "May I illustrate?" Not waiting, as if not certain of the ladies' sufficient interest in the demonstration, Mr. Blok walked with amazing agility on all fours around the room. He would have taken one round more if their shrill laughs had not brought him to a stop. He stood embarrassed and erect and looked at them reproachfully while arranging his hair and tie.

"Oh, please, Mr. Blok, don't be angry, " cried Mathilda. "It's not really you, but your trousers — Oh God!" But she was unable to continue, laughing freely now and without any effort to stop. "If not for your pants you would be the image of' a centaur. Please forgive me," she concluded after quieting herself somewhat and drying her eyes. But Blok did not listen to Mathilda as he stood there in the middle or the room and looked at Sophie, and Sophia did not even smile, trying to convey to him her feelings so far from ridicule and so close to understanding. Blok felt it and smiling gratefully said, "Lucretius, a long time ago, expressed an opinion similar to that of Dr. Lindquist when he wrote, 'For commonly it is thought that wives conceive more readily in the manner of a wild beast — after the custom of the four footed breeds — because so postured, with the breasts beneath — and buttocks then up-reared, then seeds can take their proper places.' Wasn't Lucretius a mouth of wisdom?"

Changing the subject, Sophie started to speak of Mathilda's impressions of Mexico. Blok, much relieved, took a seat in a comfortable chair and listened to her attentively. Occasionally, Mr. Blok's hand would go behind his seat and discreetly feel his trousers. But there was not a trace of worry or bitterness in him as he sat and listened, nodding at the interesting points of Sophie's story. But he was definitely in an active mood and he felt that to only listen would not be sufficient pleasure for him today; therefore, when Sophie finished and asked Mr. Blok whether he had had any interesting experiences in exotic countries, he said quickly as if he had been waiting for that opportunity for a long time. "I don't know exactly what you mean by exotic countries, but I have been in the tropics and even had some minor adventures that might be of some interest."

"Where was it?" asked Sophie.

"Have you been in Mexico?'" inquired Mathilda.

"Yes," said Blok, "but the little story I want to tell took place somewhere in Venezuela, a country far more fascinating than Mexico."

"Is that so?" exclaimed Mathilda with surprise. "Why?"

Mr. Blok smiled. "Why?" he repeated, "because I saw a tiger in the kitchen of a hotel and because I paid $39 a day in a hotel that had no bath but a rathole in the room."

"My goodness," said Sophie. "How horrible! It was not in Caracas?"

"No, indeed not," answered Blok. "It was in a city where I was almost deafened by the terrific noise of the streets, and where nobody seemed to hear or understand each other and where the horns of the cars blew with incredible persistence and force day and night, standing or moving." When Blok noticed the unmistakable interest with which the two ladies listened, he continued: "Yes, that town was full of cripples on the streets, selling lottery tickets, newspapers, sweets, or cigarettes. The more fortunate had a little stand on street corners. Their best means of advertisement was their own voice. Some individuals with legs capable of moving molested every passerby by offering lottery tickets or begging. There was one with an enormous head who followed me for eight blocks. He was so persistent and aggressive in his demands that I had to take more energetic steps to be rid of him."

"This story promises to be a very cheerful one," remarked Mathilda, but either ignoring or not noticing her words, Blok continued: "In the middle of a prettily shaped Square near a fountain with four angels on top, students held political meetings almost at any time between morning and midnight. After many speeches, which were always loudly approved by the crowd, a procession through the city would follow. In some foreign countries it would be called a minor revolution, but there it was just an everyday activity and, in a way, an entertainment. The whole population was on the streets almost at any hour of the day or night. The first impression was striking, but my eyes and ears got used to the constant noise and the masses of people with their agitated gestures and grotesque movements, and the whole picture seemed normal and natural. On the corner of one narrow street with sidewalks that permitted but one person to walk on the pavement that was covered with spit, orange peels, cigarette butts, and useless bits of lottery tickets, sat almost naked, a striking-looking man holding lottery tickets for sale. He was a peculiar mixture of Indian, Negro, Chinese, and perhaps Portuguese. His muscular body was a yellowish-dark color, and he had no legs, although by observing I saw sticking out just below his hips two duck-like webbed feet. They were so abnormal and in such contradiction to his strong build that the unexpected discovery made me shudder and want to walk away. And yet there was nothing in that creature to arouse pity — perhaps because of his powerful frame or, even more, because of his shiny and angry eyes, which did not ask for pity. They were belligerent and despotic.

"Next to him silently stood a boy of ten or twelve. He was also dark-skinned but very thin and fragile. Now and then he looked down at his owner or perhaps relative, apparently waiting for an order. And the order soon came. The boy bent down and with great effort lifted the cripple and slowly carried him away. I watched the boy cross the street with his unusual load, enter another narrow street, turn and disappear down a dirty little side street where small huts with thatched roofs stood closely in a row. They entered one of them. It was late in the afternoon.

"The next day was the much-awaited drawing of the National Lottery. The cripple must have had two unsold tickets, for I saw the boy return to the street holding the tickets in his small hand. He must have had strict orders not to return before they were sold. The boy obeyed. He obeyed always; it was his life. I saw fear in his eyes as he hurriedly passed me by. It was after ten o'clock when the boy returned. He looked anxious, and there was something of hopeless despair in the way he walked still holding the tickets in his hand. I wanted to speak to him, to buy those tickets or say something encouraging. I followed him almost to the door of the hut, but for some reason that I could never explain, I did not approach the boy but stood silently in front of the door. The dim light of a candle did not permit me to see clearly through the half-open door the exchange that took place in the room between the two of them. The cripple was too angry to scold the boy; he just gave him a sign to carry him to the street. The tickets must be sold, and there was no time to lose. The boy could not lift the heavy body of his master this time. He was too tired and too hungry, but a few furious slaps on his face made the boy ready for a supreme effort. The cripple made himself secure by putting his arms around the boy's neck, and I saw him pass with his load, stumbling toward the direction of their usual corner. I saw the boy suddenly collapse, hurting the cripple in his fall. The boy tried to get to his feet and lift his owner, only to fall again and again. With each effort the hands of the cripple tightened furiously tighter and tighter around the boy's neck. Then I heard a high, feeble shriek through the light tropical air, then the rattled sound of a choked voice followed by ghostly silence, the first complete silence I had experienced in that city.

"The boy had been strangled to death.

"The next day was a great day indeed! One of the unsold tickets was the great winner of the lottery."

Mr. Blok took a deep breath while the two ladies, impressed, waited for him to continue. But he did not utter a word, sitting with his eyes lowered. Sophie was the first to break the silence.

"Did that actually happen? Is it all true?" It took some time for Mr. Blok to answer, but then he said, "Perhaps I tried to dramatize a little, but on the other band, I felt at that time, and even today so much more than I could possibly put into words, that it seemed to me I did not succeed in retelling the story in its true dimensions."

"I think," said Mathilda, "you are a skilled raconteur, indeed. I was not bored for a second, although I understand why Sophie asked you if all you said was the truth. How, for instance, could a tiger walk about in the kitchen?"

"Oh yes," said Blok, getting red in the face. "I just omitted mentioning that the tiger was in a cage. By the way, I am not really sure that it was not a baby leopard."

"In any case," interrupted Sophie, "it does not change anything. I imagine how sorry you must have felt for the poor boy."

"I could have prevented the tragedy so easily," Blok said gloomily, "but should I add that guilt to all the others that sprang similarly from thoughtless passivity, I should carry a far heavier load on my shoulders than the heaviest and most monstrous of cripples." Looking at Sophie he guiltily smiled. He avoided looking at Mathilda, and her friendliness made him feel as though he had deceived someone innocent. Had Sophie told her what she knew of Kratki, Mathilda's attitude would be different, thought Blok. It was a relief when Mathilda, after a few amiable phrases, left.

"She is so happy, I had no heart to tell her," said Sophie. "They will get married very soon."

She said, "I am so pleased that you are back and your worries are over."

"I am more than happy, darling. You look so lovely." He walked toward her, looking caressingly. "You are so wonderful, so good." His heart was pounding as Sophie put her bead on his shoulder. Being slightly taller than he, she had to bend her knee to bring her head to the level of his shoulder. Blok noticed her discomfort and tried to stand on his toes. It threw her off balance and separated them. He wanted to say something tender, but his tongue was wooden. He feared that even the right words would never come out convincingly. "Why is it," he thought despairingly, "that instead of making love to a woman I love, I want to preach like a Caodaist priest in Indo-China, or pray, or just talk, or cry, or paint!"

Chapter XV

Mr. Kratki was not in his best mood this morning. It was true, the conversation with Mathilda the night before had been far from agreeable, but with some effort he had succeeded in making clear to her the danger of listening to that nincompoop Blok. What a noddy fellow! Or was it Sophie who'd said something. Hmm — it was unpleasant. But on the other hand, who can afford to let others look through the files of the past? Who are those who have nothing to hide? One-day-old babies already have a record, a bad record, and a cause of suffering and pain, reflected Kratki, spreading honey over the griddle cakes. It was his favorite meal, and he liked to enjoy it undisturbed and quite alone.

In many ways the morning was the best part of the day for Mr. Kratki. It was far better planned and executed than his afternoons or evenings. There was no hurry, no interference. From the moment of awakening everything went into a carefully worked out routine. And yet he never allowed the process of shaving, washing and dressing to be just a routine, for every contact with his body, every touch and thought of his own self was — a new experience — each a time of importance and joy. There was pride, significance, and self-recognition in every movement during those delightful morning hours. After all, it was his body he attended to, his face he shaved, his teeth he brushed. He felt entitled to admire and to love them.

Of course, there was not admiration only, by any means. He was not blind to certain shortcomings of his body. He was well aware of superfluous fat covering it and making his belly hang rather ungracefully, nor could he miss the big black and brown warts growing on his chest, his back, and under his arms. He was equally not blind to many other unattractive growths, flabbiness and stains on his body. But he was tolerant of it.

His butler, Albert, one morning accidentally overheard him speaking while counting his warts. Albert swore that Kratki spoke to them tenderly. "My little ones, don't I give you good care?" he'd said. "Don't I allow the lovely ladies to caress you, to play with you, and kiss you, my little Existentialists? I did not wed you to Vesta, did I?"

Albert must have told the truth, for he inquired about the meaning of the words Existentialist and Vesta and declared he could not repeat other things Kratki said in the morning, explaining that he spoke those so softly that even the cleverest of ghosts would have had difficulty in hearing him.

But there were no ghosts around Mr. Kratki for he was not their type, and this morning Mr. Kratki had to think of other things than ghosts — there were things of importance to be accomplished forcing him to modify and to shorten his morning ritual and the traditional program. There was no third cup of coffee, and even the newspaper remained unread on the table. Any minute now he expected his secretary, and he knew it would not be an easy meeting.

God knows Lucretia Shrimp was not an easy nut to crack. Kratki was bitter and angry, and his thoughts jumped like fleas searching for food. Shrimp, he thought, a shrimp that has grown to a shark, and even at that with no vitamins in the liver, and his thoughts flew to the day when she had first come to his office.

Had she been young and lovely? He did not care to remember. The truth is that he never cared for any specific type of female; their age or charm was of no importance to him. What fascinated him really in his relations with women was the situation. From the moment intimacy became established or recognized, it had to end — brutally if necessary but preferably discreetly.

Only seldom were such epilogues painless. Those bizarre beginnings more often had shocking or even tragic ends.

At first Lucretia's efficiency and discretion did not give the faintest illusion of her being anything more than a secretary. But as time went on, Mr. Kratki learned some of her other surprising and delightful qualities. It was not her perfectly molded breasts that stood so delicate and proud, wide apart from each other, or her shapely legs that began to speak to Kratki's imagination. It may seem strange, but it was her knowledge of Greek that created the first change in his attitude toward her. She was a scholar, yes, a scholar and an actress of culture and charm.

His discovery, like most discoveries, presented itself by pure chance. It was when he noticed among his papers a drawing of a frog with something in Greek written under it. She explained that it was hers and apologized for leaving it on his desk by mistake, adding that among her other hobbies were Greek tragedies and that she loved to recite and to draw the amusing personages of Greek plays.

Odd to relate, one afternoon after office hours, she entertained him by impersonating Euripides, Bacchus, Xanthias, and others from "The Frogs" in its entirety. To him even the choruses of frogs, "brekekeke-coax...... brekekeke-coax," sounded heavenly.

Though Mr. Kratki was not acquainted with Aristophanes, or perhaps because he was not, the novelty of it, the charm and humor of Miss Shrimp, fascinated him. She was magnificent as Bacchus, standing in the middle of the room clad in a lion skin, pleading with Hercules to reveal all the brothels, hostesses, and rooms where there were the fewest bugs.

As he grew fonder of his unusual secretary, the office hours were shortened and the evenings lengthened.

But as time went by, Kratki became aware of being entangled in a silly web, elastic enough to let him move but not to tear himself free. The spider was gentle and fast, and it started to eject a sticky substance to strengthen the threads and paralyze the victim and curb his will. It was not necessary for her to be over-cautious now that he was well in her power and she could even let him observe her at work. Oh, how fine her work was! She knew the things no one was supposed to know — all his personal affairs and his innermost ambitions and plans — and nothing escaped her. She became bold and fearless. She was a power, and it was too late to do anything about it. She had become a formidable adversary with whom to cope.

But was she an enemy? Not yet — not quite yet, perhaps — it all depended on what her demands were. What did she want? Money? His love? Or just power over him? A strange and dangerous creature! Was he afraid of her, he asked himself? No — no, of course not.

She bore her name Lucretia with dignity and mystery, and her ways often led him into a distant unknown world of strange and burning excitement. He often heard her giving out orders as she swam through the office with the serenity and security of a shark. He watched her silently with hate and fear.

Now, waiting for Miss Shrimp, he was again thinking of a shark and wandering in his thoughts all the way to Panama and his pal Heinrich Bulenbacher, with whom he had spent so many pleasant hours playing with the sharks at the deep coral reef hole, in whose transparent blue waters the sharks lived in dignity and peace. In peace, yes, until Bulenbacher's boat stopped above them.

"Let's play tricks on those greedy bastards!" he used to say.

It was great fun to lower a wounded and bleeding sawfish into the water and marvel at its speed and efficiency in defending itself by sawing the ferociously attacking sharks in half. It was a magnificent scene of battle that Kratki cherished in his memory. He only regretted never having seen the end of the heroic slaughter because the water was transformed from a heavenly blue into a whirl of blood.

"Luba used to accuse me of morbidity, poor darling. She, who liked her fish fried and her steaks rare," he said aloud.

There was a knock on the door, and Arnold announced Miss Shrimp. "She's waiting in the library, sir."

Kratki lighted a cigar and walked slowly toward the library. He found Lucretia standing in a corner looking at a book. She did not lift her eyes, even after Kratki's greeting. He coughed and repeated in a firm voice, "Good morning," and coughed again.

She put the book away and said, "Congratulations. Wonderful news! How do you feel as a fiancé? Or was this the honeymoon?" And not waiting for Kratki's reaction, she continued, "I always thought Mexico was so romantic; though to be frank, you should have chosen me as your happy bride. Though I would have insisted on Athens, or perhaps Rome. Yes, of course, Rome. There and only there is where we belong."

She walked nearer and facing Kratki, spoke softly, "Don't you agree, oh dear Petronius, that we belong together? There need not be a wedding, for in Rome I would be your devoted slave."

"Stop that nonsense, please," interrupted Kratki cuttingly. "Your chatter tires me. Why don't you rehearse your roles somewhere else?"

"I may, I may," she answered quickly, "find a cute little place somewhere, where I can rehearse my roles. Perhaps somewhere in Chiapa de Corzo, where the body of Fernando Gomez was found tied to a tree and devoured by giant ants. Poor Gomez! I wish it were someone else. Do you like giant ants?"

"Miss Shrimp," said Kratki officiously, "I called you here to thank you for your past services and, to express in the name of our firm, our sincere appreciation and regret at having to part with you." He paused, cleared his throat, and reaching his hand towards her, said that a letter with two month's salary would follow presently.

Lucretia did not notice his outstretched hand, and he had to draw it back. He was angry, but she just stood there and looked at him.

"Yes, hmmmm, what did I want to ask you — eh — will you remain in this city, or look for a job somewhere else? We will recommend you with pleasure, and will give you, hmmmmm — please don't hesitate to ask."

She did not utter a word.

"Well, Miss Shrimp, I must go."

As he was leaving, she stopped him and said, "Please accept a souvenir from a woman you loved." Then she opened her mouth and, removing her false teeth with both hands, handed them to him. This gesture made Kratki stand speechless, holding her wet teeth in his hand.

Taking advantage of his perplexity, she seized her purse, grabbed a revolver from it, pointed it at Kratki, said something that sounded like sizzling steak, and fired four shots at him.

When Albert entered the room, he saw Miss Shrimp sitting on Mr. Kratki's body calmly replacing her dentures.

Due to the activity of the Aristocrats of Mind Society, which took her case to their hearts, she was treated by the court with kind leniency. As far as it is known, she became a Buddhist; moved to Arizona; among other things, played English horn; and was very active in instructing some Indian tribes in classical antiquity, Hellenism, and comparative literature.

Chapter XVI

"The manner of death or the circumstances of birth of some beings have created the most lovable legends in human history," remarked Blok, looking consolingly at Mathilda.

Dressed in black, she did not react to his words as she sat silent and grim.

"Sometimes the manner of the death and its circumstances even overcome all imperfections in the past life of the person, leaving to the world only a last impression of martyrdom and sorrow. Someone said today of your deceased fiancé, 'SUA-VITER IN MODO, FORTITER IN RE.' I could not but agree, as Mr. Kratki was truly gentle in manner and resolute in execution."

Sophie made signs to Blok to stop talking, but not succeeding in this, she saw him advance toward Mathilda with the solemnity of a priest, looking up and clasping his hands as if in prayer, and heard him say, "SIT TIBI TERRA LEVIS."

There was something of theatrical affectation in Blok's bearing that surprised and exasperated Sophie. She took him by the arm and led him out of the room. When they were out of hearing distance, she stopped and said, "Can't you understand that there are moments when one should not speak? Or is it your feeling of guilt that grows to such wordiness?"

"There is no blame in trying to soothe and distract a person in mourning, is there?"

"Oh, please, please," said Sophie, "it's a strange way to distract a widowed fiancée by talking of death. And in heaven's name, what made you talk of those grasshoppers at such length? Do you imagine really that poor Mathilda has any interest at such a moment in hearing of your grasshoppers who wear their skeletons outside? — or of their marvelous chemical compound 'chitin' that resists alkali and acid capable of eating the flesh and bones of men? No, really, your lecture on insects, to put it mildly, was very childish and, you must admit, hardly fit for the occasion."

"I am sorry. Perhaps you are right," he said with submission and then with sudden warmth, "I did not speak for the sake of speaking, though I admit it will give me immense pleasure to speak now, to tell you how attractive you are." And pressing her hand to his lips, he added with fervor, "Let's go away from here, to Yankielewitch's, to Aspen, Colorado, to a bench in the Square, or just for a Coca Cola at Pinkel's — anything to be alone!" He cried with enthusiasm, "I know where we can go — do you remember our wanting to celebrate? Well, we never did!"

"Oh, then I was in a quite different mood," she declined coolly. Sophie did not want to leave Mathilda alone in her great sadness, but Blok was so persuasive with examples from the history of human behavior, regarding weeping and mourning in solitude as a fine tradition, that Sophie, despite her qualms, finally gave in to him. As they were speaking in the corridor, having taken more time than they realized, Mathilda in bar hat and coat came to say that she had to leave.

"Let's get ready."

"At what time shall we go out?"

"In an hour?"

"Good!" The minute Sophie went to her room, Blok rushed to polish his shoes and clean his jacket. He took his trousers off, folded them carefully, and placed them under the mattress. He opened the door, put his head through it, looked around, and with words half-spoken, half-sung, galloped gaily and nude across the corridor into the bathroom.

Sophie selected her prettiest dress, the one she had bought from Mme. Vionnet in Paris that refused to go out of fashion. It was simple and beautiful. Some dresses make a woman look slimmer and taller, some fatter but younger, some older yet chic, but this one, thought Sophie, is a real dress, for it makes one look better than one really does. She had been examining people the whole day long and began to feel pleased with the idea or going out.

Sophie and Blok chatted pleasantly as they walked along the street. "Where shall we go?" asked Sophie, not really caring.

"I guess we had better take a taxi," said Blok, "It is quite far." They hailed one, got in, and, driving around the Square, passed 20th Street, turned to the right, then to the left, passed the railroad station, and entered the colored section of town.

"Where are we going?" asked Sophie.

"Didn't I tell you?" exclaimed Blok. "To a very tiny delicatessen. It does not look fancy, but the food is delicious there. It belongs to Moshe Yankielewitch and is really first-rate." The taxi arrived in front of the delicatessen, and they entered the place.

"Hello, Mr. Blok. So nice to see you," Yankielewitch greeted him and, then looking at Sophie, said, "best greetings to your lady too. Well, well, Mr. Blok, we have not seen you for quite a while," and winking with one eye added, "pleased to see you with company. Mrs. Yankielewitch always said Mr. Blok would make a fine husband."

This remark annoyed Mr. Blok very much, but Yankiele-witch continued, "Yes," he repeated, "Mrs. Yankielewitch says Mr. Blok is a born provider and will make a fine father, if he would only hurry, but now I see," and he winked again, "all is just fine. I will tell Mrs. Yankielewitch, and I know she will agree with your excellent taste."

He assigned a table to them and left winking and smiling.

"What a personality!" remarked Sophie.

"He is quite a good fellow, really," said Blok apologetically. "Likes to talk and doesn't always manage to be tactful. But the food, I must say, is excellent here," and taking the menu, he handed it to Sophie. "I hope you will find something you like. For myself, I don't need it because I know it by heart. It is classical, and it never changes."

Sophie, after studying the menu carefully, asked Blok, "What is kishkis? And matzo balls?"

"Oh, it's excellent. Just try it. I will order for you. All right?"

"Very kind of you, thanks."

"Your orders, folks?" demanded the waiter.

"Make a nice plate, please," said Blok, "of chicken liver, chopped herring, some matjes herring — Mr. Yankielewitch knows the kind I like — and I assure you," added Mr. Blok, "it is not the marinated herring but the real, natural one. Please put a few big slices of onion and some lox on it — nice portions, please. After that we will have some matzo ball soup with some kasha on the side. After, if you have nice golubtzi, we will take it. If not, some kishkis. No, No, wait, please. That is not all. Don't forget to give us some nice Greek black olives and a plate of sauerkraut and a lot of those delicious nijinsky cucumbers. For our desert, we would like halvah, kissel, and above all, hamenstash. Hamenstash is absolutely obligatory."

Blok was delighted with the order, but when the waiter left, he remembered something. He ran after the waiter, caught him near the kitchen, and said excitedly: "Gefilte fish — for heaven's sake, don't forget that, and some red and white horse-radish with it. Now all is in order," said Blok, relieved, seating himself near Sophie.

"Most of the things you ordered — I mean the names of them — are unknown to me," said Sophie, "but though it is not a Russian restaurant, I was almost certain we would have some pirozhki and borscht."

Blok looked at Sophie with dreamy tenderness and said, "To see you here is like smelling a wonderful flower in a slaughterhouse. You are wonderful." Touching her hand, he said again, "You are wonderful."

The moment the food arrived, Blok started with the herring and onions, but after he ate some of it and was ready to taste the chicken liver, he noticed a man staring at him.

"Who is that man?" asked Sophie. "He must know you, the way he gazes at you. He has not taken his eyes off you since we came here."

As Blok looked at him, the man wiggled his ears in the most peculiar manner but did not smile even with his eyes. "He is frightful," whispered Sophie.

The man's head was shaved clean, giving the impression of baldness. In contrast to the hairless head, he wore a bushy beard, black mixed with white patches. His big black eyes were fiery, burning with that particular glow of a drunkard or a madman. Suddenly, he grinned at Blok. There was something offensive in his face, and yet Blok could not help finding a certain fascination in it. There was something else in it, something familiar, but even after they stared at each other for an embarrassingly long time, Blok could not recognize him.

The man stood up and moved slowly toward their table. His arms in the air as though ready for an embrace, he exclaimed, almost roaring: "My dear, dear Blok!" and only then did Blok instantly remember Edouardo de Bryn. Yes, it was he! Blok felt embarrassed, not knowing what to say or how to react. Blok must have hurt his feelings, for his arms dropped and he said, "So you, too, Blok? Just like the rest of those so-called old friends — the sons of bitches! You too are disgusted with me? Don't like my looks, eh? My behavior and the rest of it? I presume you are shocked like the rest of them, what?" he yelled.

Sophie pressed herself against Blok, terrified, and whispered, "Let's get out of here, please!"

"Let's have a drink on this wonderful occasion — a meeting of two dear friends. Let's have a drink. Well, Blok, what's the matter?" He coughed and dribbled. "What's the matter? Hell, your reception is colder than a witch's tit. Don't you want to offer me a drink? Hell, I will take even a bottle of beer; or just give me two bucks, will you? Give me a couple of bucks and the hell with you."

Blok went through his pockets, slipped the money in Edouardo's hand while quite stupidly repeating, "Was glad to see you — very pleased indeed." He grabbed Sophie's coat, moved the table and, taking Sophie by the arm, moved with her toward the exit.

Just before they walked out Yankielewitch rushed excitedly towards them. "Anything wrong? You did not have your dinner!"

But Blok calmed him. "We will be back sometime. I will pay the check later. We just forgot something and must hurry. Best regards to Mrs. Yankielewitch," and with assurances of seeing him again soon, they left the restaurant.

"I am so sorry — terribly sorry," he said to Sophie when they were on the street looking for a taxi. "I will tell you later all about that man — remarkable story, very unusual. The poor fellow. I will tell you later." He pressed her hand. "There are so many other things I want to tell you. Oh dear, Sophie, I am afraid my feelings are so... so... I really don't know how to say it. I thought my abstemious character...I mean habits and all... I am sorry, you must think I am an old fool, maybe those Germans are right. Didn't they say, 'The old wood burns the best'? They must have meant people like me." At this moment, a taxi stopped at the curb.

They entered and drove toward the center of the city.

"I have not danced since my graduation from the university," said Sophie.

"And for that matter," said Blok, "I never danced at all, but it is a good idea. Let's dance. Do you know a dancing place in the city?"

"No, unfortunately, I do not know one."

"Chauffeur," called Blok, "do you know a dance place somewhere in the city — a nice place?"

"You bet I know," answered the driver. "There is one at 20th Street, a swell place — high style — no jerks and a high-class band."

"That's splendid," said Blok. "Please drive us there."

Meanwhile Blok became conscious of the effect the raw onions must have had on his breath. It forced him to turn away each time he addressed Sophie, but when they reached the Square, Blok saw a drugstore on the corner, stopped the taxi, and with apologies rushed out and in a minute returned, with half a packet of Sen-Sen in his mouth and two extra ones in his pockets. He wished their journey would continue forever through the dark and deserted streets, but alas, in a few minutes the taxi stopped in front of a bar.

The headwaiter greeted them cordially, but before leading them inside to a table he whispered discreetly to Mr. Blok, "Your jacket is badly torn under the arm, sir." But he added with a professional smile, "Fortunately it is so dark there," pointing to the tables, "that you can easily mistake yourself for someone else. No one will take notice of your jacket, sir."

Blok ordered champagne and sandwiches just before the band took its place on the platform. It was lucky, for after the musicians, wearing cold and indifferent faces, had started to blow and to beat, the waiter could not have heard Mr. Blok's order. The noise was terrific, making all conversation impossible.

"What did you say?" screamed Sophie.

"Do you want to dance?" yelled Blok.

"What?"

"I mean," said Blok, coming nearer, "we will dance after the first glass of champagne."

The people dancing in the middle or the room were pressing each other, standing on the same spot in the overcrowded circle, only moving their bodies. "Heavens, what is all that — an orgy?" asked Sophie, touching Blok's ear with her lips.

"I love you, darling," said Blok, coming almost to her mouth and expressively pressing her arm.

"You smell like a pharmacy," said Sophie, but Blok did not hear as the music continued with increased fury and deafening noise.

"Who are all those people?" inquired Sophie, and her voice sounded like a saxophone.

"They are ghost writers rehearsing 'Walpurgis Night,'" roared Blok.

"Who?"

"I said 'ghost writers and black magicians,'" coughed Blok. "Not ectoplasmic — just amateurs and substitutes."

"I can't understand you, please repeat," begged Sophie, but at the moment Blok answered, the band suddenly stopped playing, and the whole room was filled with his forced voice. "I say they are maniacs and amateurs — witches."

It was embarrassing. People looked toward their table, but the band started again, drowning and blacking out with its noise all thinking. Sophie and Blok drank champagne and ate sandwiches and also danced once, but it was not because Sophie could not endure Blok's stepping constantly on her feet, or because of their knocking into other dancing couples, but simply because they wanted to be alone and to go someplace where they could talk.

Blok's head was weaving a little as they walked arm in arm toward Sophie's apartment, but he enjoyed the effect of the alcohol, so unfamiliar to him.

As they entered the apartment, Sophie said, "Oh, you remember, you promised to tell me about the strange man in the restaurant? The man you called Edouardo!"

"Hmmm... Edouardo.... of course, with pleasure," mumbled Blok, feeling that his thoughts were freed only partly, and gaining time to arrest the flow of all the following thoughts and jam them back in his mind, he repeated, "certainly, with pleasure."

Sophie curled herself on the sofa, speaking as if encouraging Blok, "He was frightening... those nightmarish eyes, brrr...."

"I knew him," said Blok, "when his beauty was as frightening as his appearance is shocking now. It is hard to believe but the same man was once God's masterpiece! A sardius, a perfect unity of all magnificence and beauty, so irresistible and forceful as to be placed among the Gods himself. To stand in front of this wondrous creation was very frightening indeed."

"Did he pose for you? I hope so much that he did!" cried Sophie.

"No," said Blok. "No brush would do him justice. His education was exquisite; his cultured and immensely wealthy parents enabled him to meet people of spirit and taste and be brought up in closest contact with the finest of art Europe could offer. He was loved by all and admired by many for his gifts were many-sided and of unusual stature. He wrote plays and directed them brilliantly, achieving at the same time international fame as a sportsman. Seldom was there a man whom it was more justifiable to envy."

"I am afraid I envy him myself," said Sophie, smiling, "so please don't leave me with that contemptible feeling and tell me quickly what bugs have trimmed him so viciously."

"Well," said Blok thoughtfully, "soon after the death of his father, in a sudden eagerness to live, his mother got herself a lover Edouardo's age, his former pal, and the former beau of his sister. Here Edouardo's ruin began. At first, the change was hardly perceptible, and the first shock seemingly only scratched his granite surface. He avoided his friends and moved from the house of his mother. Then there began a rapid, mad passion for self-destruction, and he marched right into the heart of all sin and iniquity.

"He was born superior, and so in the world of depravity, crime, and foul darkness, he was also the king. No one was a better addict, man whore, greater alcoholic, liar, or thief. His was the perfection of filth and destruction, and yet he was not a demon, for a demon has greatness of evil and black powerful wings while he was the fastest of crawlers and deadliest of insects. He went through many prisons and hospitals, and more than once, I was given the honor of helping him out for a while.

"Now, waiting for his final perdition, he makes me think of an apricot tree, rotten and hollow, empty inside the trunk, which I touched once with a piece of an old lead pipe to see the putrid powder of the wood stir and make the disturbed little ants run for their souls. Though rotten, that tree had enough life left in it to bear small but sweet fruit. So, Edouardo, even today, is capable in brighter moments, of reciting in the most exquisite English or French, Italian or German, the sonnets of Petrarch and Shakespeare or the poetry Baudelaire. ..."

With his head bent and his hands buried in his hair, Blok let his remembrances travel in silence, and the long pause was left to speak for itself.

Chapter XVII

"In a way, I'm sorry for your Edouardo," said Sophie unconvincingly. "But haven't you ever met just normal and simple people to be friends with?"

"Of course, I did," Blok said with a start. "Why?"

"Oh, I was just wondering."

"There have been many people that have crossed my path — simple and complicated," said Blok somewhat evasively. He smiled. "I knew a man who believed in having a different person supply each of his needs and purposes. One was perfect for a game of gin rummy, but a bore for everything else; another good to listen to only; another to speak to; one good at chess, but stupid; one good to laugh with; another to cry with; one just right to eat with; some good to sleep with; some good to run away from; some enjoyable only on Sundays; the others in the afternoon; some to fall in love with platonically; and some only to fish with; some only to sing with in the Kiawanis; some ..."

"Stop it, stop it!" cried Sophie. "You see, that is what I mean by asking if you knew just normal people."

Blok said seriously, "Poor man, he never did find one person good for all moods and purposes."

"But did you?" asked Sophie.

"Yes, providence sent me one," he looked at her dreamily.

"One so complete, so heavenly perfect, so pure, so exciting, which of all living beings, only a woman can be."

"You are so white. Are you not well?" Sophie came to him.

"Oh, it's nothing, perhaps just the champagne. I am not used to it. I… uh…. usually drink only…. buttermilk."

"Please rest on this couch." She led him to it carefully.

"Thanks, thanks, you are so wonderful," he said, stretching himself on his back and looking gratefully at Sophie, who sat at his side.

"You don't know me," she said absently. "Nothing of me. Should you know, you would never, I mean… " She continued with more determination. "I would like to tell you something that weighs very heavily on me. All my life! I want you to know! I want to confess!"

"Confession?" cried Blok, "I am in the mood to listen to a confession. I was always in favor this ancient psychoanalytic method."

"I will be brief," began Sophie. "There is no better way of telling old and long stories. Well, at the age of fifteen, I was raped by a gardener. The man who robbed me of my virginity was never punished. It is hard to explain my refusal to reveal his identity. I pretended that I did not know him. I never recovered from the shock but remained grudging silently with fear and hate, crying for vengeance but punishing the innocent, like my father and myself. I shunned all the advances of boys of my age and renounced all the pleasures of young women. I was a good student and served as an example of perfect behavior in our circle of wealthy and idle families. I tried to avoid all that was rich and refined. In my reveries I was attracted by the so-called lower class. No, no — not really, what I mean to say is, by a man, the gardener I told you about.

"The slant-eyed, yellow-skinned Kalmuck who belonged to our garden, like the old apple tree which stood at the eastern end of the lawn, could be seen from all sides of the grounds. Though ever-present, he remained unseen. The Kalmuck became a matter of habit, an object, and no one deemed it necessary to pay any attention to that silent and soft-moving master of the garden. How long was he employed? How and from where did he come? Who were his friends or acquaintances? Why did he never take free time from his work? It was very puzzling to me how feeble was the imagination of those who after one glance were not startled and fascinated by him.

"How differently I felt! How eagerly I watched from my window his springy body moving with the lightness of a cat. I watched with a peculiar and hidden excitement, as if doing something not befitting a young girl, as he cut shrubs and dead branches with a sharp knife, the shiny blade contrasting so well with his dull yellow face. Did not his roving forefathers cut the throats of the enemy with an equally sure and indifferent hand?

"His hands were fast, and greedy for work, but his reserved manner and sparseness of words frightened away the gossipy help.

"There was no doubt that he was aware of my unusual interest in him and appreciated my discretion. For many months after the crime he committed, he lived in extreme fear, and it was only this which kept him from running away in a panic and from the danger of being denounced by me.

"But how great must have been his delight when, after many months passed, he found in me instead of a menace and a victim, an accomplice. Instead of hate and vengeance, a mistress bringing favor and desire!

"He became the focus of all my imagination, leaving all other men in the dark and distant shadow. He knew it well, and though he did not dare to come near me or touch me again, he enjoyed my passion for him from afar. At night he would climb the big elm tree by my window and look through it with his slant, Asiatic eyes and watch me lying in bed. I swear, I never made him suspect that I knew of his spying on me. Though my heart was beating in fear, I would never cast my eyes toward the window. I did not need to see him. I felt his presence as one feels a mortal danger. It came through all parts of my body and touched and burned my skin and made me want to cry in terror for help, but I did not call out or move as I lay in bed with my eyes closed and heart beating fast.

"It was just like living again through that dark afternoon when I felt his hot breath on me and heard the sound of my dress ripping. Only now I felt safe in my room, free to give way to my passion and let him be witness to the sinful and shameless exhibition of love to myself.

"It was a sordid but sweet experience that lasted for a long time. The sharp-edged pleasure was never dulled during those strange years of my life. He watched me displaying my voluptuous body, ever-increasingly becoming a partner in my lusty games. I knew I was an addict and my adolescence a shame and a disgrace."

Blok nodded quietly. Taking a deep breath, she continued. "Never before have I spoken of this — this cancer, creeping and spreading, got ready to choke my brains and my heart. This is the confession! Do you understand?" And not looking at Blok or waiting for an answer, she said with great effort, "I punished myself and waited for a savior, and just after graduation from medical school, left for a long journey.... I chose to travel alone. In the Belgian Congo, as well as in Venezuela and Colombia, several rare and interesting skin diseases were found that attracted my interest. Besides this, I had a strong desire to visit remote places of the world not yet touched by our civilization, where the primitiveness promised greater wisdom than our twisted, cruel cities can offer. I was not disappointed — the beauty and grandeur of the interior of Colombia surpassed all my expectations. I wanted to stay there forever, together with those simple and attractive people who were a part of the green, luxurious spaces, who belonged like the cliffs or the forest to the hills and the mountains. But I felt like the turbulent waters of the Magdalena, imprisoned between the rocks and rushing in wild insecurity to find the way to freedom or great magnificence.

"I mean that's what I dreamed to be, while really I was like an oyster who lives in its own shell. Those beautiful places and people, like the starfish to the oyster, meant destruction to me. I fled from people, only to close the shell tighter over me.

"Wandering from place to place, I could never shake his image from my mind. I longed for him in my dreams, and the further I went in my journeys, the clearer became his image, the deeper the sensuous joys, and the sharper my guilt until I became insensitive to the surrounding beauty," Sophie cried. "I indulged my passion in Mexico, in the Belgian Congo, in Venezuela and Colombia, I masturbated on mules and in cars, in villages, on boats, in the jungle, everywhere, every time. I was a slave to myself, to the crime of my habit and could not throw it off, drown it in the turbulent waters of the Magdalena or the depths of the ocean. And I could not destroy it by fire, for I was burned by it myself. Oh God, How I needed you then! How much I need you now! For you and you alone are my savior. I trust you! I need you! I want to be your wife!"

There was a long silence, heavy and embarrassing.

Sophie stared at the unfolded pack of matches that lay on the small table to her right, reading mechanically on its cover,

"FOR PARTIES: Several Distinctive Rooms — Buffet Dance, Thursdays Saturdays - Sundays."

She read it over again, now knowing what she was reading. Then she whispered, "Please, oh please, say something!" and then, a little louder, "Do you hear?" But there was only silence.

Blok lay with closed eyes as though asleep. Then she dared to look at Blok. "You aren't asleep, are you?" she said disdainfully. Blok opened his eyes and said with great calm,

"The Kalmucks have always been expert riders, very clever on horses, and otherwise quite advanced, I mean comparing them with Venezuela's Motilones, or with the pygmies of the Amazon. One simply cannot blame all the Kalmucks because of one degenerate. Yes, hmmm —once I remember my father tried the drink they make. They call it bash-busa, or something that sounds like that. Awful stuff. My father made me taste it just before he vomited. Hmmm , what do I want to say? It is all so confused, your confession and all you had to go through, and then the proposal of marriage. It is so overwhelming, so unexpected!

"Oh darling, to be chosen by you… it is like a turtle being given wings!

"Nothing is more abused than the word and meaning of love! It is our fault, the fault of men. Love is never a man's profession; it is a woman's. They prove it by deeds and pain. An experienced hunter would shoot the lioness first, for should he kill or wound the lion before her, she would charge with deadly fury. Not so if the lioness is killed. He will only sniff the dead body and walk away.

"No, I am speaking of love that, like a deep-rooted tree, resists all weathers and storm and is not in distress because of a few broken branches and limbs — a tree which grows gradually, and dies slowly."

Holding Sophie's hand, he continued, "I will try to make you forget all feelings of guilt and shame that have tortured you so cruelly. Shame!" he repeated forcefully. "How innocent of you! Shame on Kalmuck and the others, whoever they are, but not on you, darling. Shame on them! Shame on Diogenes, who, when surprised in the act, explained "I am planting a man," no more blushing at being so caught then if he had been found planting an onion. He made love in public and even demanded the presence of bystanders.

"There are many other examples of the strangest practices and habits in sex matters to be found in the writings of monks and in the books of which would put your shame to shame and make your experience seem as mild and innocent as a child skipping rope."

Sophie listened, looking surprised at Blok as he spoke now softly, now raising his voice to passionate climaxes.

"Look at the Cynics. Read the accounts of other women, whose deeds Montaigne describes. You remember?" he continued breathlessly. "When Luna could not otherwise enjoy Endymion, she put him to sleep for several months and browsed in the enjoyment of her young lover who stirred only in his dreams. Or think of Joan, Queen of Naples, who had her first husband Andreasso hanged at the bars of her window with a cord of silk because in his matrimonial duties, she found that neither his parts nor his performance answered her expectations. Some women, like spiders, would devour a man. Shame on Luna, Shame on the Queen of Naples!" he cried, with an expression as if he'd reached reason, and looking inquiringly at Sophie, asked, "Don' t you agree?"

But Sophie did not answer as she stood there looking nowhere, the way women sometimes do in a mood of half-sadness — a mood when a woman can leave a man quickly, never to return, or say "yes" with joyless indifference. Still looking nowhere, she walked slowly to the sofa, sat on it, arranged her dress, and said, as if addressing no one, "I am not interested in spiders, any more than Mathilda was in grasshoppers. I cannot remember much of Montaigne's writings, and I am not impressed by the Queen of Naples' cruelties." And, almost inaudibly she added, "I am not interested in Cynics. I'm afraid … I'm losing interest in you…"

Blok rushed to her, fell on his knees, and begged her to forgive his insensitiveness and his inability to say the right things at the right moment.

"I am so clumsy, I always was. I never fit anywhere. I was born a stranger. You understand me? You must! I am one of a new race of uprooted people, cut in halves and quarters, who even at home have to thank others for hospitality. Home! What a wonderful word. What an unknown sensation! You are a great woman, darling! Greater than the noble wife of Seneca, who shared with him his death, or the wife of Pliny's neighbor in Italy who died in the hands of her husband, and every other woman who shared their lives with their husband's and wished to be their companions in death. Wouldn't you? Of course, I don't know how good I will be to live with … but I will be good to die with."

Only now, after bringing himself to a state of almost rapture, did he notice Sophie's eyes fixed on him with a dismal stare. "You speak as if in a trance," said Sophie, and touching his forehead, shook her head. "You have fever, you are not well. Otherwise you would not respond to my proposal with a demand for my death."

"I did not! You misunderstood, and I am not ill at all. In fact, I am thrilled and happy. Oh darling, you misunderstood, and I am not ill at all. I love you. I… I…" but Sophie walked out, leaving Blok standing in the middle of the room, bewildered and very sad. He hoped she would return. "I must see her. I want her," his lips whispered.

She put the hall lights out. It was her way of showing resolution and to indicate the break. He put his light out also and groped slowly to the hallway and to his room. He undressed in the dark and, as if obeying an overpowering impulse, stealthily walked to Sophie's door. Not daring to breath, he stood looking at the streak of light which showed under her door, but it also soon went out, making the silence almost unbearable in the dark. He felt as if Sophie knew he was standing there and could neither advance nor retreat. His heart burned with desire, defeating all other feelings and thoughts. But soon, he carefully stretched his hand to the door knob and, turning it gently, began to push the door ajar. It creaked slightly, and he stopped — listening and waiting. He tried again. and when the opening was wide enough, he peered into the dark. Not trying to hold back his heavy breathing any more, he made the first step into the room. He wanted to call to her. Yet, as he called, "Sophie, Sophie," no sound came from his mouth.

Guarding each footstep with great silence, he reached her bed and, carefully kneeling down, felt for her. But before he actually touched the coverlet, the enormity of his daring struck him and made him draw his hand away.

A feeling of fear suddenly overcame him, sinking his desire beneath a cloak of an awkwardness. Suddenly strange and fearful images crept into his mind. He shivered as if gusts of cold air whipped his perspiring, naked body. With increasing fear, he heard flapping wings over his head. He threw himself to the floor, and the strange sound became fainter. He listened with eyes closed, his face pressed to the carpet. At this moment, there was a click of the light-switch. He jumped to his feet and saw Sophie fully dressed. Speechless and stunned, blinking in the glaring light, Blok stood crushed with embarrassment. He dashed for the door, not even vaguely catching her words or her laughter that followed him into his room.

Chapter XVIII

The next morning, Blok was relieved to find himself alone in the apartment. It was painful to think of the embarrassment of last night. He felt ashamed and worried. How can I face Sophie again? The tormented questions appeared again and again. She will not see me any more… Also, to have been from his art for such a long time made him feel guilty. I have abandoned and betrayed my work. Isn't art the only thing that really matters? He walked determinedly to the largest canvas he had, adjusted it to the right height on the easel, and looked at it.

He knew what he wanted to paint, but the start — the first stroke of the brush – that was his Rubicon! In his head was a creation, but his hand? Would his hand, equipped with knowledge, be at his service, or could any realization in art be as great as it was when conceived in the head and heart of the artist?

"I will call the steam bath," thought Blok, "and ask the masseur to pose for me. Just to start. I will not keep him long. No, no. I don't need him. What I must visualize is how he massages the leper. I know the composition, the atmosphere — that's what I need. Steam — a lot of steam. Then that hard bench with the miserable body on it. What did the attendant say? Bumpy spots? Dead material?"

Blok began to work with great concentration and speed, and though the painting progressed, he was dissatisfied with it. One could hear him say, "It's not that, not that." He worked with intensity, yet his old fervor was missing. "I am too dependent on so-called inspiration, the paradise of amateurs. Give them a little inspiration, mix it with some gossipy tradition, and there they are, ready for the market and immortality," thought Blok angrily. He stepped back from the canvas, then moved very close to it, and after several strokes, moved back again, closing one eye, murmuring something to himself. The brush moved faster now, and the colors were mixed rapidly with a sure but nervous hand. "It's going," he thought smiling. But it was the smile of someone else, a stranger with a grimace on his face. But Blok did not know it; he had no time to think of his face. He was painting feverishly, clearly visualizing the moving flesh he was putting on canvas.

Now one could almost hear the masseur's hands, rubbing and beating the body stretched on the bench and see his powerful, swiftly-moving hands and hear the leprous man groaning. "It's starting to live, it lives already," he said to himself, changing brushes.

"But there is no steam. I need steam, the air full of steam. He ran into the bathroom, opened a faucet and waited until the hot water gave off steam." Then he closed the door in order to allow the steam to accumulate, went into Sophie's bathroom, and after doing the same thing there, he returned to his canvas. The sound of running water brought the atmosphere of the steam bath back to him. Its sound made him see the husky attendant with the towel wrapped around his belly as clearly as if he were standing before him. Blok was working fast, now stroking the canvas with lightning speed and exactitude, now with hand poised thoughtfully, his body always moving back and forth, his narrowed eyes examining keenly each painted line, appraising each new color put on the canvas.

His forehead was bathed in perspiration as he ran to open the doors of the bathrooms so that the steam could fill the apartment. He reached a state of ecstasy when he saw the canvas enveloped in the grayish-white steam which slowly seeped through the whole apartment. He continued working long after all the objects in the room had become lost in the thick fog. The noise of running water added to his fervent inspiration. He stood close to the canvas. As never before, there were no problems to be solved, no doubts to convince. He was aware of the great creative moment in his life, this rare and precious moment for the capture of which one must fly fast and high and then hold tightly with one's hands and heart. To find that moment, one must lose time and lose oneself. This is what happened to Blok, and that is why he was so stupefied when he heard Sophie's voice coming from somewhere out of the thick fog, "Heavens, what is all this? Damn it! Everything is ruined! The floors are full of water. Where are you?"

But he did not answer, standing as if stunned with a brush in his hand. The sudden silence was strange, and after Sophie stopped the running water, he saw her opening the windows.

"Such a fool! A misfit!" he heard her angry voice.

She tripped as she rushed past him, knocking his canvas to the floor.

"Get this out of here!" Her voice sounded to him like a crow as she flapped her way out of the room.

Blok picked up his canvas, took his hat and coat from the closet, and walked out of the apartment. He crossed 20th Street, holding the wet canvas to his side. Just as he was entering the Square, a sudden gust of wind blew his hat off.

He ran after it, but he could not reach it until the corner of 19th Street where he saw it under the wheels of a passing greyhound bus. It lay there in the middle of the street, dirty and crushed to the ground, and it no longer looked like something that had been close to him just a few minutes ago. Blok walked bareheaded and solemn toward a bench at the southern end of the Square. His head ached and a melancholy mood pervaded his soul. This execrable city and this round Square, always the same — "How tired I am of it." He heard the squealing street cars.

"How do you do, Mr. Blok?" He saw the grinning face of Mr. Snok. "How have you been?" he inquired again.

"I am just fine, thank you," said Blok, getting up and ready to go.

"What's the hurry?" protested Snok. "Please sit down. There are a few things I would like to talk over with you." Blok showed no great enthusiasm. "Much water has flowed away, and uncounted trillions of spermatozoa have been wasted since I saw you last." Then, looking close into Blok's face, Snok exclaimed, "Why Mr. Blok, your face is green! You look slightly damaged."

"Hmmm… perhaps," said Blok sourly, "though I am not nearly as damaged as a certain lady you know who was pinched to the state of maternity."

"Let's not talk of relatives and maternity," said Snok. "I owe you an apology. The A. of M. showed me the folly of suing a great artist like you."

"Oh?" mumbled Blok. "They must know what is best."

But as Snok began to say something, Blok thanked him and started to walk away. But he did not reach the center of the Square before he heard Snok calling him from close behind. "Please wait. My car and chauffeur are right there." He pointed to 20th Street. "I will take you wherever you want."

"Why should you?"

After his long insistence, Blok consented.

It was a blue, shiny limousine with a uniformed chauffer in front. Blok gazed with amazement at the rare orchids in beautiful glass tubes on the walls. Behind the driver's seat there was a television screen, and on both sides of its mahogany cabinet were crystal flasks with liqueurs.

"Under one of the seats," Snok explained, a small library was installed, equipped with an automatic book reader, and on the other seat an electric thinker, capable of correcting the reader, and giving the right interpretation if desired.

Snok was pleased with the impression the car made on Blok and only too willingly spoke of other excellences it possessed. He spoke of a barbecue grill in the rear; collapsible helicopter on top; the new model CX that at the pressing of a button unfolded; a dry-water cleansing apparatus' radar in the front that prevented collisions and also responded to green and red lights. "But the most useful gadget," he said, "is this cute-looking temper conditioner." He pointed to a round ivory switch, with three letters inserted in it, C, H, and T, for Cold, Hot, and Temperate. "But mind you," he said, "those are strictly emotion regulators and have nothing to do with temperature. As you see," he continued, "the switch is now on T, and so neither of us can feel hostility towards the other." Snok remarked, "Switch H is of great value to married people and has been proven helpful in cases of mild impotency. I admire the usefulness of this invention but feel that the use of switch H should be restricted to reliable people." He concluded then with a smirk, and looking at Mr. Blok's astonished face, he cocked his head, stretched his long, wiry neck, and said, "Didn't you want to go somewhere? We're standing on the same spot."

"I want to go home," he said.

When they reached his house, Snok said, "I am looking forward to seeing you at the Great Assembly." They shook hands and before parting, and Blok asked if the fabulous car belonged to Snok.

"Of course, it's mine," said Snok proudly.

"But doesn't it cost a lot of money?"

"It certainly does. You see," he explained, "I worked in collaboration with a colleague of mine on a formula in which certain chemicals enable any desired part of the body to fatten or to flatten and shrink at will. The green pills round the breasts, the pink flatten behinds, and so forth. The great beauty of it is that a lady can simultaneously make her breasts fuller and derriere thinner. The success of the invention is truly stupendous, as you have probably heard from Pinkel. The proof of it is that in the last couple of months, pink pills alone sold five million orders," and looking at Blok' s stomach with a calculating eye, he added, "I will send you a few dozen of the white ones. Men with flat stomachs are better understood by women." Then suddenly, as if remembering something, he resumed, "We don't yet sell facial form transformers, leaving it for the time being to plastic surgeons, but in contrast, for all that is below... Mr. Shopklang became literally a different man, making him laugh at his previous inferiority complexes caused by..."

At this point Mr. Blok, having reached his destination, stepped out of the car, and stood at the window listening to Snok's farewell. It appeared to him that Mr. Snok's neck and his nose in particular stretched and grew, advancing toward Blok's face, creeping like a caterpillar along the window with little jolts and shivers and working itself up into space making ready to jump at him. Then it suddenly became a nose again with two huge nostrils in whose deep darkness grew reddish and prickly plants with tiny rodents gnawing on them with their sharp shiny teeth and darting with their beastly small eyes at Blok. It was unbearable. Blok closed his eyes, opened them again, only to find Snok's monstrous nose touching his face. Blok caught it and snapped at it. He heard a shrill cry from Snok and saw the great limousine departing.

Entering the studio, Blok found it in shambles. Peanut-shells crackled underfoot; his one chair lay with broken legs. Torn newspapers, envelopes, dirty socks. and shirts littered the floor. He sat on his bed looking at a howdah standing near the fireplace. "Who brought that here?" he wondered.

"Beware of a lone elephant in the jungle … beware of a lone whale in the ocean … they are rejected by their herds, they are tormented … and mad … they are dangerous … So am I, so am I … only I am not dangerous, only tormented.

"Oh God! There I go again, said Blok to himself with disgust … a bavardeur stays a bavardeur even if alone… Away with the chatterers! Away with the clumsy romances! Away with all of them!

"I will work. I will not give in to vagaries and will not let clouds descend and envelop me until I evaporate! The work one loves is salvation to all. I will work hard. Harder than all painters who hanged themselves or died in bordellos, who knocked out their brains in search of originality, or cut off their ears, or were pursued by the demon of their genius to their glorious doom — to remote islands, or into mental hospitals.

"I will submit to the laws and sanity of nature, and like her I will not give all only to people. Don't they already have more than they can digest? I will paint animals for animals. I will look at the bird with cat's eyes and paint the bird. I am resolved, I will leave people in peace splitting their atoms and studying their conditioned reflexes and behavioristic psychology…

"I'm covered with dust from the roads I have tramped. I'm all covered with it, —my brains, flesh, and glands…I will sweep it clean with my brush and put what is beneath it onto the canvas."

With these thoughts, he picked up a bunch of letters and carefully opened the first envelope. It was from Boys' Town, asking him for support; enclosed he found a card indicating Honorary Citizenship of the Town. The next letter was from the United Jewish Appeal, and then one from the March of Dimes, followed by the American Oncologic Hospital, the Kiwanis Club, the Red Cross, and the Friends of the Boston Symphony. He wrote seven checks, put them in envelopes, and rested for a while, praising the private initiative and good will of citizens. He read appeals from the fire company, Boy Scouts, the Catholic Church in Teyton, the Metropolitan Opera Company, the Public Health Association, the Children's Hospital, the Actor's Mutual Aid Society, and the Foundation for the Blind. There were many other appeals for equally noble causes, mixed with numerous interesting bills, but their lack of imagination tired Mr. Blok and made him feel sleepy. But he did not really mind that dull feeling of tiredness, preferring it to the upsetting emotions that are so annoying if they occur too often. "There is even some good in apathy. God knows we have no need to be pepped up in this century," reflected Blok scribbling something on the back of an envelope.

Oh Energy, Ambition —

Have mercy on the anguished,

On victims of your power.

Cease, subdue, yield your strength

to me who still chants of love

Who dares not withstand.

Let my doom not be your victory,
Let not vanity be my bride.
The gentle thought is my only harbor,
My only speed is melody.
Oh spare me, unholy energy,
Have mercy for the timorous and proud,
It does not scan, it does not scan, scan, scan.
Sincerely yours,
Blok

Chapter XIX

Mr. Blok, having lost the habit of freedom, soon found a different kind of freedom in his self-imposed seclusion. At first he was bitter and lonesome, alone with his thoughts and painfully conscious of his failure with Sophie. But soon his palette and canvas, as so often in the past, came to his rescue. He plunged into his work with passion and tenacity, making the days pass almost unnoticed. Though exhausted and hardly able to stand on his feet in front of the easel and with greedy fanaticism, he would make one more stroke — then another. The last one, he would say to himself, and it would lead him into an ecstasy again. Though tired, he was tireless, exhausted, yet bursting with inspiration.

During these days he did not answer the telephone and opened the door only when he would hurry out for his supplies. Only once did he make a quick and furtive visit to Elsa, but he felt ashamed of his relationship with her and as if he had betrayed Sophie. It was joyless, and he doubted whether he would ever see her again.

Returning to his studio from one of his shopping trips, he found a woman waiting for him. She demanded to see him with such resolution that he had to bow to her will. Sitting on his bed and listening to her strange orations, he was irritated and cross. And yet, he still could not find out the motives of her visit or who she really was.

"Yes, it is a crime to prevent an artist from working," said Blok.

"But you said yourself, Mr. Blok, that you are exhausted from working. Didn't you say that for ten straight days you hardly took any time to sleep!"

"It's true, perhaps I work too spasmodically. Before you came, I wanted to take stock of my work. It's important for balance. "

"You're not a juggler."

"Also, not a rubber ball to be tossed about," said Blok with visible aggravation.

"Please do not be angry. The anger on your face is as unfitting as a cigar sticking in the mouth of a cherub. And please, I beg you, never repeat the word crime to me negligently."

"Why not? Are you so guiltless?"

"You know very well."

"No, I don't. For the last two hours you have been telling me 'you know, you know' What do I know?"

"Crime! That's what you know."

"I? No, it's really too much. How dare you."

"You see, you see," she spoke quickly. "Didn't I warn you? You see the affect it has on you?"

"Oh, God, why don't you leave me alone?" said Blok with exasperation. "I hate to be impolite, but you must understand I don't even know who you are."

"You will know soon enough. By the way, did you prepare a speech for the Assembly? You know it is tonight. They have chosen you as their IDOLS. Every five years a new idol is chosen for the Great Assembly. I believe all the previous idols have died or have been forgotten — most probably both."

"How cheerful," grumbled Blok.

"It is cheerful, I assure you. Don't you agree that all Idols are boring? Even the Aristocrats considered abandoning them for good. They hope this example will be followed by the rest of the world."

"They were so good to me," said Blok reminiscently.

"Their aims are universal, too big to understand. They live by contradictions. And yet, all of humanity seeks the guidance of this glorious body of noble thoughts and deeds. You will see for yourself tonight at the Assembly. The last time, it was some conglomeration — actually representatives – of everything walking on two legs."

"Don't understand a thing," said Blok.

"The better for you. The greater will be your surprise tonight."

Blok paced the room nervously.

"I never imagined you to be so nervous," she said. "You need a vacation. Arizona is the place for you."

"One can perish from too much advice. Why can't I live alone with my art?" said Blok nostalgically, speaking as if to himself.

"Your bad humor has made it difficult for me," said the lady, "to thank you for the lovely gadget you sent me as a present, considering that you didn't even know me personally then."

"I still don't know who you are."

"Really?" Her eyes protruded.

"What gadget?" asked Blok.

"That cute little revolver, of course."

"Revolver? I never gave anyone a revolver!"

"Is that so? "

"I never possessed one. I never held one in my hand. Will you tell me what you are driving at? It's getting rather tiresome," Blok said, raising his voice.

She also seemed irritated. "Mr. Blok, please do not pretend. It's not very brave."

"I'm not brave, and I do not pretend!"

"Oh, maybe it is just a weakness of your memory," she said ironically. "The less one is impressed, the easier it is to forget."

"Impressed with what?" Blok nervously plucked a hair from his eye brow.

"With the death of Mr. Kratki."

"Kratki? What do I have to do with his death?"

"Didn't you want him to die?"

"I did not love him."

She suddenly burst into laughter. "Oh, you should have seen his face as he held my dentures in his hand. That was the last thing he saw in this world."

Blok approached her. "You must leave me now, do you hear?" And suddenly he thought of the prowler. "It's a nuisance. I resent people to intrude like this… "

As she finished laughing, she said through her teeth, "So, you had nothing to do with his death? How innocent! They took the revolver away from me. I would have loved to keep it as a souvenir."

"I demand an explanation," Blok screamed in rage. "It is ridiculous."

She got up and with a theatrical bow said a long phrase in Greek and then announced, "My name is Lucretia Shrimp, and the revolver was brought to me with your compliments by a certain Mr. Miller. If not for your present, Kratki would still be alive today. I loved him, but you hated him. He took Luba away from you and Mathilda too."

''Mathilda?" shouted Blok.

"That's right, and you took his life," she rasped. "I was silly not to know it right away. You are the killer! A miserable cowardly killer." Her bony face hardened still more, and the pupils of her eyes almost touched each other as she advanced toward Blok staring at him angrily. Her words rolled out with great force. "I came here to tell you that you are the true murderer. YOU ... you ... you!"

"You're insane, crazy," Blok shouted and ran out of the studio. It can't be. "She is out of her mind. No, no, perhaps she must prove someone else guilty. Maybe her case will be reopened. Oh, what a cauldron. Why did Miller do a thing like that? That idiot with a grip of iron." Blok cussed running across the Square. "Could it have been because he lost his job on account of me? That shrapnel of a woman — called me a murderer. Ridiculous, absurd." Oh, never mind. He tried to brush the whole thing off, but the thoughts persisted.

"Perhaps I am a murderer! Didn't I kill him a thousand times in thoughts and dreams? I did things I couldn't dream of doing, and I did things as in a dream. I am a killer, though I did not kill directly. But what she said could be the truth. I spoke too much sometimes. What was the first thing she said when she came? Didn't she ask if 1 had received a summons? Also, if I know how the lottery ticket peddlers die in South America? What was she insinuating? A dangerous woman! She looked at me so strangely." He remembered hearing Van Horn mention to Miller something about Kratki. Didn't he also hear the name of Shrimp then?

"How can I go to the Assembly in such a state? My nerves — it's a sham." He looked at the time. "I should be there now," he thought. Arriving at the Assembly Auditorium, he paused before the entrance to try to collect himself. He combed his hair and fixed his tie. He looked at his shoes, took a yellow handkerchief from his back pocket, and while the elevator operator watched him with great interest, he wiped the dust off his shoes. Blok folded the handkerchief and placed it into his pocket and with a deep sigh headed toward the elevator.

"Are you the Idol of today?" asked the elevator man with respect.

"I am a guest," murmured Blok, confused.

"You must be Mr. Blok," said the man. "They are all waiting for you."

Blok walked into the great Assembly Hall. He was late. As soon as he reached the presiding table, the whole assembly arose paying respect to the honored guest. Mr. Blok bowed politely, and after taking a seat, Mr. Van Horn rose from his chair and read lines from Lao-Tse:

> "Throw away learning
>
> Cast off excess knowledge
>
> reap thus a hundredfold gain.
>
> Banish cumbrous benevolence
>
> And interfering righteousness:
>
> Then will people return
>
> To filial love, to brotherhood.
>
> Void the ideals of scheming and getting.
>
> Robbers and thieves will disappear.
>
> Education has failed,
>
> Hold fast to intuitive good!
>
> Be simple, be natural -
>
> Check ambition; curb desire."

After these words, the great Assembly was officially launched. Only for an extraordinary occasion such as this were the iron doors that separated two halls removed to make an immense and truly imposing auditorium. "No wonder," thought Blok, "it is known as the largest and best equipped auditorium in the world." The very long presiding table covered with green cloth faced nine much smaller tables that formed a horseshoe. All tables stood on a slightly elevated stage that was in the center of the two halls. The vastness of the room made the tables and people seem astonishingly small. The voice of the speaker sounded higher than normal and reached every corner and ceiling of the empty room. Blok thought it had the sound of a radio left on high volume and was not human.

Except for Mr. Ellis and Ondra, who got on both sides of Mr. Blok, and Mr. Van Horn a few chairs away, no acquaintances occupied the table with him. Along the walls hung many striking paintings, but though Mr. Blok recognized his own work, it in no way made him less conscious of being a stranger among these earnest and solemn people.

Since his arrival he had not stopped fretting. "After LaoTse we always let five minutes of silence transform all carnal emotions into spiritual ones," said Ondra in a whisper. "That silence is dreadful," thought Blok. Mr. Ellis tried to catch Blok's attention.

"Did she come to see you?" he asked when Mr. Blok turned his face from Ondra. "They will try me now. Here are the judges." It came to him with a premonitory chill.

"Who?" Blok tried to be calm.

"Shrimp," said Ellis. Blok nodded. "I thought so," said Ellis. "Does he know? Murderer, Idol, Shrimp," rang in his head. "Idiot, blockhead," he heard himself saying and felt Mr. Ondra's hand touching him.

"Be careful of what you are saying."

"I thought of myself," Mr. Blok lied quickly.

"No, you looked at him." Ondra pointed his eyes at a man whose extremely narrow forehead was completely covered with hair. "I hope you have not offended him," said Ondra softly. "It is Mr. Cheezis."

It was a great relief to everyone when the Aris Superior got up and commanded North, South, East and West to proceed to the center. Mr. Blok made a motion to stand up but was held back by Mr. Ellis and Ondra. "It is not for you," they said. Mr. Blok saw four men walking in line toward the Superior and in turn, all kissed him on his forehead, his chin, and both cheeks.

"Did you notice the third gentlemen?" whispered Mr. Ellis. "Yes, why?"

"Nothing" said Ellis, "I just wondered if you observed anything unusual. It is maintained that he is an infant."

"He has a moustache." reacted Mr. Blok.

"Exactly — that is the trouble. He matured too quickly. Remarkable. Yesterday, he celebrated his sixth birthday. You see? Look! He is fed guava jelly by hand."

"It is true," remarked Mr. Blok with astonishment.

"But mentally he is a giant, " said Mr. Ellis admiringly. He wanted to speak more but at this moment, the Aris Superior struck the gavel several times and put a velvet hat on his head. He spoke. "In the name of noble thoughts and deeds, I welcome you here, my friends, Aristocrats of the world. As always in the past, we will also at this great Assembly acknowledge our defeat and fiasco in all matter of aesthetics and the pursuit of beauty by human civilization. Yes, we admit our traditional defeat, but we must rejoice in our tenacity.

"Gentlemen, let's forget all the bloodhounds of violence, all rascals of greed, all criminals of intolerance, vanity and ignorance. The joy of our meeting today shall be unclouded and pure. In ancient times whips of leek or shallot were used in certain rites in which ceremonial scourging took place." Surprisingly Blok saw a smile on the Superior's face as he proceeded.

"How innocent in comparison with the auto de facto cremation of millions of innocents alive in this so-called modern
civilization. How gratifying shall be our rites of bestowing the
highest honor upon this great man and artist," and the Superior
pointed majestically at Mr. Blok. "I am proud to pronounce
you our Idol #49, or as we have voted, Idol the Last."

"Miss Shrimp told me the truth," thought Mr. Blok, as the
garland was ceremoniously put on his head and a scroll handed
to him.

After several speeches, all short and to the point, the
Chairman, Mr. Van Horn, changed places with Ondra. While
the meeting, he said to Mr. Blok, would attend to business and
formalities, splitting into groups of four and five, he would ac-
quaint Mr. Blok with the few important personalities present.

"It will help you in your coming address," he explained.

"Where is the bathroom?" asked Mr. Blok. "I would like to…"

"Impossible." Mr. Van Horn looked shocked. "You will
create a precedent — completely impossible." Looking at Mr.
Blok's worried face, he said with softened tone, "There will
soon be empty guava jelly containers." Mr. Blok said nothing.
"Look at the Assistant Western Aria," said Mr. Van Horn. "Even
he holds himself back." Mr. Blok did not share Mr. Van Horn's
sentiments and listened silently. "The man on the infant's left
— do you hear him speak French?"

"I can't hear him," said Mr. Blok.

"Oh, never mind. He is so conscious of the beauty of
the French language that he does not give a farthing for what
he says. He is very moody but proved to be valuable at all
our intervals. The gentleman on his right is a general. After
his retirement from active duty, he was appointed Ambassador to the country he helped to defeat. I have been told he
learned Finnish. The gentleman a little farther down knows

250,000 quotations by heart from Koran, Homer, Shakespeare, Schopenhauer, and eh —" Van Horn wanted to continue but was interrupted by Mr. Blok.

"Must I know them all?" he asked. "I can't wait. Will the jelly be served soon?"

"They are noble minds, but I warn you they may become inquisitive, and should any of them start to question you it is in your interest to get acquainted."

"What questions?" asked Blok.

"One never knows," said Van Horn vaguely. "Miss Shrimp, that preposterous and unpredictable woman, will appear here mingling with the guests and will speak to every Aris separately.

"I gave orders not to let her in, but I am afraid it will only complicate matters. She should have stayed in Arizona," he concluded gravely and patted Mr. Blok on the shoulder.

"Who is speaking now?" asked Blok.

"I am pleased," said Van Horn, "that you are beginning to take an interest. He is the head of Patriotic Department. Due to the fact that the patriotic sentiments are not a monopoly of the natives or naturalized citizens of each respective country, he developed a technique or patriotism quite unique, I must say. But we have no time to waste. Mr. Ellis and I will speak to you simultaneously."

"Ellis":	I'll introduce everyone to your left.
"Van Horn":	On your right is a Portuguese poet.
"Ellis":	Is a gentleman of Morocco.
"Van Horn":	Mr. deSeixas
"Ellis":	He is the victor over the notorious, nefarious Marius.
"Blok":	Marius?
"Van Horn":	Wrote short lyrics – very beautiful.
"Ellis":	The gentleman next to him

"Van Horn":	The gentleman next to him
"Ellis":	has rediscovered
"Van Horn":	is a new manager of a Fry festival
"Ellis":	A matter thought irretrievably lost.
"Blok":	You both are stuffing me like a turkey.
"Van Horn":	And the gentleman next to him due to not entirely salubrious...
"Blok":	Shut up.
"Ellis":	Formerly was a judge
"Van Horn":	What I mean, he is a judge
"Ellis":	Calcium deposit in his joints forced him to resign.
"Blok":	Oh, where are the empty guava jars?

"Superior": "Gentlemen, honored friends — I would like to express my gratitude forkeeping me as your Superior. My joy is pure and complete, and in my heart there isn't a trace of doubt left. I only wonder does one from number one stop or begin to count?"

"His phraseology is delightful," said someone. "He strives for the top but is interested mostly in the middle — his own and otherwise," remarked the same man.

The Superior continued. "This man, whom you see before you, does not really need an introduction, for he is as familiar to us as all these animals and birds created by his unfailing hands that you see on the walls. Look, gentleman, at the proud vicuna! — or next to it, dingo, the wild dog of Australia!... Do you hear its terrifying bark? Do you see its sharp hungry teeth? Well, the vicuna of the high Andes is not afraid of it. They like each other's company on the wall and live with the fennec, with the desman, eland, and grebe in peace and harmony.

"Let us gentleman, and fellow Aristocrats, pay due tribute to the man who introduced to us the barbirusa of Celebes and gave us 400 pounds of arapaima, the Brazilian fish, as a present. Let's thank Mr. Blok for notornis, the grison and guanaco," cried the speaker pointing is hand first at the paintings and then at Mr. Blok.

"Hear! Hear!" cried a few Englishmen, others following with "Bravo," and some French with loud "Encore."

The hall was filled with voices and enthusiastic applause. Mr. Blok was besieged with demands that he address the Assembly. He responded and arose nervously. "The aims and activities of your society," he said, "do not need recognition and praise, as the universe does not need or ask recognition or approval. It simply is!"

"Wonderful!" someone cried out.

"People limped and crawled miles behind the mighty steps of victorious nature for thousands of years. Well, now we are still crawling behind it, but only in moral and esthetic matters; in some others we are driven by great powers. We are flying and speeding in incredible haste as if running in terror from nature rather than following it at a respectful distance. You can move your misery from place to place faster and faster — while man remains the same.

"Gentlemen," cried Blok with inspiration, "I know you agree with what I have said, but I wish you to admit that the path followed by our spirit – since its birth until our day — has proven a tragic failure. We failed to feel and thus did not progress." There was a deeply felt silence, and looking up, Blok saw Mr. Van Horn signaling him to sit down.

"Now," said Mr. Van Horn, "I see by the agenda the program of this meeting will continue with an exchange of thoughts and general discussion. As always, we will start from the end and proceed to the beginning — but considering the difficulties of starting anything from the end and leading it all the way to its beginning, I suggest that you feel free of all regimentation and say or ask anything, provided it is of some interest.

"Splendid," exclaimed the man on Blok's left. He got up and repeated, "Splendid! Mr. Chairman, being rather precise, I would like to pose a question to Mr. Blok. In your admirable speech," he said, "you stated that people walked or crawled miles behind nature. May we know how many miles? That's all," he concluded with the air of demolishing something with the strength of a breath and sat down. All looked at Blok with expectation, while he just stared at the man. The conduct of Mr. Cheezis was unanimously found persnickety and offending, and he was made to apologize, after which the Superior announced the panel discussion scheduled for the entire week.

He then went on to enumerate the various groups of expected guests who would arrive after the first intermission. This included all those who were invited by the Special Committee for the Defense, as well as the general public and followers. "Please converse with one another in whispers during the intermission," he concluded.

There was a short silence followed by the light stroke of a gavel and an announcement of recess. Ellis graciously invited everyone to partake of the Benedictine and loquats that were being served on either side of the iron doors.

"I wonder what a loquat is?" murmured Mr. Blok rushing to the rest room.

Chapter XX

"Honored guests," boomed the loud speaker, "this is the largest audience in the history of our society. Doesn't it prove that humanity is not crippled in disunity? Let us stay close together. Not an inch or space shall separate us. Your cooperation is needed. Please stand more closely together so as to make room for the procession that shall begin at once."

In response to this request, there was a tremendous amount of motion as the regrouping of participants for the procession took place. If it hadn't been for the extraordinary good will of all concerned, there might have been a disaster. But as it was, the damage was slight. It is true that several individuals unable to endure the extreme pressure fainted, and that a few more resistant were injured. But they were very ably revived and taken care of by several surgeons and particularly by the masseur, who during his efficient manipulations caught sight of Mr. Blok and winked at him with great friendliness. The quickness with which order was achieved and the path for the procession was made, considering the great hazards of movement at this point, was truly admirable.

Though Mr. Blok made attempts to come nearer the exits, he was only bruised and swept in the tumult still further away. In spite of the fact that he was bruised and found himself in unfavorable surroundings, twisted and squeezed by strangers of both sexes and various weights, he was still pleased to find himself better placed to view the proceedings than the multitudes whose view of the procession had been completely obstructed.

With great surprise Mr. Blok watched the first group pass by that was led by Mr. Snok heading rows of celibates and divorced eunuchs. Mr. Blok thought that their soft quasi-singing voices were euphonious and deserved better text, which he understood to be something like, "We are not harmed by being disarmed, for we still have desire which keeps us entire." Mr. Blok was quite impressed with Snok's transformation from aggressive viciousness to a calm submission.

As soon as the eunuchs passed, a small choir of bereaved fiancés led by Mathilda, garbed in billowy black lace, sang during their procession a short and deeply moving threnody. Mr. Blok sincerely regretted it was of such short duration. The light now became silvery and caressing, making faces look soft and content, preparing a perfect setting for the parade of Holy Rollers and the Swiss followers of Zwingli, behind whom he saw Mr. Shopklang with the inspiration of the Faith of Baha U'Llah on a small shield.

"No, it's not Shopklang. He couldn't have walked out on his youth so soon," murmured Mr. Blok faintly.

"Most of us do." He heard a muffled voice as if from someone's stomach. As Mr. Blok looked for the voice, a school teacher whispered, "You won't find him. He's a wicked vagabond of Cracow, shameless magician and ventriloquist."

"Psst, be quiet," said a man from behind his bushy beard. "We want to listen to the wonder rabbi of Arkansas."

Mr. Blok stretched his neck trying to follow the parade. His eyes became strained and tired as the temperature in the hall climbed past 100 degrees. Being unable to move or raise his hands without causing great inconvenience to everyone around him, he almost envied the person he saw wiping the perspiration from his face by rubbing against the beard of his neighbor. "Oh, what a luscious beard," he thought. "Aren't the shaved men of today as ridiculous as a featherless peacock or a mane-less lion?" The moment that his eyes left the beard of the man, his attention was called to the head of the man who stood directly in front of him. It was completely bald and covered with small rivulets of water that from time to time he shook off, sprinkling Mr. Blok's face and suit. Considering the great heat in the hall, it was a pleasant relief.

As the procession continued, he found himself wearied by it. His splitting headache and bruised ribs caused him to give it in completely to his exhaustion. He could scarcely keep his eyes open, and the effort to stand on his feet seemed beyond his endurance. Relaxing his muscles and bending his knees, he discovered he could stay upright by leaning on all the people who surrounded him. Resting in this manner, he was about to shut off his mind from all the disturbing elements of the Assembly when he felt a very soft velvety touch on his back. Its insinuating softness caused a new sensation. It was so different from the pressure he had been accustomed to. "It's the touch of a woman," thought Mr. Blok, wanting to turnaround to verify this. This was quite impossible. It was unmistakable in the way she rubbed herself against his back that she must have found pleasure in his nearness. She seeks to establish contact, thought Blok, closing his eyes. Blok felt her thighs vibrating against his body in intimate but controlled excitement, caressing and teasing with scarcely noticeable motions. As in a dream, Blok gave himself to this strange experience. He was abruptly brought back to his senses by a shower from the bald head of the man. It made him angry. "Whoever you are who stands in front of me, stop squirting me," he said "It gets on my nerves. I am not a plant."

"I know you aren't," answered the man angrily. "I didn't come here to perspire and to be handled by people behind me. If you want to know the truth," he said trying to turn his head, "I find this whole meeting atrocious." As soon as he said this, his body seemed to be first lifted, and then to fly in circles high above the heads of the people until he disappeared, probably through one of the ventilators.

After this curious incident, all the ventilators were turned on, and all the fire sprinklers in the ceiling were opened. It refreshed everyone and lifted Blok's spirits. Since the disappearance of the bald-headed man, there was more space in which to move and even to turn and raise one's hands. Before Blok changed his position, he saw with admiration, that Mrs. Chonkey's cactus hat had started to bloom. How wondrous, after only a few drops of water. Then he turned and saw a woman in front of him, rather a woman's back. He asked her to turn around, but there was no response. He leaned as far as the free space allowed. He was puzzled. "Please," he asked her again. "I would like so much to see you." She stood deaf to his pleading. "It is unfair," he whined. He turned her around and found she had no face. He turned her again and again, but he always found only her back. "Don't you have a front? Isn't there another side of you? Where is your face?" he demanded desperately, now turning her with violence. He shook her by the shoulders, but there was no answer. He demanded, he begged, but to no avail. He looked around him hoping to find an explanation, but no one seemed to see him or the woman. How could they be indifferent to such a striking phenomenon? He despised their indifference. He wanted to insult them, but he knew it would be senseless. They would not listen. He looked again at the woman who drew him with the force of a magnet, but he could not move. He did not breathe as he stood overwhelmed and trembling. Looking penetratingly at her, he seemed to see a dark cave-like opening. With fear and fascination, he looked at its protective walls and had a sudden urge to enter.

At this moment many soft-spoken voices tried to reach him. He felt them flying low above his head, circling and trying to enter his ears. He knew they were frantically trying to warn him from entering. Then everything went dark. He heard a voice speaking intimately and yet as if addressing the entire universe. "You are still a little boy," she said. "No one who comes from within me ever grows up. Don't be ashamed of not being mature. No one is. Not even I, who am a mother."

"You sound like someone I know," said Blok.

"I know dear," the voice interrupted. "I sound like Sophie. Yes? And perhaps like all the other women you knew."

"She is a symbol and an axis around which the world circles." Suddenly Blok heard the powerful chorus. "She is our comfort and our agony. Our reality and myth," the chorus sang. "She is the beginning of all, creating only new and unknown. Each who emerges from her is unique and the only," spoke the chorus repeating the lovely refrain, "unique and the only, unique and the only." The choir was interrupted by the shrill, shrieking voice of a woman.

"I demand justice. Arrest this murderer. Help. Mr. Blok is a killer." The searchlights circling the hall picked up the figure of Miss Shrimp who was weaving her way through the procession and choir that stood still in the dark during the change from the chorus. Blok looked nervously as she quickly advanced toward the podium. The lights stayed on her. "Here is proof." She waved a canvas. "It's his. It is Mr. Blok's. The murderer, the strangler of this innocent boy carrying an invalid.

The same hand who painted this strangled the boy. At this moment, Mr. Blok saw bodyguards rushing in seize her, but before they could reach her, she hurled the canvas at them, emitted a deafening shriek, and taking a small pill from her ring, shoved it far back in her throat. She began to choke and gasp, and her words sounded as if they came through a sieve. Cursing humanity and defiantly flinging open her kimono, she threw a Condesa de Sastago rose at the Superior. "The great Amateresu, Great death. I follow with joy. Oh, you spirited eagles. I — me — vive la Arizona. Ghhh … fooooo … um… um… um… " And she fell dead to the floor.

"Remarkable," murmured Blok, petrified.

As she was carried into a corner, the loudspeaker stated, "Please, we beg your kind indulgence for this unfortunate interruption. We will hear now from the great Arture Pavaroni." Mr. Blok saw a mighty figure of a man tearing himself from the procession of critics toward the platform. Mr. Blok thought his face resembled that of Pinkle's. The performance which followed was very impressive. The vibration of his powerful voice was truly unbelievable. It shattered two windows and one door from its frame, and the dramatic expression of his interpretation pushed three hearts and one brain from the bodies of four listeners. The performance evoked great enthusiasm and, though no one applauded because of the lack of space, cries of bravo, encore, fabelhaft, and even skel rang throughout the hall.

"Christ, what an artist," admired one man.

"You must not compare artists to Christ," Mr. Blok heard someone say and pull at his ear. "Stop pulling my ear. I didn't say anything," groaned Blok. But the man went on unconcerned.

"Why shouldn't I? All artists belong to the public, like museums and lavatories in railroad stations."

"Shut up," hissed Blok.

"Dear, you are very tired and nervous," he heard the melodious voice and felt the warmness of the faceless woman again. "Soon you will be able to rest and lie down," she said rubbing gently against him.

During the formation of the new procession, there was a brief broadcast of two governors from a jail, and soon after one saw silhouettes of critics, sullen and whimpering, passing on stilts. Following them marched champions, town fathers, yogis, brain trusters, and others in a long line. But even the goose-steps of the disciplinarians and the cries of debaters as well as the wild gossip circulating throughout the room drew Mr. Blok's attention. He found himself drawn to the faceless woman with such force that he felt completely fused with her. "You are the peace of my passion. You are the end of my guilt," he whispered to her as a strong searchlight dancing and hitting the walls stopped in all its trill brightness on him. Blinded, he tried to elude the blazing torch but stunned and helpless, he could not move. He felt all eyes piercing him and heard weird voices recalling his deeds of the past, advising, praising and cursing with ever increasing force until all joined in frantic unison screaming out every syllable in short and cutting rhythm. "His mission is accomplished. He must go back into the womb." Inciting each other to a state of ecstasy, they sang and screamed again and again, "Back into the womb."

In fear, clinging still tighter to the woman, he felt himself lifted together with her by the hook of a crane and hoisted into the air. After completing a semi-circle high overhead, their unresisting bodies were lowered and laid on the edge of the stage. "No seed would be needed to plant him again," he heard voices and the sound of a gong. Some people were turning and searching for the face of the woman, while others pulled the shoes off of Mr. Blok's feet and undressed him until he was nude.

"It's an orgy. It's violence. Oh, those hideous voices like hammers hitting my head," he complained vehemently. As if responding to his bitterness, all sounds died out and all stepped aside to let ortho-psychiatrist, accoucheurs and experts on symbolism to come closer to Mr. Blok and observe a process that everyone believed would be a rare spectacle of great significance. The dead silence only increased the great tension. As if in a trance, all stood around Mr. Blok and waited.

They waited for the surgeons, who holding a huge transparent placenta in their gloved hands, were approaching the platform. The surgeon's assistant, dressed in white, began at once to sterilize the upper parts of Mr. Blok's body while the nurse took care of the rest. He felt an agreeable touch of their hands, and the scent of the liquid he found delightful. Equally enjoyable to his skin was the feeling of the warm breath of the accoucheurs and the nurses with which they dried his body. Mr. Blok could not help regretting when this process was through and the disturbing rolling and wrapping into the placenta began. It made him giddy, and the smell of the rubber-like substance was sickening.

"Strange," he thought, "it's like perishing by one's own will," and he tried to help the accoucheurs with their task. As if everyone felt the solemnity of the occasion, they watched in silence and awe the fearful and unique process of sliding a man back into the embryo. When Mr. Blok was up to his neck, he pronounced a beautiful prayer and drank in abundance the last of his tears.

The expert hands of the accoucheurs and movers lifted the swollen body of the woman and placed it inside a double-bass. Suddenly, thick fumes streaming from the bass arose heavily in the air and made people cough and rub their eyes as they moved frightened, pushing and choking toward the exit.

"Attention, attention, please — stop! It's just a trick," yelled Mr. Cheesiz through the loudspeaker. "Silence, please, calm. It is only a magician's trick."

"Order, order," shouted Ellis. "Don't you here? Fools! Fools! Mr. Blok is right there in the corner asleep in the double bass. He ate some anthropological grass that was sent him from Basel. Stop crowding."

"Those damn antinomianists," said Mr. Cheesiz, whose voice became hoarse. He rattled some other words to himself, trying to stop some who rushed by in panic, but nothing would stop them. Mr. Cheesiz himself gave up and joined the rest of the perspiring and cackling crowd who like a huge mound of living flesh were fighting their way to the street.

Mr. Blok was awakened by the tremendous commotion and climbed out of the bass. Since he found himself quite nude, he snatched the kimono off of Miss Shrimp whose body was lying in the corner next to him. As soon as he stood on his feet, he was carried along with the wild current that emptied itself finally into the street.

With many deaths and injuries, thus ended the fateful and wondrous Assembly.

Chapter XXI

Not until Mr. Blok reached the Square did he feel safe and alone at last.

"See how the break of day sneaks out of darkness. Is it afraid to offend the grave pompousness of the night with its too brisk victory?" thought Mr. Blok looking up to the sky.

Daylight began to break more daringly now, but there was no joy of awakening life in it. Cold and numb, Mr. Blok sat on the bench. He wanted to rub his eyes, but his arm, curved and stiff, did not obey. He wearily cast his eyes on the shrubs and dust covered flowers that he thought would never grow in the Square by their own choice. He observed that they, like his fingers, were also stony and stiff. It struck him that his fingers did not look like fingers at all, but like the icicles that sometimes grow overnight on his window at home. "Oh, it was too long ago. What happens to time when it runs away from memory? Does it become never?" mused Blok, playing with his fingers. He listened. "They make the sound of breaking glass. I must be careful." He remembered once when splitting icicles a few sharp chips penetrated his skin. Now, as if he felt pain again, he blew on his hands. "Mother used to stop pain that way always ... she would say ..."

A loud voice cut into his reminiscence. "What are you doing here at this hour?"

He saw a policeman. He bent toward Blok. "Haven't I seen you somewhere before?"

"No," said Blok, "I just came from Russia a second or two ago."

"But I thought I saw you in this city," remarked the policeman, playing with his holster."

"Hmm — perhaps at the Assembly..."

"Let me smell your breath, sir."

Blok got up. After examining him, the policeman said, "You were not drinking, it's true. Strange..." and then strictly, "Where do you live? What's your name?"

"I wish," said Blok, "my address would be Heaven or Hell. No matter, as long as it would not be in this civilization."

"I don't understand you, sir," said the officer.

"How could you, you who are trained to catch drunkards and murderers."

"Come along," said the policeman, taking hold of Blok's arm, "and show me your identification papers."

"Always papers as though you can see spirit in them. I expect to be recognized by my style," answered Blok, somewhat hurt.

The policeman stopped at the lamppost. "Where are your papers?"

"At home," said Blok. "I live just around the corner. I shall be glad to satisfy your curiosity," and looking reproachfully at him, he added, "Don't you see that the kimono I'm wearing has no pockets?" And with his teeth chattering, he told the policeman, "They took my clothes off at the Assembly, and if it were not for the suicide of a lady Buddhist, I would still be lying there naked in the double bass."

"Il est complement fou," murmured the officer to himself.

"No, no, I am not, not at all — it's true. She swallowed the pill and dropped dead," said Blok as they approached his studio.

"You are not feeling well?"

"Why?" asked Blok.

"You're walking like an old horse harnessed to a hearse," said the officer.

"No wonder," agreed Blok, "after all that I have gone through." They entered the studio. The paper he showed the policeman was an honorary degree bestowed upon Blok by the Art College of Bocquet. It satisfied the officer completely.

Blok offered him a glass of buttermilk.

"Au fond, il n'est pas vraiment detraque," Blok heard him say.

"Your French is excellent," Blok complimented.

"Oh, you understand French!"

"Yes, I do."

"In that case, I will ask you not to mention my French to anyone," said the officer quickly, and then confidingly, "You see, sir, I don't want them to know my origin at the station. They would not understand — as my father, Marquis de la Goddard, never understood. I mean he would not believe that my passion for playing policeman as a child would last forever. Parents never trust games. He wanted me to become a replica of himself," he shrugged, "Such a foolish and conceited idea. You should have seen him! Anyway, I resisted his will well enough, as you see." There was an expression of healthy satisfaction and a proud smile on his face, but it changed as his eyes fell on Blok's feet.

"Why," he said, "where did you lose your shoes?"

"Hmm… my shoes," said Blok, looking at his toes. "They took them off. One of my accoucheurs happened to be a shoe fetishist. He kept them."

"I see, I see," said the Marquis de la Goddard. "You better put on woolen socks."

He walked out somewhat abruptly, thought Blok. Gently shutting the door and locking it, Mr. Blok took off the kimono, smelled it, walked resolutely toward the fireplace — threw it in — and began to search for wood. But except for a few frames he found nothing with which to make a fire. He stood in front of the fireplace and spoke to himself the way singers do when trying their voice. "If it were for art, I would, like Bernard de Palissy, burn all my furniture, but just to warm my own body, no! It would be as ugly when warm," he observed, looking at his goose pimples.

It was cold in the room, and he was tired, too tired, to do anything about it. In such a state his body was curiously and absurdly in discord with his mind, which seemed to be doubly charged with energy.

"I am standing as though my feet were nailed to the floor, like Soutine's chicken," thought Blok. "Poor chicken. He should not have done that, the crazy fellow."

He saw his knees bending under the weight of his body. "I must move from the spot. Is it true that African elephants can stand for centuries on their feet?" He moved insecurely, rumbling and sighing to his bed, and curled up in it. "I must look like a fetus in a bottle of alcohol," he mumbled. His thoughts again went back to his childhood. "Brr — rr. It's cold here, — darker, — dirtier, — than those building on that cursed street that I passed from my home into the city of Moscow. Those stubborn buildings, are they still there?... with their unpainted walls outside and their smell of poverty inside ... waiting for something?"

Blok shivered as he lay in the bed with haunted thoughts from afar. He turned and heard as if dry snow were crunching under foot. It was the only sound that broke the silence as he passed in his thoughts the same streets and buildings... on that gray morning when his blood had turned to ice. No one looked through the frosted windows as he walked by... Perhaps later after the sun had risen on the same windows, the snow would shine as in a fairytale. Only then the snow had been blue, purple blue like the lips of the drunkard he dragged once from the Volga river. He was not pretty, the drunkard, but the river was...

"Stop thinking... Oh, Jesus... Buddha... Solomon... my thoughts speed like a speeding squid, the sperm whale will catch it and tear is to pieces. But I am not a squid, I have not tentacles, you hear?" screamed Blok, "I don't live in the depths of an ocean — I am Blok, Blok, Blok. All my life I have been on the surface."

"Who, you?" someone beamed and made Blok turn in his bed. But he could not open his eyes; they were locked with three iron locks on each eyelid. Blok said into the dark, "Please call a locksmith," and turned over.

"Is it you who live on the surface?" the voice repeated with a laugh. "No sir, you are an inhabitant of wet clay, don't you remember? ... the walls of the ditch are mighty protective, aren't they? You remember now?"

"I do, I do," groaned Blok.

"No, you don't. You think you climbed out of there, but you are still there, dreaming out things — sometimes very funny ones, ha, ha — pranky! do! ... I'll bet you don't even know who's talking to you right now, do you?"

Blok did not answer.

"All right, then, I will tell you. My name is Sober T. Reality," wheezed the stranger. Then he asked politely, "Are you asleep?"

"Leave me alone," Blok rattled.

"Shhh, you're alone here. Do you know what? I suspect, of course, it's only a suspicion — and hardly a flattering one for me — that I am you. How do you like it? Ha, Ha." Then with a shriek, "Don't try to scratch me! Oh, Oh, you miserable stray cat!"

Blok like a child asked for forgiveness. "I did not want to hurt you. I really did not intend to."

"I am glad," uttered Sober Reality, "that you are coming to your senses and are willing to pay for your sins gracefully. By the way, what I said before was just a joke. I like to crack a good joke occasionally. Hmm … what I want to say is that I am I, and that you are … a fop, … and a fake …" and, as if in a hurry, "Listen and don't interrupt me with your ugly groans, … I want to refresh your memory. It will be just a short, weird promenade. Will you? Just to the door of your parents whom you deserted. Hmm. You don't like it?"

"Alright, no objection. Let's look up at your teacher, to whom you owe all you have except your talent. Let's see the good old man whom you betrayed so elegantly. But don't get excited, most students betray their teachers. And don't groan! It gets on my nerves!" he hollered. "Come on! Or I'll drag you straight to your sister with whom you played doctor in the basement. You don't like that either? Alright. Do you remember calling your father a stud? No? You were just a kid. You still are. That's what's nice about you. Helpless and impotent. Honestly. Wouldn't a baby be a monstrosity otherwise? No one could possibly call you a monstrosity. You hear? Nobody! And certainly not Sophie with whom you blundered so oddly and completely. She still loves you. I wonder if she knew of your unadvanced age. Hmm… Did she serve you with diapers during your leprosy? Who cares! She knows you are happy now and safe as an embryo."

"Shut up!" cried Blok.

"May I unlock your eyes and start the fire, or perhaps start the fire first?" asked Mr. Reality.

Blok heard him moving away, and, in a minute or two through the crackling of burning wood, the man's voice came as though through a shroud. "Can you recognize your painting by the sound?" And, not waiting for an answer, "Those are only the drawings. But listen now! It's something oily and thick. There it goes."

"Must be my sunflowers," doubted Blok.

"Not at all," said the voice, bustling around the fireplace. "It is one of your earlier potboilers. See, it burns fast. I will add 'The Lady in White' … here it is … and some newer ones, which made you so famous… They give a bright flame. Good you didn't waste your talent on ceramics. They would be useless for such cool day." Then he said to Blok officiously, "Soon we will have some bacon and eggs at the fill-up counter. Come here to the fire and sit on this lovely howdah."

"I don't want to ride on a camel," sniveled Blok.

"Don't be splenetic," said Sober, throwing more pictures on the fire. He coughed and cursed. "That dreadful kimono doesn't burn! It's like some old traditions," he said pleasantly.

"Some spendthrifts get a kick out of burning their money." Blok heard him gurgle. "We here have much better fun, burning ideas, efforts and knowledge. I love it. I would burn Drachma, Quetzal (not the sacred bird), Pengo, Lempira, Rupees, Lat, Litas, Kran, Zloty, and Cordoba like straw, and with no feelings whatsoever! Listen… watch… that 'Mouse and Pigeon' perishes like a stoic. God bless it!" And then, "Dear, dearest, divine Mr. Blok, you remember a nest of newborn mice that you threw in the Bocquet river? They were so tiny, perhaps only a day old, and already swimming so efficiently — you did not see them drown — or did you?

"It was court and the farmer threw them into the river," corrected Blok groping to the fire and settling himself in the howdah, perspiration running in streams down his body and forming a puddle under his feet while some of it leaked into the fire and made it sputter.

"Don't put the fire out," said Sober.

"And you please don't call me divine," said Blok, playing with the iron locks.

"Why not? I think you are divine, no less than the priest who initiated you into Christianity. Remember? When you converted? But perhaps you were too small then and too busy, playing with the lovely little cross you got from your brand-new godfather to remember the priest's face at all. I wonder where the cross and the priest are now? They must have gotten lost." Sober reflected melancholically, "I guess we all become losers as time goes by. We lose teeth and hair, enthusiasm and orgasms..."

"Please stop this rancid rhyming," cried Blok with hostility.

"Why should I?" Sober shrugged. "You yourself tried your hand at poetry, remember? You even read some of it to a Hollywood writer, but after he did not show the expected admiration, you scolded him, I must say, with exaggerated severity."

"I?"

"Yes, you. You called the poor fellow a scavenger and a plot-hunter. He answered you quite justly that Jesus Christ's grammar was not better than his and walked away."

"Obtuse prattle," murmured Blok. "It's you who ought to shut your mouth with those iron locks."

"But gladly — wish nothing better," said Sober pleasantly. Bending over Blok's eyes with swiftness, he took off the locks.

"Oh, how wonderful to see again!" thanked Blok, rubbing his eyes, looking at the fire, and then turning his head, "Where are you? Hey, you!"

His eyes swept the empty room. "Yoo-hoo, yoo-hoo, where are you?", he called, but his voice came back to him emptily.

"Where is he hiding, that insidious fellow?" he asked puzzled and got up. He searched all the corners, went into a big cupboard and opened two chests of drawers.

"Some people like to crawl under the bed," he murmured, getting ready to throw himself on the floor, but at this moment there was a knock on the door, and Sophie entered.

"How wonderful that you are alive," she said with feeling, and after a pause, "Why, you are naked again!"

Blok apologized and, confusedly covering his maleness, explained, "I was quite ill; my eyes were locked. Also, I was engaged in an incongruous conversation with an upsetting personality who burned my pictures. I couldn't..."

"What?" she said.

"Hmmm..." hesitated Blok, "I haven't even had time to dress myself." Then he added hurriedly, "Oh, please sit down. I will be with you in a minute," and turning his back he quickly disappeared into a large Biedermeyer cupboard. He did not let her wait long.

"Lovely fire," Sophie said when Blok emerged.

"Yes, isn't it," he agreed. He found her seated on the howdah, rubbing her feet. "At the Assembly," she said, "an uninhibited Russian, presumably from one of those icebreakers, stood on my feet during the whole procession of critics. A brute!" she complained while Blok watched her with great concentration.

"It's not Sophie. It's not the woman I loved and knew. It's a stranger, cold and indifferent," he thought. It appeared that the woman he was looking at was much bigger than Sophie. "She is enormous," thought Mr. Blok.

"What are you thinking of?" he heard her metallic voice.

"You have changed so much," said Mr. Blok.

"I watched you at the Assembly," said Sophie.

"She is still growing. Now her shoe looks like a boat," thought Mr. Blok in terror.

"I saw you there with a woman," Sophie said. Now Blok found that her voice resembled Sophie's. There was a note of tender pain in it.

"I never saw her face," Blok said defensively.

"Her face?" Now her voice again sounded metallic and hard. "I know she had no face. She had something else. Something you always craved for." She stood up and spoke with great scorn. "I saw you go into her — into her womb. I could have saved you, but I did not want to. I hated you. I hate you now. You hear? I was glad to lose you." Her dry burning eyes seemed to scorch all her body and heart. Blok did not move, as though not daring to interfere with some mystic miracle that a saint or a witch was about to commit.

"You betrayed me. You trampled upon my feelings and me. And now you are lost. You are perished and lost forever."

Blok tried to say something but could not find words. "But... but...I... I'm here. You can see. It was a mirage — mass hypnotism. I am as before. You can see it. I am in nobody. I am the same old..."

And then something happened. Something frightful and strange. He saw a gigantic mass of hard flesh approach. He felt himself lifted and placed in her palm. He crouched, tightening his muscles for fear of being crushed like a bug. "You, you as before?" Her whisper almost blew him off her hand. He was deafened by the thunder of her laughter. "You are an embryo; just an embryo. Do you want to see yourself?" He felt himself carried to the mirror. "You see?" Not trusting his eyes, he moistened and wiped the glass. He stared in the mirror and then closed his eyes in horror. He stared again and again. "It's true, it's true," he shrieked, but no sound came from his mouth. She dropped him on the floor. Someone kicked Blok in the ribs.

"Get angry with her, you fool. Move out of here quick. Run from your doom." He heard the familiar voice of Sober Reality. Then Blok saw himself running from the studio into the street and straight to the Square. He wanted to follow a straight line, no matter in what direction as long as it was straight but crossing the Square he had to turn left. He did not walk around but took the middle walk and so arrived at the other end. Then he turned to his right and this time went all the way, never changing his course, always around to the right. Right… right… right… circling to the right.

He was panting and wet, but not once did he step on the pigeons or squirrels that ran under his feet. His thoughts were also running and also were right; for there were no problems and all was right. He passed 20th Street twenty times without counting, and it was twenty times exactly, precisely, like the fruit of his life and as clear as his fame.

"Oh, oh, … isn't it hard to make a stop when on the move?" he asked himself, panting and turning to the right…

"Oh, God, stop me," he prayed. "Have mercy!" He saw a tricycle coming at him. Was it a colored boy speeding so madly? He felt a hard blow from the front wheel and hit the ground and rolled into a ditch. There was a sharp pain that passed almost instantly.

"Father, father," he heard a boy cry. "He is not hurt, father. He's just very old." Blok opened his eyes. "Mr. Blok," he heard the man say.

Blok recognized him. "Mitchell Wrinkley?"

There was a long silence. Mr. Wrinkly said, "No, son, Mr. Blok is not old — he is dead! He's surely dead. Let's get out of here before someone comes." Blok heard them hustling away.

"It's a pity, I would have liked to see him," Mr. Blok thought with great sadness.

Lying on his back in the mud, his eyes closed. It was soft and warm, and the marvelous quiet made him feel almost grateful and glad. How amazingly simple it is to be dead. The transition is so painless, it is hardly perceptible. "Oh, nature is kind," he admired quietly.

"Such a short distance from life and such quietness. If people knew, they would never be frightened of death, never — never. Perhaps later I will find a greater difference on this side, if there is any. No wonder so many people don't know they are dead. It is good to get rid of one's body when the best in one still remains. I can still think... muse... oh, if only it wouldn't be so dark here. I have lost all conception of time. Probably there is no such thing here. When was I killed? Since when am I dead? Hmmm, utterly unimportant. It's like fainting. A drunkard who passes out must feel the same. Hmm... no... no... he can't. A real true death is a sober death that can reason and remember. I can. With many beautiful recollections, the life of a corpse can be fine."

He heard steps overhead. "Someone is coming to welcome me here."

"Hello... blo... blo... greetings." Mr. Blok did not answer. He listened.

"If there is such a thing as hell you will not know it. Congratulations!" the voice continued. "I can always tell one new boarder from the other."

Mr. Blok could neither see nor speak.

"The ditch — grave — even the urn after cremation are recognized channels to enter this place, but I was not as lucky." The voice began to speak in fast tempo. "I came straight from the electric-chair, and before I could say blo… blo… I became a Short Wave. Blasted cabbage! What a life!

"Jerking convulsively in fabulous speed without a second of rest, intercepting messages, codes, mostly broken parts of them, sent in queer languages, delivering them God knows where. Finally, I am going to be promoted to a Long Wave — it's a cinch." Blok heard steps vanishing into ethereal silence. He turned on his side. "What was that? Queer!" He felt pain in his legs. He moved his arm. "Am I alive after all? Strange." He took a deep breath. "Oh, my chest, my neck!" He opened his eyes full on the dribbling wall. "Am I again in the ditch? Where is Wrinkly?" He remembered. He tried to get up, but his feet seemed soft and jointless, stuck in the dirt. He burrowed his hands in the ground and forced his elbows and arms to lift his heavy back until he could sit leaning against the wall. While resting and composing himself, he listened to the steps of people passing on the sidewalk overhead. "They trample on me. Not these. These steps are light. Must be a nice person — a woman. Why does no one stop and look into the ditch? Every step has a different character — a different meaning. They are more telling than faces. They did not learn to lie."

He tried to visualize each person. All of a sudden, he wanted to listen to his own steps. "I must get out of here. Didn't Wrinkly say exactly the same words? Hmmm, he ran away from murder." He looked at his soiled suit. "I must be quite a sight," he murmured half-jokingly. "Brainy and interesting men are seldom good-looking." With this thought he got to his feet and brushing dirt form his jacket tried to climb out of the ditch. After many attempts he finally emerged and, supporting himself against the wall of a building, was glad to stand and rest for a while.

The passersby hardly payed any attention to him. Blok took their indifference for kindness. "There are multitudes of truly fine people in this world," he said to himself, slowly advancing toward the Square. It was a beautiful starless evening.

He must have had a smile on his face, for a lady, as if in answer, smiled also. When she passed, Mr. Blok turned and watched her fragile and anxious figure as though in search of friendliness disappear into the dark. Strolling along the Square, Blok's thoughts touched only vaguely on the recent occurrences and his mind was not preoccupied with the immediate needs of the day. "I feel like newborn, and maybe I am. Don't those who really live, live anew? Feeling and seeing the new in the old? They never know boredom." He wanted to travel to Turquoise Creek and stay there among the Havasupai. "I always wanted to stand there on a red cliff and look at the blue water cascading over inaccessible rocks down the slopes. Where was it? In Arizona? I think it is." He arched his eyebrows. "Miss Shrimp wanted me to go there. I would rather visit Ulrich. He was such a good fellow." This brought Mr. Blok back to Chicago when he had urged his friend to start a new life. "He grows grapefruit in Texas now. Hmm, it was a mistake. He should have grown dates, instead. I would. Perhaps I will. I will," said Blok to himself and began walking faster. "Date trees are really wonderful. I will start with twenty young couples, no — more. Perhaps with thirty male and female trees. Somewhere in the desert. They should not be pollinated by hand; it's unnatural. The Syrian fly must do the job. The dates over there grow more tender and sweet. The skin of the fruit must never be hard. I will import Syrian flies. I will breed them in great quantities in an oasis in the desert. A colony can be started there. An artists' village. First the village, then the town, a city, then the world. Everyone can be an artist. Everyone has talent for something.

"Hmm, it is true. Everyone is superior in something. I never met anyone who was not my superior in something. Even Gordon the farmer. I thought he was inferior. Everyone knew of his complete inefficiency, until his great love for bugs was discovered. He loved them. He knew them. Now he has become a valuable advisor to the National Forestry Board. Or look at that old Chinese artist who painted nothing but crayfish until the supply of fresh models suddenly stopped, and to his astonishment, he learned of the bloody war raging in China for the past three or four years. Odd fellow! Narrow, wasn't he? Though his crayfish on paper, I must admit, look far more attractive to me than the prettiest models on a canvas."

His thoughts came to his friend, the cobbler in Vienna. Also, a great, a true artist. "Where is he now?" wondered Blok. "He refused once to cut shoes for a princess. He didn't like her feet." Blok smiled. So sunk in thoughts, half dreaming, half-awake, he approached a bench. Just as he was about to sit down, someone touched his shoulder. Blok saw a stranger. "You are great."

He pumped his hand vigorously, then patted him on the back and shook Blok with his two hands. "You don't know me," he said with great enthusiasm, "but I know you. The whole world knows you. Isn't it an agreeable feeling?" he said and burst into laughter. "Sure was happy to meet you. You are just great. Goodbye. Bye, bye, so long." He left as briskly as he had appeared. Blok watched the bulky back of the stranger who had disturbed his trend of thought.

"I love spontaneity and enthusiasm, and I believe in their constructive duty; but why must they express their emotions physically?" he grumbled. "I do thoroughly disapprove of those habitual shoulder-patters, hand-shakers, laugh-bursters, eye-winkers, cheek-kissers, tearjerkers, chin-ticklers, tongue-clickers, as well as shriekers, cryers, feet-stampers, coughers, spitters, sneezers, hair-pluckers, throat-clears, whistlers, gurglers, ear-scratchers, wheezers, sighers, groaners, pimple squeezers, just squeezers, program rattlers, whisperers.... " There was a big smile on his face. "Smilers... etc.... etc.... etc.... etc...."

About the Author

Gregor Piatigorsky (1903 – 1976), the famed Russian cellist, was born in Ekaterinoslav (now Dnepropetrovsk), Ukraine. After leaving home as a little boy, he became the principal cellist of Moscow's Bolshoi Theater at the age of 15. He escaped from the Soviet Union in 1921 in the aftermath of the Bolshevik Revolution, crossed into Germany and became the first cellist in the Berlin Philharmonic under Wilhelm Furtwängler. Subsequently, he concertized extensively, married the French Jacqueline de Rothschild, had a daughter, Jephta, and came to the United States when France entered the war in 1939. He settled in Elizabethtown, New York, had a son, Joram, and became an American citizen. Renowned as a teacher, he taught at Curtis Institute of Music in Philadelphia before moving to Los Angeles in 1949; he ran a master class at the University of Southern California and turned out many of the leading cellists of the time. Piatigorsky died in Los Angeles in 1976; he is considered a legendary cellist of the 20ᵗʰ century.